Also by Rachel Shukert

STARSTRUCK

LOVE ME

LOVE ME

Rachel Shukert

DELACORTE PRESS

Text copyright © 2014 by Rachel Shukert
Jacket photograph copyright © 2014 by Michael Frost

All rights reserved. Published in the United States by Delacorte Press, an imprint of
Random House Children's Books, a division of Random House, Inc., New York.

Delacorte Press is a registered trademark and the colophon is a trademark of
Random House, Inc.

randomhouse.com/teens

Educators and librarians, for a variety of teaching tools, visit us at
RHTeachersLibrarians.com

Library of Congress Cataloging-in-Publication Data
Shukert, Rachel.
Love me / Rachel Shukert.—First edition.
pages cm
Sequel to: Starstruck.
Summary: "All the glamour and glitz of the Golden Age of Glam is back, except
this time Margo, Gabby, and Amanda are going to receive an even greater dose of
reality about Hollywood and their place in it"—Provided by publisher.
ISBN 978-0-385-74110-1 (hardcover : alk. paper)—
ISBN 978-0-375-98985-8 (glb : alk. paper)—
ISBN 978-0-375-98426-6 (ebook)
[1. Fame—Fiction. 2. Actors and actresses—Fiction.
3. Hollywood (Los Angeles, Calif.)—History—20th century—Fiction.] I. Title.
PZ7.S55933Lov 2014
[Fic]—dc23
2012047071

Printed in the United States of America

10 9 8 7 6 5 4 3 2 1

First Edition

Random House Children's Books
supports the First Amendment and celebrates the right to read.

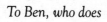
To Ben, who does

ONE

Movie people were used to being up at the crack of dawn.

The lucky ones—that is, the ones who actually had jobs—were already hard at work at the studios by the time the dazzling California sun came up over the scrubby, green-dotted rock of the Hollywood hills: dressing sets, calibrating lights, tapping out rewrites, stumbling into the makeup department to have their imperfect, human faces carefully assessed, erased, and replaced before the daylight could expose anything the dream factories would rather keep hidden. The unlucky, unemployed majority had seen out the long night and their last dollar in the twinkling row of restaurants and ballrooms lining the Sunset Strip, dining and dancing and drinking away the choking fear that the long-awaited lucky break would never come.

And then there were the others, somewhere in the middle.

1

Not quite successful but not quite ready to give up, not quite famous but not quite unknown.

They were the ones who were trapped. Caught in a web of work and worry—not to mention the pills, which made the work possible—through which sleep could never quite find its way. Winding up in Hollywood purgatory, a kind of eternal sophomore slump: that was the greatest fear of everyone in the business.

And it was exactly where Gabby Preston found herself now.

Or maybe more accurately, *again.*

It was four-thirty in the morning, but Gabby was still wide-awake. She paced the floor of her bedroom in the house on Fountain Avenue in a well-practiced path, placing one slippered foot in front of the other all the way down the frayed edge of the rose-colored Oriental carpet to the dressing table, where she'd pause to yank up her pajama top in front of the mirror, checking to see if her exposed stomach looked any flatter than it had a minute ago. A quick rearranging of the perfume bottles and lipstick stubs, then over to peer inside the door of her wardrobe, as though some new and exciting purchase might have magically materialized among the collared blouses and sensible skirts hanging in neat rows from the matching hangers.

Next came a desultory shuffle through the albums resting in an untidy stack on the polished cherrywood surface of the RCA all-in-one wireless/record player. It was quite a luxury to have one of those babies all to yourself, but as Gabby's mother, Viola, had told the keepers of the Olympus purse strings, given the amount of music the studio expected Gabby to learn every week, it was a necessary one.

Finally, she'd flop back on her quilted satin bedspread, where

2

she'd take a few deep, hopeful breaths before the thrum of her racing heart told her it was no use and the whole pattern began again.

How long had it been since she'd slept? Really properly slept, with dreams and everything, and without needing blue pills to make her eyes close and green ones to open them up again? A couple of months at least. Maybe—probably, if she was being very, very honest—even longer. And the blue pills were barely working anymore. She had gobbled four of them before bed-time last night—her last four—and gotten no more than half an hour's light nap, tops. It would be hours before the pharma-cies opened and she could send Viola out for more.

Gabby picked up the empty glass pill bottle off the dressing table and held it up to the light. A fine residue of blue powder coated the base. She couldn't stick her finger all the way to the bottom to reach it, let alone her tongue, but if she filled it half-way with water and let it dissolve, she could drink it.

Maybe that would be just enough to push her over the edge into a few precious hours of sleep.

Of course, the powder would be a whole lot more effective accompanied by a nice big glug of gin, but Viola had put the liquor cabinet under lock and key. *Ironic*, Gabby thought, *considering it's my five-hundred-dollar-a-week salary that's paying for it all, right down to the padlock.* How would Viola feel if Gabby started rationing the food in the icebox?

Or better yet, if I slapped my own padlock on the door of her closet? Ever since Gabby's mother had gotten a load of the bounty in the trunks Amanda Farraday had moved into the spare room—the delicately jet-beaded evening gowns, the close-fitting Paris suits with the raw-silk linings and hand-stitched

3

seams so tiny and neat you practically needed a microscope to see them—the packages had been arriving from the most exclusive department stores in Beverly Hills. Smart striped hatboxes and stacks of shoe boxes and tissue-paper parcels yielding piles of complicated underthings in slippery French silk. Gabby couldn't bear to imagine what the hell her mother—who at forty-five was positively *ancient*—thought she was doing with that kind of stuff. She liked even less to think about how much it was costing.

It'll all be different as soon as I turn eighteen, Gabby told herself. Then she'd have control of her money, and her life, and Viola would find herself on a budget so fast it would make her curly little head spin. *That is, if I don't tell her to take a hike altogether.*

It wouldn't be much longer now. Two years, maybe less, if she could figure out some way to dig up her original birth certificate. Viola had always been a little vague when it came to birthdays, ever since the vaudeville days, when the Fabulous Preston Sisters were known for conveniently being whatever ages the theater bookers and press agents thought would sell the most tickets. According to her official Olympus Studios publicity bio, Gabby Preston, singing starlet of stage and screen, had turned sweet sixteen on Christmas Day, the only birthday Viola had ever let Gabby or her older sister, Frankie, celebrate, since "if it's good enough for the Baby Jesus, it's good enough for the Preston girls" and the double billing saved on presents in the lean years besides. In reality, Ethel Ellen O'Halloran, as Gabby had been named at birth, had to be at least a year older. Maybe even eighteen already.

Still, she couldn't do much without the papers to prove it,

and Viola had probably thrown those in the fire years ago. There wasn't much Gabby's mother wouldn't do if it meant an extra year with her hot little hand in Gabby's pocket.

Margo Sterling would never have this problem, Gabby thought.

True, Margo didn't talk about her parents much—or at all. But Gabby was a close enough friend to know that the incandescent blonde all of Hollywood—hell, all of America—had anointed its latest big-screen queen had grown up with pretty much everything a girl could ask for: a big, beautiful house in Pasadena, a top-notch education at some fancy-schmancy girls' school, a place in Society (the capital *S* signifying the kind of rich people who would never willingly admit showbiz types into their rarified midst). And that was all *before* she'd seemingly done nothing but shrug her slim shoulders and step straight into the coveted role vacated by Diana Chesterfield in the box-office smash *The Nine Days' Queen.*

Honestly, Gabby thought, *it's like she just said "Oh, all right, I guess I'll be a movie star today."*

Margo's romantic life had seemed similarly effortless. She had broken the heart of Jimmy Molloy, Olympus's biggest star and the man Gabby had desperately wanted for herself—or at least, everyone thought she had, which was the important thing. Now Margo was practically living with Dane Forrest, who was just about the handsomest actor on the planet. Her picture had been on the cover of every magazine in the country. And this morning, by the time her maid had delicately sliced off the top of her soft-boiled egg, Margo was probably going to have an Academy Award nomination for Best Actress. *Talk about a charmed life.*

It wasn't that Gabby was jealous of Margo, exactly. It was

5

just so unfair that it had all been so easy for her. Worst of all, nobody else seemed to mind. You'd think the anxious strivers and class-conscious immigrants who ran Hollywood would resent the entitled nonchalance with which the newest star in the Olympus Studios constellation seemed to grab every available column inch, but no, they just lapped it up as if they were kittens at a saucer full of cream.

That's the trouble with arrivistes, Gabby thought. *They always have way too much awe for those who never needed to arrive.*

This was supposed to have been Gabby's year. Last spring she'd been all set to headline in *An American Girl,* the picture Harry Gordon was going to write for her. It was supposed to have been the big one, the role of a lifetime, the picture that would finally make her a big star. She was the one whose phone was supposed to ring at sunrise this morning with a call from Larry Julius in the Olympus press office. She was the one who was supposed to have a truck pull up outside with one of the six-foot-tall foil-wrapped Oscars Mr. Karp, the head of the studio, was said to have specially commissioned from his personal chocolatier in Beverly Hills for every Olympus nominee. She was supposed to have stacks of congratulatory telegrams from the likes of Clark Gable and Spencer Tracy and Claudette Colbert, and weeks' worth of consultations with Rex Mandalay, the famously tempestuous (and tight-panted) Australian who was Olympus's most revered costumer, about the gorgeous gown he would design just for her.

But none of that was going to happen now. Those dreams had died that horrible night when Harry Gordon had told her he was taking the part—*her* part—in *An American Girl* away from her. It was a wound that hadn't quite healed, and Margo's inevitable nomination would only pour salt in it.

There's always next year, Viola would say. Everybody would say it. But Gabby had been in Hollywood long enough to know that the more people said those things, the less they believed them.

And besides, they weren't even making the picture now. *An American Girl* might have been the role of a lifetime, but it was dead as a doornail as far as production was concerned. That was some small consolation. If Gabby couldn't play that part, at least nobody else would.

"Gabrielle."

The low whisper came through the keyhole. This was Viola's latest affectation, conveniently forgetting that "Gabby" wasn't short for anything, that it wasn't even a real name. "Gabrielle, are you awake?"

The door swung open before Gabby had time to decide what her answer would be. Her mother stood framed in the doorway, her stout body wrapped tightly in a lavender chenille dressing gown, her newly hennaed hair protected by a large square of white silk pinned over the tight marcelle waves. For years, Viola had had plain brown hair, just like Gabby's. Then the hairdressers at the studio had started putting a chestnut rinse in Gabby's curls and suddenly, Viola had decided she needed a reddish tint too.

"I saw your light on," she said, pushing one of the pins at the edge of the silk back into place. "Don't tell me you've been up all night again."

"What does it matter if I'm asleep? I'm resting, aren't I?"

7

Sighing, Viola sat down on Gabby's neatly made bed, making a face as she ran her hand over the pale satin of the bedspread. She had spent what seemed like hours in the linens department of Bullocks trying to talk Gabby into buying what she termed a more "age-appropriate" cotton coverlet printed with pink and yellow strawberry blossoms, but Gabby had refused to budge. Now Viola hated the bedspread for the same reason her daughter adored it: it represented one of the only arguments Viola O'Halloran Preston had ever lost. "You need sleep. Why didn't you take a pill?"

"I did. They're all gone."

"*All* of them? There were six left in the bottle when we finished dinner last night."

Six? "No. There couldn't have been that many."

"Gabby, I counted them myself."

The last time Viola decided Gabby was taking too many pills, she'd ripped up her prescription, and Gabby had spent the whole week feeling as if bugs were crawling under her skin, eating her from the inside out, until Dr. Lipkin, the studio doctor, had saved the day. *Think of something*, Gabby thought desperately. *Anything.* "Amanda must have taken them."

"Amanda?"

"I know she's been having trouble sleeping lately," said Gabby as sincerely as she could. Delivery was important with Viola; she had been blessed with what she liked to think of as a peerless nose for bull. *Lucky I'm such a good actress*, Gabby told herself.

"That girl," Viola groaned. "That girl is becoming a *problem*." A dangerous rasp had crept into her throat.

"It's not Amanda's fault." This was the trouble with telling

8

even one lie to someone like Viola. You always had to tell so many more. "I said it was okay. She wouldn't have taken them otherwise. It's just a misunderstanding."

"Gabrielle, those pills aren't *jelly beans*. You can't just hand them out to be friendly. They're your *medication*. What Dr. Lipkin and the studio have decided you need to take to be able to *work*."

"But Amanda—"

"Amanda's career isn't my concern," Viola interrupted. "Frankly, I don't care about her one way or another."

That's not how it used to be, Gabby thought bitterly. When Amanda Farraday first started hanging around the house on Fountain Avenue, looking for a hot meal and a shoulder to cry on in the wake of her breakup with the red-hot screenwriter Harry Gordon, Viola had seemed quite swept off her feet. Gabby had watched with a mixture of bemusement and jealousy as her normally curt mother stayed up late into the night sitting at the kitchen table with the glamorous redhead, drinking hot tea with whiskey while poring over the latest issues of *Vogue* and *Harper's Bazaar* and tearfully commiserating over the awfulness of men.

Sometime between Thanksgiving and Christmas, when Amanda started complaining about the hotel she'd been staying at since Harry left, Viola, in a fit of sudden holiday spirit, had invited her to stay in the spare room for as long as she liked.

She hadn't even bothered to ask Gabby first, although it wasn't like Gabby could object, since Amanda's broken heart was just the teensiest bit her fault. Gabby had gotten so mad when Harry Gordon told her he was thinking about getting the starring role in *An American Girl* reassigned to his girlfriend that Gabby had accidentally-on-purpose-but-mostly-on-purpose just happened to tell him Hollywood's best-kept secret: that the ravishing Amanda had once worked for the notorious Olive Moore, the self-styled "concierge" of Hollywood's most infamously lavish house of ill-repute. *Oops.*

Harry Gordon had reacted just like Gabby thought he would. For all his radical-socialist utopian bluster, he was a pretty traditional guy at heart, already a little worried about just how he was going to present a bombshell like Amanda to his little Jewish *mamaleh* back in Bensonhurst. The news that until fairly recently, the property of which he considered himself the sole occupant had been widely available for rent hit him like the proverbial ton of bricks. It was all he could do not to hit Amanda with a literal one.

Their relationship had been doomed from the start. Anyone with half a brain could see that. Still, Gabby had been startled by the volcanic force of Amanda's grief.

"You'd think a girl like Amanda Farraday would have a whole army of understudies waiting to step into the newly vacant leading-man role," Jimmy Molloy had said, after what was supposed to have been a fun group outing to the movies ended abruptly with Amanda crying her way into a full-fledged asthma attack when she caught a whiff of a man in line for the theater wearing the same aftershave as Harry. "But whaddya know? Turns out she really loves the guy."

The whole thing made Gabby feel uncomfortably—not to mention uncharacteristically—guilty. Not to the point where she'd actually considered fessing up, because what good was that going to do anyone? But letting Amanda, aka the world's sexiest watering can—who, Gabby was pleased to note, was

10

covered head to toe in a coating of very imperfect freckles when she didn't bother to dress or put her face on, which these days was frankly most of the time—hide away in her spare room and help herself to the remnants of the icebox seemed like the least Gabby could do.

Besides, the truth was Gabby kind of liked having Amanda around. It was nice to have another girl in the house, no matter how mopey she was. Someone to talk to, to make little jokes with, to deflect some of Viola's suffocating attention. It was almost like when her sister, Frankie, had been around, before she'd gotten so sick and tired of the Fabulous Preston Sisters and their not-so-fabulous vaudeville gypsy life that she'd run off with Martini the Magnificent, the magician who opened for them on their double bill, and left Gabby all alone.

Figures, Gabby thought, taking note of the malevolent sparkle, hard and all too familiar, that had come into her mother's eye at the mention of Amanda's name. *Just when I get used to having Amanda around, Viola's going to run her off. So long, Amanda Farraday. Nice knowing you.*

"Aren't you listening to the broadcast?" Viola dropped Gabby's hands abruptly. The *Viola Preston Nurturing Mother Variety Hour* was over for another day.

"What broadcast?"

"Gabrielle, *please*. You know exactly which one."

"It's not on for another hour at least."

"Still, I don't know why we bought you that expensive radio if you're never going to bother using it."

"You mean the radio *I* bought," Gabby said hotly. "And I do use it. Just not in the middle of the night. It's called having consideration for other people. You should try it sometime."

11

Viola shrugged, but there was a crafty gleam in her eye. "It's not because of that Sterling girl, is it? Because honestly, Gabby, you're going to have to get over that. It only makes you look small. Margo Sterling is going to be nominated for the Oscar this morning, and when the newspapers call, you're going to tell every one of them how thrilled you are for her. After all, the two of you are the best of friends, and there's no reason why you shouldn't be. It wasn't Margo who stole your part in *An American Girl*, was it?"

Gabby felt her jaw clench. Viola always knew how to land a punch.

"No," her mother continued, answering her own question, "*that* fast little piece is right here, sleeping under your very own roof."

"And you invited her."

"God knows what I was thinking." Viola sighed. "I've got too big a heart, I guess. Never could refuse shelter to a stray, that's me."

"Right. You're a regular Christian martyr."

"But there's no telling what she'll have up that Paris-cut sleeve of hers next," Viola continued. "I just think it's an unnecessary risk. Why keep her around, soaking up the spotlight?"

Gabby felt an angry flush spring to her cheeks. "You think I can't hold my own next to Amanda?"

"I know the cheapest rhinestone sparkles more than the rarest pearl," Viola said calmly. "It's only once you've taken it home that you realize it's worthless. I'm simply thinking of what's best for you. You're the real talent, Gabby. I just want to make sure you get your chance to shine."

Viola's eyes were shining now, bright with unshed tears, and not for the first time Gabby thought her mother was the one who should have been the actress. *Deep down, I'm pretty sure she thinks the same thing.* "Me too."

Smiling beatifically, Viola fixed her moist gaze on the clear glass vial of green pills on Gabby's vanity. "I don't suppose you're going back to sleep, are you?"

Gabby snorted. "I don't suppose so."

"Where's that Eddie Sharp record? The one the studio sent over?"

Shrugging, Gabby pointed toward the stack of records on the polished lid of the cherrywood radio. Viola rummaged through them until she found the one she was looking for, buried near the bottom.

"Gabby!" she exclaimed, holding up the brown paper sleeve accusingly. "It's still sealed! You haven't even *opened* it."

"So what?"

"So *what?*" Viola's eyes blazed. "You think Olympus puts any old bandleader under contract? They know what they're doing. Eddie Sharp is going to be the next big thing. Bigger than Glenn Miller. Bigger than Benny Goodman."

"So what?"

"Say 'so what' again, Gabrielle, and I'm going to knock you one, I swear it," Viola hissed. "You may think you're too high and mighty to care about him, but believe you me, Leo Karp cares. And if Leo Karp asks you to sing at the Governor's Ball, whether it's with the New York Philharmonic or some jug band they dug up out of the swamp, you better care about that too."

The Governor's Ball. It was the most glittering evening of the Hollywood social calendar, an invitation even more coveted than one to the awards ceremony itself. Gabby had imagined making her grand entrance in the Crystal Ballroom of the Biltmore Hotel with a golden statuette gleaming in her hand. Instead, she was going to be crouched in the darkness in some hastily arranged backstage holding area, waiting to be shoved in front of the glamorous crowd to perform like a trained monkey. "He just asked me to sing a couple of songs," Gabby said. "It's no big deal. It's not like it's an *audition*."

Viola gave a short bark of a laugh. "Oh, but, my dear, that's *exactly* what it is. That room is going to be filled with every important person in Hollywood. Powerful people. People who could give you everything you've ever dreamed of, or take it all away for good." She seized a silver letter opener from the leather blotter on Gabby's unused secretary desk and shoved it roughly into her daughter's hand. "Open that record and get to work. You're rehearsing with him tomorrow, and you'd better know the music."

"But I want to get some sleep," Gabby said. "I'm tired."

"Oh, darling." Viola flashed her most charming smile. "So what?"

TWO

"And the Oscar goes to . . ."

On the rose-covered stage of the cavernous ballroom of the Biltmore Hotel, Spencer Tracy stood in an immaculately cut tuxedo, flashing a mischievous grin at the audience as he broke open the fateful missive's golden seal. He read the name inside, gave a knowing little shake of his head, and took a deep breath before he lifted his famous, grinning face back to the camera.

"Margo Sterling, for *The Nine Days' Queen*."

The scream of joy bursting from Margo's throat was almost completely drowned out by a deafening sea of applause. All around her, friends and colleagues were leaping to their feet, their faces jubilant. Leo Karp, the powerful chief of Olympus Studios. Larry Julius, the head of the omniscient press department and the man who'd discovered her. Raoul Kurtzman, her beloved director, and Harry Gordon, the brilliant screenwriter, cheering proudly as they held their own statuettes aloft. Jimmy Molloy, Olympus's biggest box-office star (and its smallest in stature), standing on his chair, whistling with two fingers in his mouth. Her friends and rivals, Gabby Preston and Amanda Farraday, looking simultaneously thrilled and like they'd been sucking on lemons.

And in the middle of everyone, as clear as though they had a spotlight shining on them, Lowell and Helen Frobisher, Margo's parents. She hadn't seen them since they'd angrily disowned her when she'd forsaken stuffy Pasadena society for a chance at Hollywood stardom. No daughter of theirs was going to be anything so disreputable as an actress, they had declared, and if she was going to be one, then she wasn't going to be their daughter anymore; it was as simple and as terrible as that.

But here they were, their cheeks wet, their arms outstretched. Cheering her as loudly as anyone, as though they couldn't be prouder of her, as though this had been their dream all along.

Margo felt tears course down her own face as she rose to her feet. Slowly, she made her way to the podium, where the beaming Mr. Tracy held the Oscar out to her. . . .

Somehow, she didn't seem to be making any progress. She felt as if she'd gotten stuck on the same conveyer belt as Charlie Chaplin in *Modern Times*. The ground beneath her was rolling, keeping her from moving forward, no matter how many steps she took. Margo looked down.

The entire floor of the Biltmore ballroom was covered in oranges. Hundreds, maybe thousands of them. Sticky juice pooled around her feet, seeping into her satin evening slippers. She tried to yank her trailing skirt out of the pulp, but her gown had mysteriously disappeared, replaced by the voluminous green bloomers of the famously unflattering gym uniform of Pasadena's Orange Grove Academy for Young Ladies. *My old gym suit?* Margo thought, frantically. *I just won an Oscar and I showed up in my gym suit?* The roar of the crowd was getting louder, less distinct, filling her ears until she thought her brain would burst out of her skull. . . .

Margo's eyes flew open as she sat straight up in bed. The room was flooded with early-morning sunlight; the rushing sound in her ears was nothing more than the waves of the Pacific Ocean crashing against the Malibu coastline. *It was a dream,* she thought, her heart pounding. *Just a dream.*

Beside her on the bed, Dane twitched. "Margo," he muttered thickly.

"What?"

"Go back to sleep."

"I can't."

"Try."

He pulled her body toward his, burrowing warmly against her. Forcing her eyes shut, Margo took a few deep breaths, trying to find her way back into slumber with the safe, familiar feeling of his strong arms around her, the pressure of his chest against her back.

It was no use. "I told you, I can't. I'm too nervous."

Dane let out a guttural sigh. He'd been filming a Western for the past few weeks, and the deep tawny suntan he'd acquired during the long hours spent in the sun made his eyes look more vividly green than ever.

"Margo, there's no point," he muttered. "There's nothing you can do. Driving yourself crazy isn't going to change what happens."

17

"But Larry Julius said he'd call either way," Margo insisted. "Maybe he already did and we missed the call. Maybe George is still asleep."

George was Dane's butler, or "house manager," as he preferred to call himself, thinking it was a title more suited to his station. There was no one to tell him otherwise. Apart from Gloria, a skittish girl who came in twice a week to clean and spoke not a word of English, Dane Forrest employed no other servants. The private strip of sandy Malibu beach that served as the backyard needed no gardener. He drove himself everywhere, and having painfully traded a large chunk of her savings for a new silvery-blue 1939 Plymouth convertible, Margo did the same. On the rare evenings they found themselves dining in, they ate the simple meals—scrambled eggs, cold sandwiches, baked beans cooked hobo-style in a tin over the fire—Dane prepared from the single box of groceries George ordered each week.

"After all, I'm just a no-account farm boy," Dane said, only half jokingly, when questioned about the simplicity of his life-style, so at odds with the opulence with which most picture stars surrounded themselves. "Who needs a swimming pool when you've got the ocean? Who needs a ballroom when you've got the stars and the sand? I don't want to forget where I came from."

But in the five months—almost six—since they'd officially been a couple, Margo had begun to draw a different conclusion from the strangely silent beach house with its careless bachelor ambience and conspicuous lack of visitors: Dane Forrest, one of Hollywood's most popular leading men and bon vivants, didn't like having people around very much.

Except me, Margo thought firmly. *He likes me.*

Sometimes it was still hard to believe it had all really happened—that it *was* happening. Almost exactly a year ago, Margo Sterling had been Margaret Frobisher, a starstruck schoolgirl on the other side of the mountain in Pasadena, sleeping with Dane Forrest's picture over her bed. Now, every night, she was actually sleeping in his.

And not just sleeping, either. Margo and Dane had done things Margo was raised to believe she would only do once she was married—if then.

Except for one thing. One very important thing.

You could take the young lady out of the Orange Grove Academy it seemed, but you couldn't quite take the Orange Grove Academy out of the young lady. At least, not all of it.

God knows I want to. After all, this was hedonistic Hollywood, not prudish Pasadena. Sex was just par for the course.

Yet somehow, Margo just *couldn't*. She'd try to relax, to let herself go, but some part of her would just clamp up, until the whole exercise seemed much more painful trouble than it was worth. *Funny,* she thought. Back when she thought Dane was in love with Diana Chesterfield, she would have done anything to make him happy, would have given herself to him in a heartbeat, no matter the cost. Now that she had him and wanted to keep him, something inside her just couldn't . . . well, couldn't *unclench.*

But it would. It had to. Dane hadn't gotten around to mentioning marriage yet, but surely it was just a matter of time. Even in Hollywood, you couldn't just invite a girl to practically *live* with you for months and then *not* marry her. And as soon as he did—as soon as Margo knew she was *safe*—she'd open up just like a flower. "Remember, girls," Miss Schoonmaker had once said during one particularly excruciating Poise and Presence class, "the ring is the key that unlocks the treasure chest."

Dane's shoulders were bare. The new muscles hewn from weeks of roping cattle bulged beneath his smooth skin.

Let's just hope the ring comes very soon, Margo thought.

Dane groaned. "Margo, George gets up at the crack of dawn. Before, even. When it's still dark."

"Maybe he stepped outside for a minute," Margo suggested. "Or went to the bathroom. Or maybe he did answer the phone and he just didn't put it through because he didn't want to wake *us* up."

With another groan, Dane propped himself up against the headboard, the white bedsheet tangled around his bare chest like a Roman toga. Rolling his eyes at Margo, he reached for the house phone on the nightstand.

"George," he muttered into the receiver. "Yes, we're awake. . . . Have there been any calls this morning? . . . Well, if there are, could you let us know right away? Poor Margie is practically eating her own skin off with nerves."

Margo winced inwardly. Try as she might, she couldn't quite get used to the informality with which Dane spoke to the help. It was almost like he didn't realize that George worked for *him*.

"All right. Thank you, George." Dane hung up. "He said he'll put it straight through as soon as it comes. Feel better?"

"Not really."

"Well." Dane turned toward her, the exasperation in his face giving way to a naughty twinkle. "In that case, maybe we can think of some way to keep your mind off it."

"Oh, can we?"

"Mmm. We'd better think about it very seriously. Very, very seriously indeed."

Giggling, Margo arched her back, pressing her body against his as she met his kiss. The long, lingering mornings in bed were really the best thing, the best part of being with Dane. Even if you couldn't quite get rid of the voice that told you nice girls didn't go all the way, there were still plenty of things you could do. *No wonder they don't tell you about any of those in school,* Margo thought breathlessly. *If they did, you'd never want to do anything else.* She just hoped they were enough for him. She explored his mouth hungrily, trying to kiss away her doubt, feeling herself begin to relax into his embrace. *Maybe this is it,* she thought, sighing at the feel of his calloused hands on her skin. *Maybe this time it's all going to come together.*

The phone rang.

Dane was up like a shot to answer it. Eyes widening, he turned to Margo, covering the receiver with his hand. *"It's the studio."*

Margo sat straight up, her heart beating so hard she thought it was going to burst out of her nightgown in a bloody mess. This was it, all right. Just a different kind of *it.*

"Yes." Dane nodded. "Yes, I see. Well, thank you so much for calling. I appreciate it." He hung up the phone.

"What?" Margo practically shouted. "What did they say?"

"That was my line producer. Seems I'm off today. Some kind of problem with the locations, so they have to rejig the shooting schedule."

"Oh." Margo felt cold. *How dare they call with something like that, this morning of all mornings?* "Oh, I see."

"I can't say I mind," Dane said sexily. "Now. Where were we?"

He dropped his face back to Margo's. His kisses were growing more urgent now. In spite of her nervousness—or maybe because of it—Margo felt her breathing grow shallow as Dane's warm hands began creeping their way back up her nightgown, exploring what was underneath. . . .

The phone rang again.

Margo froze. "Answer it."

Dane's lips were buried in her neck. "Oh, baby, come on. It's just my producer again. If he changed his mind about me going in today, I don't want to know about it."

"*Dane.*" Margo jerked roughly out of his embrace. "*Answer it.*"

Dane seized the receiver. "*Yes?*" he snapped tersely. "*Oh.*" His breath caught in his throat. "Larry. Hello."

Larry! Margo stopped breathing.

"No, no, of course I didn't forget," Dane was saying. "No . . . oh." His eyebrows shot up. "Oh. Well. I see. No, that's . . . that's quite something. . . . Yes. Of course. Well, thank you for calling. . . . Yes. I appreciate that. I'll see you soon."

Dane hung up the phone. Margo lay motionless beneath the covers, too terrified to move. "Well?" she gasped finally. "What . . . what did he say?"

Dane didn't seem to see her. His face was deadly pale and his eyes looked as wet and unfocused as a newborn's.

"It seems," he began, in a soft, small voice, "it seems I've been nominated for an Academy Award. For *The Nine Days' Queen.*"

You? Margo wanted to scream. *What about me?* "That . . . that's incredible," she stammered instead.

"I can't believe it." Dane's hands were shaking. He looked

22

down at them stupidly, as though they belonged to somebody else. "I just can't . . . I mean, who would have thought?"

Not me, Margo thought meanly.

Not that Dane hadn't been perfectly marvelous in his five scenes as Lord Guilford Dudley, nearly all of which had been filmed prior to Margo's being cast in the leading role of Lady Jane Grey after the original star, Diana Chesterfield, had disappeared without a trace. But he'd barely been mentioned as more than a "typically handsome presence" (*The New York Times*) who "puts his matinee-idol profile to good use" (*Variety*) in any of the notices, let alone in any of the lead-up speculation about just who might have a chance with one of the little gold men who were suddenly the hottest date in town.

"Dane," she ventured carefully, "that's wonderful, and I'm so happy for you. But . . . Larry didn't say anything about me, did he?"

Dane looked at her with surprise, as though he'd forgotten she was there. "You? No. He didn't say anything about you."

Margo's heart was racing. "Nothing" was hardly the same thing as "no." Maybe he'd just gotten the news about Dane first and didn't want to wait until the full nominations were in. Or maybe Dane had hung up the phone in shock before Larry could finish talking. Maybe he was going to call back any minute. *Or maybe . . .*

"He doesn't know I'm here!" Margo shouted, her face flushed. "He's probably been trying to call the bungalow! He must have been calling for ages and wondering why he didn't get an answer."

"The radio," Dane said at once. "They announce the nominations on the radio."

23

"What time is it? Oh God, they've already started!"

With a shriek, Margo leapt out of bed and ran out the door and down the long corridor to the kitchen. For reasons that had never quite been made clear to her, Dane insisted on keeping the only wireless in the house in the pantry "for George to listen to." Dane padded behind her, still looking stunned as he pulled on his robe.

George jumped in astonishment at the sight of the house's nominal mistress bursting into the pantry unannounced in a transparent nightgown, her hair standing on end like a wild woman's.

"Marg . . . I mean, Miss . . . Is there something . . ."

"The radio," she croaked. "I need the radio."

She shoved him out of the way, wrenching the dial from the sedate breakfast program he liked to listen to in which a couple of British people bickered pleasantly over the merits of marmalade versus jam, until the static gave way to the familiar voice of Frank Capra, the director who was currently serving his final term as president of the Academy of Motion Picture Arts and Sciences.

"And now, for the acting nominations."

Mr. Capra's voice was ebullient as usual, but it hit Margo like a splash of icy water to the face. She drew her breath in sharply.

"For the Academy Award for Best Actor, the nominees are as follows," he continued. "Spencer Tracy, for *Boys Town*. Charles Boyer, for *Algiers*. James Cagney, for *Angels with Dirty Faces*. Dane Forrest, for *The Nine Days' Queen*."

"Mr. Forrest!" George jumped about three feet in the air. "My God! We have to celebrate! I'll make a special breakfast; we'll open a bottle of champagne—"

"George! Be quiet!"

The house manager's face fell.

"Sorry, pal," Dane said in a loud stage whisper, shooting him an apologetic look. "The dame's a little antsy, what can I tell you?"

"I said, be quiet! That goes for you too."

". . . and Leslie Howard, for *Pygmalion*. And now, the nominees for the Best Actress award."

Margo felt her blood run hot and cold all at once, like a tornado was going to start swirling inside her. Dane reached for her hand, but she swatted him away.

"Bette Davis, for *Jezebel*." *No surprise there.* The whole town had been saying Davis was a shoo-in for a nomination, if not the big prize itself, for more than a year, since Margo was still mooning over movie magazines at the soda counter at Schwab's.

"Fay Bainter, for *White Banners*." That was more unexpected. Bainter was a character actress with the kind of face, as studio bigwigs like to say, that had "Best Supporting" written all over it. Usually cast as kindly mothers and spinster aunts, she was hardly the kind of glamour puss for which the Academy liked to reserve its highest honor.

"Wendy Hiller, for *Pygmalion*."

"That's the British girl," George chimed in knowledgeably. "I thought she made a spectacular Eliza Doolittle. She played the role on the West End as well—they talked all about it on *Breakfast with Irene and Roger*. Apparently, she's a special protégée of the great Mr. Shaw himself."

Well, bully for Wendy Hiller, Margo thought. Anyone could be swell in a part they'd already played before. And George Bernard Shaw might be the Greatest Living Writer in the English

Language, but after a grueling semester listening to Mr. Overstreet, the frustrated former actor who taught English literature at Orange Grove, read *Caesar and Cleopatra* in a phony British accent, Margo found his work a little pedantic for her taste. Caesar and Cleo didn't even wind up together, or come to a tragic end. *Give me Shakespeare any day.* At least *he* knew how to write a proper romance.

"That's good." Dane squeezed Margo's hand, in spite of her earlier rebuff. "Howard got the nod too. It means they're putting up costars this year. It's a good sign."

"Norma Shearer, for *Marie Antoinette.*"

"Well, of course," Margo said aloud. They couldn't let the year go by without heaping accolades on Irving Thalberg's widow, even in a part she was at least fifteen years too old for in a movie that was dull as dirt. It was time for some fresh blood at MGM, all right. Garbo, Crawford, and Hepburn, their three other huge female stars, had all been labeled "box-office poison" last year. As for Shearer, well, Sainted Irving, the boy genius, had been dead since 1936. How much longer was it going to take for Louis B. Mayer to admit to himself that the woman simply could not act?

". . . and Margaret Sullavan, for *Three Comrades,*" Frank Capra finished. "Now, onto the supporting categories. For Best Actor in a Supporting Role, Walter Brennan, for . . ."

Quietly, Dane reached over her shoulder and switched off the wireless.

They didn't pick me.

It hit Margo like a bucket of ice water in the face. She'd been so sure. Everyone had been so sure. Larry Julius's office had already written her gushing, tastefully tearful "it's an honor just to be nominated" statement for immediate release to the press. Rex Mandalay himself had begun preliminary sketches for her gown. The studio had spent thousands of dollars ordering and distributing prints of *The Nine Days' Queen* all over town, so every Academy member could have the luxury of watching Margo Sterling's star-making performance in the comfort of their own private projection rooms. It didn't matter. It hadn't worked.

Except, Margo thought darkly, *except for Dane.*

And somehow that made it all so much worse.

Margo felt her face flush. Her vision grew blurry, and a moment later, the fat, hot tears spilled down her face, slowly at first, then in floods. Before she knew it, she was wailing, sobbing like a baby denied its bottle.

Dane's arm was around her. "George," he said quietly, "please fetch Miss Sterling's robe from the bedroom. Margo, come with me."

The house manager gratefully fled. Still blinded by tears, Margo obediently let Dane lead her out of the kitchen and down the hallway to his small, dark study. He settled her on the leather chaise and poured a glass of brandy from the cut-glass decanter set carelessly on a pile of important-looking documents on the paper-strewn desk. "Drink it," he commanded Margo.

"Dane, we haven't even had breakfast yet."

"I don't care. Drink it. All of it."

Margo drank. The brandy burned a fiery path down her throat, spreading warmth through her chest.

"Better?" Dane was watching her closely. "Need another one?"

She shook her head. "I'm afraid I'll be sick."

"Fine."

Running a hand through his mussed hair, Dane briskly paced the length of the room before coming back to stand in front of Margo on the chaise.

"Now listen carefully, sweetheart, because I'm not going to say this twice. This is *one* year. *The Nine Days' Queen* was your first picture. You'll have plenty of chances. The studio picked up the option on your contract, you've got two pictures in the can . . ."

"Girlfriend parts." Margo sniffed. "Silly schoolgirls, simpering debutantes. And nothing on the horizon. They're talking about that *Madame Bovary* remake that Kurtzman wants to do, but . . ." She shook her head furiously. "I swear, Dane, it's like I'm going backward. One minute I'm playing the lead role in one of the biggest dramas of the year, the next I'm standing around in some snowball of an evening dress, batting my eyes at Jimmy Molloy while I tell him how swell it is he wants to put on a show in Grampa's barn. Not that there aren't plenty of good parts around, but they're sure not giving them to me. David Selznick wouldn't even see me for Scarlett O'Hara. My God, he must have tested every hatcheck girl and taxi dancer in town, and he wouldn't so much as let me read!"

"And why should he have?" Dane asked. "Because you hit the jackpot the first time you played the slots? That makes you lucky, Margo. It doesn't make you good."

"You don't think I'm good?" Margo felt her eyes start to swim again.

"Of course I think you're good. We wouldn't be here if you weren't good. You don't think I let the lousy actresses stay for breakfast, do you?"

28

Dane grinned. Margo didn't crack a smile.

"But we both know you've still got a lot to learn," he continued, "and because you're lucky, you're going to get a chance to. A chance a million girls would kill for, and not metaphorically either." His tone softened. "I'm sorry, baby. I know how much you wanted this, but you're going to have another chance. This just wasn't your year."

Margo wiped her nose. "Do you think the studio is terribly disappointed?"

Dane gave a short grunt. "I don't think, I *know*. That's why everything you do from now on is so important. No matter how you feel, Margo, you've got to go around for the next four weeks with your head held high. You're going to go out every night, laughing and dancing as if you were the happiest girl in the world. When the reporters ask you, you'll tell them how thrilled you are for all the nominees, and how you can only dream of one day even being considered to join their august company. You're going to float into that ceremony at the Biltmore on my arm looking so gorgeous that no one is going to give a second glance to Shearer or Davis or whatever dried-up bag of bones they give the goddamn statue to. And you're going to do whatever Rex Mandalay or Larry Julius or Leo Karp tells you to. You've got to keep them all on your side." Gently, he took the empty glass from her hand. "The clock had to strike for Cinderella sometime, Margie. You've been in Hollywood long enough to know that all the real acting happens offscreen."

Margo's mind felt fuzzy. On her empty morning stomach, the brandy had gone straight to her head. She nodded carefully, as though she were trying not to dislodge anything that ought not to move. "I understand."

"Good." Dane walked behind the scarred mahogany desk. "Look. There's something else, something I wanted to . . ."

He trailed off, looking down at the piles of papers. The blind over the single window was closed, but even in the dim light Margo thought she saw a blush creeping up over his neck.

"I don't know if this is the best time," Dane continued, "but what the hell. Maybe it'll cheer you up." He slid open a drawer and retrieved a small object. Smiling shyly, he held it out to Margo.

It was a square velvet jewelry box.

The kind that only meant one thing.

Margo's mouth flew open. Could it be? Had he been planning this all along?

"Oh, Dane . . ."

"Open it," he urged. "Go on."

With trembling hands, Margo caressed the little box, wanting to make the moment last as long as possible, imagining the tears that would spring to her eyes, the delighted gasp she would make as she caught her first glimpse of the diamond that would sparkle on her finger for the rest of her life—or a good chunk of it, anyway. She lifted the lid.

It sparkled, all right. But it wasn't a ring.

It was a brooch, no more than an inch square, of pavé diamonds in the shape of the Imperial State Crown of England. A minute gold cross set with pearls emerged from the top. A cabochon sapphire gleamed from the center, where the Black Prince's Ruby would be, and when Margo looked closely, she could just see the faint shimmer of the star winking in the center.

"Oh," she said numbly. "What a lovely thing."

30

Dane beamed, clearly mistaking her confusion for genuine awe. "I've been hanging on to it for ages. I ordered it especially from Cartier; apparently they do all the ice for that Mrs. Simpson, the one who married the king of England. I thought maybe it could replace that little one with the pearls that you always used to wear, the one that got lost?"

The pin that got lost.

The little gold-and-pearl circle pin had been her favorite, a family heirloom given to her by her parents for her sixteenth birthday. She'd worn it as sort of a good-luck charm whenever she needed to feel particularly brave—which in Hollywood was a *lot*—until it went missing on the lawn of the Pasadena Country Club that horrible night at her former friend Doris Winthrop's coming-out party when Phipps McKendrick, her former beau, had tried to force himself on her.

Luckily, she'd been rescued in the nick of time when her driver, Arthur, heard her scream, but there had been a terrible scene. The crowd had rallied around Phipps—who after all was the son of one of Pasadena's most prominent families, while Margo had shamed her family by running off to become an actress, which as far as they were concerned was no better than being a whore—and Margo found herself cast out of the world into which she had been born once and for all.

It was sweet of Dane to recognize how much the pin had meant to her, but what he didn't know was that it wasn't lost at all. It had been anonymously returned to Margo, tucked into a blank envelope along with a brief, cryptic note, unsigned and in an unfamiliar hand. Margo had never found out who sent it. Even the thought of making inquiries dredged up memories of things she'd just as soon forget. As for the pin, she'd never worn it again, could barely even look at it. It was too potent a reminder of her old life, of a world in which she was no longer welcome. Any good luck it had held for her was gone. Still in its mysterious envelope, it now lay—along with her old school tie and unused yellow autograph book—out of sight in the back of her closet in the studio bungalow, buried in a shoe box like a little cardboard coffin.

"I wanted to give it to you at the premiere," Dane said, "but it wasn't ready yet, so I figured I'd wait until a special occasion. Now's as good a time as any, I guess. Do you really like it?"

It's a funny thing about letdowns. They're always so much worse than never expecting anything at all. "It's lovely," Margo repeated. "Really lovely."

"Good." Dane beamed. "Now let's have a real drink. I just got nominated for an Oscar!"

THREE

Dear Harry,
I've written so many letters to you by now, you'd almost think I'd have run out of things to say.
But I haven't. In fact, with every letter I write, I

"Ugh," Amanda Farraday said, crumpling the vellum notepaper and tossing it to the floor in disgust. Chewing her bottom lip, she twirled a lock of copper hair around her finger and reached for a new sheet.

Dear Harry,
Congratulations on being nominated for the screenwriting Oscar. I can't tell you

how proud it makes me to write those
words. I only wish you would let me be
there to

No. Amanda started again.

Harry,
You once told me that the sole
responsibility of a writer is to be clear.
Well, you've done a good job, I guess.
You've certainly made it clear over these
last few months that you don't want to
see me.
Now let me be clear: I don't care. I
don't care if you don't want to talk to
me, if you never want to set eyes on me
again. There's only one thing I care
about. That I love you, and I always will.
And I know, deep down, that you

Not right either. With a sigh, Amanda folded the unfinished note and slid it into the bulging packet with all the others.

How many letters were there now? At least a hundred, maybe closer to two hundred. She'd been writing them to Harry Gordon for months, at least one a day since he'd left. Amanda had explained everything in the uneven scribbles on those sheets of paper, things she'd never told another living soul. What had made her run away from her stepfather's farm in Oklahoma when she was fourteen years old, and why she could never go back. How she'd finally hitchhiked her way to Hollywood with no more than fifty dollars sewn into the hem of her dress, and just what she'd had to do for them. How she'd lived when she got here. About just what a person could do, if they were scared enough and hungry enough. How long days spent hustling for a scrap to eat and long nights spent searching for a bed could make a certain kind of girl think that working for someone like Olive Moore was like stumbling on a little piece of heaven.

She'd written her whole life into those letters; they could fill an entire book. *If Harry only read them, he'd understand everything.*

But Amanda had never sent them, not after the first one came back unopened and practically broke her heart all over again.

Yet she kept writing them, and after a while, she started being less afraid that Harry wouldn't read them and more afraid that he *would*. There were some things she wasn't ready for anyone to know yet. Maybe she never would be. A girl like Amanda needed her secrets to survive.

Survival. How had she gotten back here again? From the moment, almost a year ago, that Amanda had proudly scrawled her signature on the dotted line of the standard Olympus Studio new player's contract, she had thought that that part of her life was over. That the scrambling and desperation and shame were things of the past; that for the first time in her nineteen years, she would be free.

Because she would be *safe*. Freedom and safety—weren't they really the same thing?

But that, she saw now, was about as much a pipe dream as becoming a star. Oh sure, she still had the contract. The checks still arrived every other week at the Olympus post office, smelling of ink and ready for immediate deposit at the Olympus bank.

But for how much longer? The twelve-month option on her contract was almost up, and soon she would have to face the very real possibility that it would not be renewed. After all, girls like Amanda didn't get by in Hollywood on their talent—at least, not in the traditional sense. She should have been painting the town red every night at La Maze and Vendome and the Cocoanut Grove, always on the arm of a different man who was famous or powerful or preferably both, getting her picture in the gossip columns and full-color photo spreads in *Photoplay* and *Modern Screen* and *Picture Palace*, until the public expected— rather, *demanded*—to see her on movie screens as well.

But falling in love with Harry had put the kibosh on that. He wanted her all to himself, and she'd been only too happy to comply. *And I got screwed*, Amanda thought bitterly. *In all senses of the word.*

Broken heart aside, even if by some miracle the studio decided to pick up the option on her contract, it wouldn't solve any of her problems. As much as Amanda hated to admit it, her old boss Olive Moore had been right: seventy-five dollars a week was less than nothing when you had hair and nail appointments and needed a new evening gown every time you so much as went out to dinner. Paris fashions didn't come cheap. An anointed studio princess like Margo Sterling could borrow whatever she needed from an ever-obliging wardrobe department. As for the rest of the hungry young starlets occupying considerably less lofty places in the Hollywood firmament . . . well, that was what buying on credit was invented for.

And boy, have I become an expert on that. The pale blue en-

36

velopes from the Olympus payroll department were almost crowded out of her P.O. box by notices from Saks and Bullock's and I. Magnin, informing her that her bills were mounting, her accounts past due, asking in increasingly threatening language when they might expect to get paid.

At least, she assumed that was what they said. Lately she'd taken to stuffing them, still sealed, into an overflowing hatbox at the bottom of her wardrobe. Or rather, Gabby's wardrobe. That was one good thing about not having her own place. You couldn't have creditors banging down your door if you didn't have one.

And now there was this: an envelope she couldn't leave unopened. It had been stuffed under the bedroom door early that morning while she feigned sleep. Even if she hadn't noticed the way her hostesses suddenly seemed to drop their conversation to a whisper when they caught sight of her, or how Viola fixed her with a Stare of Death every time she opened the icebox for so much as a drop of milk, Amanda was pretty sure she knew what was inside this envelope too. You didn't live the life she'd led without knowing an eviction notice.

Sighing, she slipped her finger under the flap and drew out the note.

Deer Amanda, it read, in Gabby's childlike, uneasy scrawl that no amount of intermittent government-mandated instruction at the Olympus schoolhouse had been able to correct. I am so vairy sorry to say this, but I gess you knew it was coming some day. Viola says you have been here long enuf and that it is tim for you to find another place to say. I am really sorry and I hope this is okay. I also hope we can stil be frends, if you want. I hope so. Love, Gabby.

Typically, Gabby had signed her name with a flourish, not so much a signature as an autograph, identical to the one the studio press department stamped on the publicity shots they sent to fans. Amanda almost laughed out loud. *Poor Gabby*, she thought. Her name was probably the only thing she could write without major deliberation.

Sighing, Amanda started taking her things out of the wardrobe and laying them on the bed. *So many beautiful clothes*, she thought, *and so much beautiful money*. Every piece really ought to be left on a hanger and stuffed with tissue paper to preserve its shape before it was packed, but Amanda couldn't be bothered. *That's how depressed I am. I can't even care about my clothes.*

There was a soft rap on the door.

"Come in."

Gabby pushed the door open shyly. In a plaid jumper, twisting a chestnut curl around her stubby finger, she looked about eight years old. Her huge brown eyes followed Amanda's movements around the room. "I guess you got my note."

"Obviously."

"I hope you could read it. I'm not a very good speller."

"Don't worry. I got the gist."

"Viola was going to write it, you know, but I made her let me. I thought she wouldn't . . . well, I thought she might say something that wasn't so nice."

"I appreciate that."

Gabby sat down on the bed. "You don't have to go right now, you know. You can wait a few days."

Amanda frowned at the feathered hat in her hand, trying to

remember which hatbox it belonged in. "I don't know. I think it's better this way."

"But where will you go?"

"A hotel, I guess. Or a friend's house. Don't worry."

"Maybe the studio will put you up. Maybe you could stay in Margo's bungalow. She's at Dane Forrest's house all the time now anyway."

Amanda laughed. "I don't think anyone had better let the studio know about that."

"I'm awfully sorry, Amanda, really." Gabby looked stricken. "It's Viola who wants you out, not me. Believe it or not, I like having you here. Like I said, I hope we'll still be friends."

"I know." If anyone had told Amanda a year ago she'd be hearing these words from that snotty little Gabby Preston, she'd have laughed in her face. But looking at the girl now, gazing up at her with those puppy-dog eyes, Amanda knew she really meant it. That was one of the good things about Gabby; she was too high on the intoxicating cocktail of pills and her own self-importance to say anything she didn't mean. She might be a self-obsessed, spoiled little brat, but at least she was an honest one. "I know," Amanda repeated.

Gabby gave her a smile of heartbreaking sweetness. "Good. I'm glad." She reached into the pocket of her skirt. "Here. I thought you might want to see this."

Amanda took the folded sheet of paper from Gabby. It was a page torn from a movie magazine—*Picture Palace*, from the typeface—bearing the boldfaced headline:

Tinseltown's Most Eligible Bachelors!

She sighed. "Really, Gabby?"

"Just read it." Gabby was already nosing around the wardrobe. Apparently, she felt Amanda's reassurance of their continued friendship had given her license to rummage through her things. "I didn't have time. I just saw the picture and ripped it out for you."

Smoothing out the creases, Amanda scanned the page. It had been ages since she had picked up a movie magazine. She knew they were designed to distract people from their troubles, but somehow the giddy superficiality, the endless gossip, the breathless Q&A's with hopeful young stars whose answers were so identical and relentlessly positive—"What do I love most about making movies? Everything!"—because they'd been scripted by a bunch of junior studio flacks in between bourbons at the Brown Derby, made Amanda feel so much worse. How could life go on when her world had been shattered? How could anyone be happy when her heart was so irreparably broken?

But this story was different. Because of one little thing:

Bachelor #3: Harry Gordon

Amanda let out a gasp.

Recently nominated for his first Academy Award for *The Nine Days' Queen,* the flick that made him one of the hottest writers in town, our Black-Eyed Brooklyn Boy ought to be on top of the world, or at least on top of any number of starlets, if you catch our drift.

Amanda caught it, all right. She winced at the thought.

"This is pretty," Gabby said, holding out an old black cocktail dress with a sweetheart neckline and diamond buttons at the back. "Is this Mainbocher? I always wanted a Mainbocher dress, but Viola says they're too expensive."

"Keep it."

"Really?" Gabby squealed

Anything to get you to be quiet. "Sure. I can't take everything with me."

"It won't fit me now. But it will. I'm going to see how it looks with my red hat."

"There's a black one that goes with it. And gloves. You can have those too."

Gabby rushed off to her bedroom with a squeal of thanks, clutching her prizes to her chest. Amanda read on:

But ever since his trip to Splitsville with Titian-haired Olympus sexpot Amanda Farraday (where's she been, anyway?), young Mr. Gordon has been seen in a number of Party Palaces for Picture People looking noticeably downcast . . . and with a noticeably empty escorting arm. Hopefuls of Hollywood, speaking to you as a Starstruck Sister, can't you find an open spot on your busy dance cards for poor wittle Hawwy? Who knows? Liven up his lonely nights and there might even be a part in it for you . . . just steer clear of the mysteriously missing Miss Farraday. Redheads have a temper, you know.

That was all Amanda needed to see.

Gleefully, she planted a huge smack on the smudged leaf of

paper and laid it on her pillow as carefully as if it were a sleeping child. Then she walked back to the wardrobe and took a good, long look in the mirror for the first time in weeks.

Her figure, always fashionably slim, looked scrawny. Her bright hair was disheveled and desperately in need of a wash. Her once creamy skin was deathly pale, and there were violet bags under her eyes from endless tears and sleepless nights.

But, she thought as she hauled her battered Louis Vuitton monogrammed steamer trunk from under the bed, *all that can be fixed.*

She'd eat a few big meals, rich with butter and cream. Her hair would be perfumed and set. As for her famously gorgeous face, all it needed was a little rouge and powder and a few nights of good sleep.

And I'll sleep now. Wherever she wound up that night, she'd sleep like a baby.

Because everything was going to be all right. The evidence was right there, literally in black-and-white.

Harry Gordon was still hers.

And all she had to do was turn herself back into the girl he'd fallen in love with. She'd make him forget all about her past. She'd make him remember that she was the answer to all of his prayers.

It wasn't going to be easy.

But like her old flame Dane Forrest had once told her, "In Hollywood, all the real acting happens offscreen."

fOUR

"How come you never let me drive?"

"Because," Viola Preston said tersely, struggling to pilot the unwieldy Preston family Cadillac along the winding road that led to the gates of the studio. "You don't know how, and you don't have a license."

Gabby pouted at her reflection in the rearview mirror, smoothing her unruly curls with her hand. "I could get one. I'm sixteen. And I *do* know how to drive. I had to drive that old jalopy in *Farm Fancies*, remember? All I'd have to do is go down and take the test."

"And when are we supposed to find the time to do that?" Viola shook her head. "You're scheduled to the hilt as it is. The only time you've got free for months is the middle of the night, and I'm pretty sure the Department of Motor Vehicles isn't open then."

"We could ask them. You never know, they might make an exception for an Olympus star."

Viola chuckled indulgently. "An Olympus star doesn't drive herself. An Olympus star has a chauffeur."

"I suppose that's you. In which case, where the hell is your little hat?"

Viola smiled. "Just remember, Gabrielle, to keep your eye on the prize. We're just about there."

They were turning onto the studio lot now, and Gabby marveled, as she often did, at her mother's uncannily cinematic sense of timing. Even now, there was something about entering Olympus, about being waved through its glittering pink stone gates with their famous iron doors wrought with an elaborate motif of stars and moons and lightning bolts, that made Gabby feel like it was all happening, like everything was suddenly within her grasp. Like all of her dreams were about to come true.

Especially today. Today, she was going to sing for the first time with Eddie Sharp.

It made her laugh now to think what a bitch she'd been about listening to his record. Because the moment she'd gotten over herself and plunked it on the turntable, it was as if her entire world had changed. Gabby closed her eyes for a moment, savoring the memory of the first time she'd heard the plaintive, almost human wail of the clarinet, of the drumbeat that sounded so much like a racing heart. The swinging numbers made you need to dance; the slow ones made you want to weep. It was like the music she'd been waiting for her whole life.

There was a lot Gabby didn't know. She had never really been to school, could barely read and write, couldn't do much

44

with numbers besides figure out how to deduct an agent's percentage. Sometimes she thought she didn't really get *people* very well, didn't understand why they would tell a lie or why they got so mad when you said something aloud that everyone already knew.

But Gabby Preston knew music. She understood it the way she understood that she was happy, or sad, or hungry. She could tell when it was right and when it was wrong as effortlessly as telling green from red or as someone—someone who wasn't her, anyway—might recognize the letter *B* and know what sound it made. And she could tell that Eddie Sharp understood it that way too.

So they would understand each other. They were going to be *incredible* together. Already Gabby had listened to that record, *Sharp Turns Ahead,* twenty, maybe thirty times, working out harmonies and counterpoints, going crazy over how perfectly the velvety tone of her voice blended with the warmth of Eddie's clarinet. It was a match made in music heaven. There was a Jewish word she'd heard Mr. Karp use when he was in one of his sentimental moods, saying how something was destined, ordained by God—*beshert,* she thought it was. He'd been talking about the budget for the latest Jimmy Molloy musical, but it was a good word nonetheless, a good word for how she felt.

Gabby and Eddie were meant to be. It was fate. He'd see that right away, she was sure of it, and maybe when his band went on tour that summer, he'd take her with them.

God, wouldn't that be something? On tour with a band, traveling on her own, playing a million different clubs in a million different cities. Big clubs with women wearing diamonds and men wearing black tie; small clubs that were no more than a couple of field hands drinking corn whiskey in overalls at a splintered table—it didn't matter. For the first time in her life, Gabby would be doing exactly what she wanted to do, which was *sing*. No more hideous dance rehearsals that started at dawn and didn't end until every muscle in her body was screaming with agony. No more hair ribbons and ringlets and frilly little-girl dresses; no more pills to keep her thinner than was humanly possible. She'd be doing the one thing she could do better than anyone else. She'd be a star, and when—*if*—she finally came back to the picture business, it would be on her terms, as a woman who'd traveled, had adventures, had lovers (the fact that the picture of Eddie in last month's issue of *Picture Palace* seemed to get cuter every time she looked at it didn't hurt any either). Hollywood would look at her and see a woman who had *lived*.

Not, Gabby thought darkly, *a girl who has to have her mother drive her everywhere.*

Viola unsteadily piloted the big Cadillac down the narrow brick street lined with jacaranda trees that led to the rehearsal complex behind the studio commissary. A burly man with the build of a gorilla greeted them at the doorway.

"Miss Preston." He nodded at Gabby, dropping ash from his cigar all down the front of his spread-collared sport shirt. "They're expecting you. Go right in."

"Thank you."

Viola started to follow her through the doorway. The man held up a meaty hand. "Not you. You can't come in."

"What?" Viola's eyes, lined with the same heavy kohl she'd been wearing since the Roaring Twenties, when the Egyptian vamp look was the bee's knees, narrowed with rage. "What are you talking about?"

"Just what I said. This is a closed rehearsal."

Viola sputtered, "But . . . but don't you know who I *am*?"

"Lady, I don't care if you're Eleanor Roosevelt, Eddie Sharp rehearses with musicians only. If you ain't a musician, you ain't coming in. Them's the breaks."

"Well." Viola looked around, as though at any moment she expected someone to come bursting out of the bushes to tell her this was a prank. "Well. I want to speak to the music department. I want to speak to Herman Steiner."

"Talk to whoever you want," the man said, in as airy a tone as a six-foot-four gorilla could muster. "I don't know about any Herman Steiner. I work for Eddie Sharp, and how he wants it, that's how I fixes it."

"Well," Viola repeated. "We'll see about that. Come along, Gabby."

Gabby snatched her hand out of her mother's grasp.

"I would, but it's getting late, Vi. Why don't you just go? I'm sure it's only a misunderstanding. By the time you get back, we'll be all rehearsed and you can tell us how swell it sounds."

With a final scowl, Viola stormed off in the direction of Mr. Steiner's office. She was wearing a net hat dotted with small white blossoms that stood out vividly against her bright red hair, making her look for all the world like a plump spotted mushroom from a Walt Disney cartoon. The gorilla stepped aside to let Gabby through, and as she squeezed past him, she could have sworn she saw him wink.

Meant to be, Gabby thought. Wherever he was, Eddie Sharp understood her even better than she dreamed he would.

Studio 16 was one of the larger practice rooms on the Olympus lot, big enough for a rehearsal piano with plenty of room to tap, but Gabby had never imagined what it would look like playing host to a twenty-piece orchestra. The scene inside was chaos. Black instrument cases were stacked haphazardly on every available surface; a forest of metal music stands, some overturned, spilled reams of annotated sheet music onto the floor. The musicians, seemingly oblivious to the mess, stood around the room in groups, thick blue clouds of cigarette smoke forming as they talked and laughed and argued, occasionally bringing an instrument to their lips to tootle out a note or two, as if to prove a point.

But which the hell one is Eddie Sharp?

Smoothing her dress nervously, Gabby spotted a tallish figure at the far end of the room with his back to her. He sported a black porkpie hat tilted at a rakish angle and had a thick blue winter scarf made of some kind of fuzzy cashmere material wound snugly around his neck. He was speaking animatedly to a group of men clutching brass instruments. They seemed to be hanging on his every word.

Bingo, Gabby thought.

Her excitement mounting with every step, she walked toward the broad back and cleared her throat loudly.

The man turned around. Gabby gasped. Clearly, she had made a mistake. First of all, this guy was holding a saxophone, and Eddie Sharp didn't play the sax.

Second of all, Eddie Sharp wasn't black.

"Gabby Preston!" the man exclaimed, flashing her a smile that made his eyes crinkle around the edges in a way that was disconcertingly adorable. "You're here. Sorry, you're catching us on one of our breaks."

"That's all right," Gabby said, flashing her dimples to try to disguise her surprise—the last thing she wanted to do was to make the poor guy feel self-conscious over her mistake.

Yet surprised she was. Not at seeing a Negro sax player— God knew there were plenty of those. But here at Olympus, it wasn't exactly your usual bowl of chicken soup, so to speak. . . . Olympus, like all the major studios, put famous black performers into its so-called race pictures, designed for Negro audiences. Some producers, like David O. Selznick, had even begun to give them bigger roles in mainstream films—word on the street had it that Hattie McDaniel was going to be so good in his *Gone with the Wind* that she might even be in contention for an Oscar next year . . . that is, if the Biltmore would allow her to attend a ceremony. But to have a black performer play a servant in the film adaptation of a bestselling book was one thing; to have one playing alongside white musicians in a band was quite another. Not that Leo Karp had anything against Negroes. But like practically ever other studio head in Hollywood, he was a Jew, and in the eyes of bigots like Father Coughlin and the Ku Klux Klan, that already made his products suspect, so Mr. Karp, with a worship of Traditional American Values that bordered on fetishistic, was even more wary of integration than most. As far as Leo Karp was concerned, politics were politics and business was business, and he was in the business of giving people what they wanted and making money doing it. An integrated picture might be banned from playing in half the theaters in the country, and if it couldn't play in the South, it might as well not play at all.

"That's all right," Gabby repeated. Her smile was starting to stiffen. She tried to refresh it by thinking about things that made her happy, like her acting coach had taught her when she first came to Olympus. *Puppies,* she thought. *Driving lessons. Lemon meringue pie. Singing. Gershwin. Eddie Sharp.* "That's perfectly all right."

"Glad to hear it." The man's smile didn't look the slightest bit feigned. "Well, I think we've been breaking long enough. We can get this party started any time you want. Your song's all set."

"My song?" Gabby's rictus smile crumbled. She hadn't told them what she planned to sing—hell, she hadn't decided herself. "What do you mean, my song?"

"The one Eddie marked up for you." He shuffled through a packet of paper on a nearby music stand and handed her a creased sheet. "You read music?"

"At least as well as I read English."

Technically true. Gabby snatched the paper from him, willing herself to make sense of either the tangle of notes or the tangle of letters dancing before her eyes on the page, with no hope of her brain ever catching up to them.

"Aw, you know it." Almost as though he could sense her frustration, the guy broke easily into song. *"First you put your two knees, close up tight . . . then you swing 'em to the left and you swing 'em to the right."* Lifting his horn to his lips, he played the next couple of bars.

"Ballin' the Jack," Gabby snapped. The knowing look in his eyes was getting on her nerves. "Of course I know it. Why would I want to sing that old thing? It's kid stuff."

"Maybe, but so is 'A-Tisket, A-Tasket,' and Ella Fitzgerald did pretty well for herself with that. Eddie thinks you sound like her."

Gabby pulled herself up to her full four feet eleven inches. "Watch it, buddy. I'm Gabby Preston. I don't sound like *anyone*."

He laughed. *Why the hell is he so damn smiley?* "Believe me, if someone says you sing like Ella, I'd take it."

"Where is Eddie?" Gabby said. "I want to talk to him."

"Oh, Eddie never rehearses with the guest vocalists. That's my job."

"Oh. Well, who are you?"

"Dexter Harrington," he said, tipping his hat. "Lead horn, side man, and second in command, I guess you could say."

"Well, I want to talk to Eddie," Gabby demanded. "If I have to sing with Eddie Sharp, then I want to rehearse with Eddie Sharp."

"I told you, baby, Eddie's not here," Dexter Harrington said. "Eddie's gone."

Baby? Gabby was furious. Just who did this Eddie Sharp character think he was, anyway? First he wanted to make her sing that stupid song, and then he didn't even have the decency to be there to sell her on it.

Figures. Just when you got your hopes up about a guy, he turned out to be a louse like all the others. And as for this Dexter Harrington, well, no side man was going to call her "baby" and get away with it. Not at her studio.

"Fine," Gabby said. "Then I'm gone too."

Turning on her heel, she started to march toward the door, kicking over a music stand for good measure. It fell to the ground with a heavy thud, practically crushing the feet of a couple of trombone players standing nearby. *Good,* Gabby thought meanly. *Maybe now they'll notice I'm here.* She kicked over another one, scattering paper and pencils all over the floor.

"All right," Dexter called after her. "I get the point. But suppose this: before you rip the place apart any worse than you already have, suppose you tell me what you want to sing."

In her fury, the reasonableness of his request took Gabby by surprise. "Is this some sort of trick question?"

He held up his hands, sax and all. "No trick, I swear. Come on. What's your favorite song to sing? If you could sing anything in the world."

Gabby blinked. "I don't know. 'I Got Rhythm,' maybe. Or 'Someone to Watch Over Me.'"

"Gershwin." Dexter nodded seriously. "Now we're talking." Without taking his eyes from Gabby's face, he sat down at the piano and, betraying not even the slightest hint of hesitation, brought his hands down into the first crashing chords of Gershwin's famous *Rhapsody in Blue*. In spite of herself, Gabby closed her eyes for a moment as the music enfolded her, letting the sensual yearning of the familiar melody shut out everything else.

"Poor George," Dexter said sadly, shaking his head. "I felt like they ripped my heart out when I heard he passed. They don't make 'em like that anymore. And the nicest guy you could ever hope to meet."

"Wait—wait a minute," Gabby stammered. "You knew George Gershwin?"

"Sure." Dexter's fingers never left the keys. "That's tragedy for you. Tumor of the brain. Cut down in the prime of life. Sure, look at everything he accomplished, but there could have been so much more. And like I said, that cat was the genuine article. A genuine Grade-A genius. But I guess I don't have to tell you."

"Where did you know him from?"

"Paris," Dexter said easily. Without missing a beat, his fingers tripped seamlessly into the opening of *An American in Paris*. "You know." He winked. "That city they keep over in France."

"You were in Paris? With George Gershwin? *George Gershwin was in Paris?*"

"Of course. Where do you think he wrote this?"

He had skipped ahead a bit now, to the part of the opening movement that reminded Gabby of a bunch of forgetful soldiers scrambling to their places on patrol—da-da-da-da-da-dee-*duh*, da-da-da-da-dee-*duh*. "So what do you say, Gabby Preston?" Dexter continued. "How about we put these lazy bums here to use and give 'Ballin' the Jack' a try? Okay?"

Okay, Gabby wanted to say. The other musicians had slowly advanced on the piano, instruments in hand. What was it she'd heard that British actor say on the radio, about music having charms that could soothe the savage beast? Gabby knew she could be a beast, all right, and she also knew that if Dexter could play this way, she wanted desperately to hear the rest of them. She wanted to sing, to let loose and match them note for note, to really show them what she could do.

And maybe she would have. If she hadn't at that moment turned her head toward the window and seen a gleaming white limousine pull up outside the wardrobe department across the street. A uniformed chauffeur hopped out to open the passenger door, and out came Miss Margo Sterling herself, wearing a beatific smile and about a thousand bucks' worth of blond fox fur that perfectly matched her golden hair. Rex Mandalay, the temperamental genius behind the Olympus fashion machine, leapt out of the doorway to greet her, practically kneeling before her custom-made alligator pumps as he bent to kiss her hand.

Like she's a goddamn princess, Gabby thought. Viola's words swam into her head, the very ones Gabby had repeated so many times herself, not least of all to Margo Sterling herself on her very first day at Olympus: *If you want to be a star, you've got to act like one.*

She turned back to the hopeful face at the piano. "No dice, Dexter," she said regretfully. "Tell Eddie Sharp I'll see him at the Oscars. Until then, I'll be in my dressing room. Don't forget. I'm a star."

FIVE

The splendor of Rex Mandalay's domain on the top floor of the Olympus wardrobe department rivaled that of any couturier's atelier in Paris.

The walls were painted the most delicate shade of lavender, decorated with snow-white moldings as ornate as the lacy trim of a gingerbread house. The enormous three-way gilt-framed mirror was designed to look like the unfurled petals of an orchid; the special pink lightbulbs in the antique chinoiserie lamps emitted a flattering rosy glow. Scattered across the plush lilac carpet were the famous tufted sofas and ottomans, upholstered in bright yellow velvet, upon which the maestro would sometimes be photographed for publicity purposes, displaying his latest round of sketches to an appropriately appreciative star.

This was the inner sanctum, the Holiest of Holies. Rumor had it that even Mr. Karp had never been allowed inside to see exactly the kind of luxury his money—or rather, New York's money—was financing. Nothing must be allowed to interfere with Rex Mandalay and his process of creation.

And what creations! There on a rack in the middle of the room hung some of the most beautiful vestments known to God or man. A ball gown of Vermeer-blue silk with a bouffant skirt of thousands of tiny individual petals, like an enormous hydrangea blossom. A shimmering halter gown as sinuous and liquid as though it had been fashioned from molten gold. Hooded white crepe with jet beading; rich red lace; a shocking-pink silk taffeta column with a matching capelet held in place with a hand-shaped clasp sporting an enormous—and very possibly real—diamond ring. All gorgeous, all virtually price-less, all one-of-a-kind.

Margo couldn't fit into any of them.

"Come on, darling!" Rex commanded, tugging at the zipper of a bejeweled forest-green satin, grunting like a man trying to push a boulder up a steep hill. Wardrobe assistants in white gloves pushed the emerald-encrusted bodice together on either side of her. "Suck in!"

"I'm sucking!"

"Suck harder! Come on!"

Margo felt her face turn purple as she tried valiantly to expel every last puff of air from her lungs. The wardrobe assistants threw their entire weight against her, pushing so hard Margo was sure they were going to crush her ribs.

"No," Rex groaned finally. He released his grip on the zipper, flinging himself on a yellow divan, his face flushed with exertion. "It's no use. For God's sake, Margo, you're going to have to reduce."

"Me?" Margo yelped. "I haven't gained an ounce. You must have made them too small, that's all."

"Darling." Rex flipped a curling lock of hair, bleached to an almost platinum shade of blond, back into place. "In my atelier, I have a dressmaker's dummy custom made to the exact proportions of every important Olympus star. And every creation you see before you was fitted to the one marked *Miss Margo Sterling.* Believe me, her measurements haven't changed."

"And I'm telling you, neither have mine."

"Well, you've got exactly two weeks to prove it. Unless you want to wear a burlap sack to the Oscars."

"I suppose it doesn't matter anyway," Margo muttered darkly. "I mean, it's not as if I'm going to be onstage, am I? Nobody will be looking at me."

"Don't be defeatist, darling. It's very 'supporting player.'" Rex snapped open a gold cigarette case, took out one of the slim black cigarettes he smoked, and inserted it into a carved ivory holder. The scent of its distinctive tobacco, a kind of perfumed musk tinged with apple, filled the room.

"Can I have one of those?"

"You *may* not," Rex retorted. "They're imported from Egypt, and if Europe persists in this idea of having a war, who knows how many more I'll be able to get."

He took a deep drag and blew a couple of languorous smoke rings before he turned back to Margo, his voice all business. "Now. Don't look so glum. Black coffee and grapefruit until the ceremony, a couple of cleverly placed hooks and eyes, and we'll be back in business. Unless . . . there's something you're not telling me?"

"Like what?"

Rex narrowed his eyes. "Well, you're not pregnant, are you?"

Margo's mouth fell open. *Pregnant?*

"Darling, it's hardly an unreasonable question. Everyone knows you've been shacked up in Malibu with Dane Forrest. Oh, don't look so horrified. This is Hollywood, not Hicksville. I'm not exactly going to start sewing a scarlet A across the fronts of your dresses. I just want to make sure you're being careful, that's all. Careers have been ruined by less, you know. Just look at what happened to the last one."

He's talking about Diana, Margo thought with a stab of horror.

So much time had passed since the scandal of Diana Chesterfield's mysterious disappearance that Margo had almost forgotten how a lot of pretty important people had believed that Dane had had something to do with it. Maybe they still did. After all, to most of the world, Dane and Diana were the Great Star-Crossed Lovers of the Silver Screen, cruelly driven apart by forces and passions greater than themselves. Only Margo knew that Dane and Diana had never been in love at all, that it was all a show for the cameras and the magazines.

But if people knew that, they'd start to ask why, and if the truth ever came out, it could ruin Dane. Picture people, fans and professionals alike, might tolerate a lot from their stars, but acting for years as though you were passionately in love with your own sister might be a little too much for them to take. It might not exactly be incest, but it wasn't wholesome either.

"Diana was sick," Margo said stubbornly. That was the official studio line, and she was sticking to it.

"Yes," Rex mused, "but sick with what, exactly?" Deep in thought, he blew a few more smoke rings and waved them into a perfumed cloud. "Oh, it doesn't matter. Out of sight is out of mind, I suppose, and rightly so. In the meantime, you'd better run along and leave me to my labors. I've got some rethinking to do, just in case the black coffee and celery doesn't work."

"You said grapefruit," Margo said, grateful for the change of subject.

"I reserve the right to change my mind. Now shoo. But leave the fur," Rex instructed. "Maybe I'll get inspired and whip up some kind of Russian evening stole." He arched an eyebrow as he poked the end of his ivory cigarette holder into the soft golden pile. "You never know. It could be fabulously . . . *concealing.*"

"Whatever you say," Margo said.

And I've got to do it, she thought as she walked down the stairs and back out to the car. *Just like Dane said. If I want to stay at Olympus, I've got to be exactly the girl they want me to be.*

"Duchess! Over here!"

Squinting through the bright sun—she realized, too late, that she'd left her sunglasses along with the fur—Margo instantly recognized the small man bounding toward her, his gait as cheerily choreographed and expertly spontaneous as if it were backed by an entire studio orchestra.

"Jimmy!" she exclaimed. "What are you doing here?"

"Oh, you know. Photo shoot. Earning my keep. You?"

"Fitting," Margo said, gesturing toward Rex Mandalay's tightly drawn curtains.

"Real top-secret stuff, huh?" Jimmy grinned. "All done now? I'm starving. What say we go down to the commissary and grab a bite? A little bird told me they've got Boston cream pie on the dessert cart today."

Reflexively, Margo's hands flew to her stomach. "I'd better not."

"Oscar diet?" Jimmy chuckled knowingly. "You and everyone else in town. That's why God invented the fruit plate."

"Rex is serious this time," Margo said. "He's probably alerted the Olympus secret police by now. When we get to the commissary, I'll be lucky if some rebel waiter lets me have a spoonful of milk in my coffee."

"Well, in that case, why don't we do something *really* crazy?" Jimmy's eyes twinkled. "Why don't we leave the studio lot?"

"I love the Brown Derby," Margo said happily as the maître d' made a big show of seating them in the booth under Jimmy's caricature, which grinned toothily, oversized top hat in hand, from between the inky likenesses of Katharine Hepburn and Adolphe Menjou. "It always makes me so happy to come here."

"Me too," Jimmy said. "It's one of the only places in Hollywood that makes you feel like you're actually living in the movies."

"Absolutely."

Truthfully, what made her the happiest was the attention she and Jimmy seemed to be getting. It had only been a matter of months since they'd been a studio-approved, loudly feted item, and if almost everyone in the restaurant knew, as Margo did, that Jimmy generally preferred the romantic company of men, they also knew that in Hollywood, the way things looked in public meant a whole lot more than anything that happened behind closed doors, and how things looked in the press meant the most of all.

And there would be press. A couple of photographers were loafing around the entranceway; Louella Parsons, Margo was pleased to see, looked alert as ever trundled into her all-seeing perch in the back. *Well, let them look.* It was good to be noticed. And if some headline tomorrow about her and Jimmy made Dane stand up and pay some attention to her again, so much the better.

It wasn't as though Dane had been *mean* lately, just a bit distant. The unexpected Oscar nod seemed to have propelled his career into a realm it had never quite reached before. Right after the nominations were announced, he'd been awfully attentive, maybe even—Margo thought guiltily—downplaying his own happiness so as not to make her feel bad.

But that had only lasted a couple of days. Now he seemed to spend hours on the phone with his agent, or in meetings with Larry Julius and Mr. Karp, or holed up in his study reading the spec scripts he kept getting from independent producers like David Selznick or that new hotshot director from England, Alfred Hitchcock. She was happy for him—she *knew* she was—but still, she couldn't remember the last time Dane had taken her to the Brown Derby. She couldn't remember the last time Dane had taken her anywhere.

"So," said Jimmy, picking up a menu. "How are things with the old man?"

It was if he could read her mind. "He's fine."

"Not too high and mighty?"

"About the nomination?" Margo asked innocently. "Naturally, we're both thrilled."

"Cut the crap, duchess," Jimmy said, putting down the menu with a bang. *It was just a prop anyway,* Margo thought. Jimmy

61

had a disconcerting habit of turning the most commonplace activities into portentous stage business. "It's me, Jimmy, your old friend. I've been around long enough to know that there's nothing like a lopsided awards season to wreck a happy home. Dear old Oscar is the deadliest femme fatale there is."

"Everything's fine," Margo said. "He's been busy, that's all. It's natural. Although . . ."

"Although what?"

"Rex mentioned Diana today. During my fitting."

Jimmy let out a low whistle. "Jeepers creepers. How'd *she* come up?"

"I don't know." Margo couldn't bring herself to tell Jimmy what Rex had really said, although she wasn't sure what was more embarrassing: the weight gain or how he'd assumed it had happened. *Or the fact that the way he thought it happened is impossible.* "Just . . . just in relation to Dane, I guess."

"Well," Jimmy said, twisting his mouth in a wry smirk, "Hollywood loves a comeback."

"What's *that* supposed to mean?" Margo asked hotly.

"Nothing, duchess. Just that what's out of sight doesn't always stay out of mind. Sooner or later, everything old is new again."

"Stop talking in riddles," Margo said crossly. "You sound like you're in a Charlie Chan movie."

Jimmy reached across the table and squeezed Margo's hand. "I'm sorry. I'm not saying any of this to hurt you. But I meant what I said. This kind of thing can be awfully tricky for a pair like you. Just to give some unsolicited advice: if you love Dane—"

"And I do!" Margo interrupted a little too quickly.

"Then don't make him choose between this"—Jimmy swept his eyes over the sea of world-famous faces grinning cartoonishly from their frames on the wall—"and you. Believe me, even if you win, you'll lose. You understand?"

"Sure I do." Margo gave him her most reassuring smile. If he didn't believe her, at least he dropped her hand and picked up his menu. "So," she continued, still grinning perkily, "have you got a date for the big night?"

"I believe I'll be escorting the ravishing Miss Preston to the ceremony," Jimmy said drily, "since Larry Julius seems fanatical about arranging the red-carpet arrivals by height. Afterward, who knows? I'm up for anything."

"What about Roderigo?" The words were out before Margo could stop them. She and Jimmy had never spoken of the silent, handsome boy she'd accidentally discovered in his bed at the Chateau Marmont on the night that had effectively ended their "romantic" arrangement, but she wanted Jimmy to know that he could confide in her, that she was his friend. "Is he still . . . in the picture?"

"He's gone back to Mexico," Jimmy said. "His mother's not been very well, you see."

His expression remained studiously pleasant, but a slight edge had crept into his voice, letting Margo know that this was not something he was prepared to discuss. Not now. Maybe not ever. And certainly not with Louella Parsons in the vicinity.

Margo was scanning the room, desperate to find a change of subject, when her eye fell on a familiar-looking redhead in a chic black suit at a table nearby. "Oh my God. It's Amanda Farraday."

Jimmy peered over the top of his menu with interest. "So it seems. In the flesh."

"God, I haven't seen her for ages," Margo said, noting with more than a pang of envy that Amanda appeared not to have gained so much as a stray ounce in the intervening period. If anything, she looked even *thinner*. *Maybe it's the suit,* Margo thought as Amanda lifted an enormous forkful of what appeared to be the Brown Derby's signature pork chop smothered in apricot glaze to her dainty lips. She made a mental note to buy herself a plain black suit at the earliest opportunity. "Where the hell has she been?"

"Holed up at Gabby Preston's, if you can believe it," Jimmy said.

"You're kidding." Margo's eyes widened. As far back as she could remember, Gabby had never had a nice word to say about the gorgeous redhead—and if you wanted to know why, you just had to look at the adjective in front of the noun. "How did that happen?"

Jimmy shrugged. "Maybe times are tough and they're taking in boarders. Maybe our little songbird has finally grown a heart to go along with her ego. Maybe she just thought Amanda might have a good line on some under-the-table prescriptions. Who knows?"

"Gabby's still on the pills, huh?"

"Duchess," Jimmy said, "everyone in Hollywood's on some kind of pills. The difference is that Gabby *likes* them." He sat back in his chair. "Anyway, it's all over now. Rumor has it Viola's kicked Amanda out."

"Why?" Margo asked, ears pricked.

"Once again you are asking me to comment on the motives of the inscrutable Preston women," Jimmy said. "It's a task you couldn't ask of the almighty Leo Karp himself. But in my humble opinion, I think the old lady probably didn't relish having another younger redhead around. The kind with a carpet to match the drapes, if you get my drift."

"Don't be vulgar. Who's that she's having lunch with?"

Jimmy peered at Amanda's companion, a heavyset fellow in brown pinstripes eying his lunch date with the calculated appreciation of a man who knows he wants to buy a car but clearly means to hold out for a damn good price. "I have no idea. But that's no surprise anymore. Ever since Selznick, the town is lousy with independents trying to set up shop, thinking they'll strike gold on their own, studios be damned." He shrugged. "Personally, I think the jury's still out on *Gone with the Wind*. Don't forget what Irving Thalberg said: 'No Civil War picture ever made a nickel.'"

"What about *Birth of a Nation*?"

"That was a silent," Jimmy said dismissively. "This is a whole new era."

"Shhh. I think she sees us."

Sure enough, Amanda's lovely oval of a face was turned in their direction, her hand half raised in greeting. "I think she's going to come over and say hello."

"Not to us," Jimmy said gently. "Look over there."

Margo looked.

Harry Gordon had just entered the room.

Surrounded by an entourage of stone-faced Olympus bigwigs, Harry appeared to be as careless and rumpled as ever, although closer inspection revealed a number of small but significant changes. The sloppy sweater was now of the softest cashmere, the scuffed shoes molded perfectly to his feet, the cheap glasses replaced with genuine tortoiseshell frames.

Like he's been turned into a Central Casting version of Harry Gordon, Margo thought.

Amanda stared at him, her face white, looking as beautiful and terrified as Margo had ever seen anyone. Harry stared back, unmoving but trembling slightly, as though every muscle in his body was clenched. An electric hush fell over the room as every diner at the Brown Derby leaned forward in his or her chair, not wanting to miss what happened next.

Amanda's lips parted. Her eyes glowed. Harry's body lurched forward; for a moment it seemed as though he was going to run across the room and into her arms.

Then he turned on his heel and went straight out the door.

"Oh," Jimmy breathed. "Oh no."

Amanda's eyes were unnaturally bright. Two dark red spots blossomed on her pale cheeks as she shakily murmured some excuse—clearly inadequate, from the look on her lunch companion's face—and dashed toward the comforting oblivion of the ladies' room.

Margo, to her surprise, found herself reflexively scooping up her purse. "I'm going to talk to her."

"No, Margo." Jimmy reached out to stop her. "Leave her alone."

"But she's upset," Margo protested. "I can't just leave her. Remember how she helped us at the Cocoanut Grove that night Gabby was sick? It's the least I can do to return the favor."

"And I'm telling you, let her be. This isn't some drunk little girl throwing up in the bathroom, Margo." Jimmy seized her hand, looking gravely into her eyes. "This is a real broken heart."

A *real broken heart.* And there, in the corner, was the real Louella Parsons, gleefully writing every bit of it down.

SIX

He cares.

The words thrummed through Amanda over and over again, like a heartbeat. *Harry still cares.*

Sure, maybe storming out of one of the most famous restaurants in town in front of a veritable title sequence of Hollywood's Who's Who was not the usual way of showing it. But Harry had never been the sort to do things the usual way. Truth be told, if he had done anything else, she would have been worried. A "civilized" man, a suave Dane Forrest type—someone like that might have handled things differently. That man might have been able to nod a greeting from across the room, even pop by her table for a cordial, if impersonal, chat.

But Harry Gordon was not that man. Harry Gordon was no Dane Forrest. *And thank God for that.*

Harry could never hide his feelings or separate his heart from his head. It was one of the reasons why Amanda loved him. From the look in his eyes when he saw her, she could tell her feelings were far from unrequited. When she'd run to the bathroom crying—not her most poised moment, true, and one that had certainly pissed the hell out of that poor schmuck she'd been having lunch with, who'd disappeared while she was gone and stuck her with the bill—the tears streaming down her face had been ones of joy, not despair. She'd been crying with gratitude, because Harry still loved her.

And now, right in front of her, was the evidence. Once again in black-and-white. Ink, that is.

Amanda took a long drag from her cigarette—smoking, she thought ruefully, being just one of the seemingly unbreakable bad habits she'd picked up during these last terrible months. Gingerly, she laid it still smoldering on the side of the cracked bathtub and reached for the newspaper on the floor. Careful to keep the precious pages from falling into the tepid perfumed water, she began once again to read the words she had by now practically learned by heart:

Like Something Out of the Movies

The song says life is just a bowl of cherries, but lunch was much more than just a Cobb salad for Tinseltown's own Romeo and Juliet, Harry Gordon and Amanda Farraday. 'Tis in the fair Brown Derby that we set our scene, where the two star-crossed lovers held each other's burning gaze across a dining room filled with the grandest grandees in town. You could have heard a pin drop . . . and you'd have wondered if that pin was from a grenade, the atmosphere was so combustible. They don't call it chemistry for nothing, chickens!

Alas, they went their separate ways with nary a word exchanged . . . but to this humble observer, they might not be separate for long. Maybe we're sentimental, but nothing would make us happier than to see a happy Harry go home Oscar night with a sexy little gold man in one hand and a sexy little redhead in the other. This story isn't over yet, kids. But let's just hope Olympus's hottest scribe can come up with a happier ending than that mopey old Bill Shakespeare.

"Hey, sister!" There was an angry pounding on the bathroom door. "Open up in there!"

"Hold your horses, will ya?" Amanda yelled back. "I'm just finishing up."

"You've been finishing up for forty-five minutes. Open the door or I'm going to call Mrs. O'Malley."

Amanda sighed. That was all she needed, for the landlady to get involved, when she was already late on this week's rent. "All right, all right." Reluctantly, she heaved herself out of the water and, teeth chattering, pulled on her black lace peignoir. *I really need to buy a nice thick toweling robe,* Amanda thought, *or maybe cashmere. Something warm.*

Pulling the thin wrapping of silk tighter around her body, she lit a fresh cigarette and tucked the newspaper under her arm before she opened the door to find Mildred, her down-the-hall neighbor, tapping her foot impatiently, her wide mouth twisted into a snarl.

"Took you long enough." With her yellow hair wrapped up

tightly in curling rags, she looked like Medusa with a head full of live snakes. *Mildred has probably turned a man or two to stone in her day.* "Thought I was going to have to take a leak right here in the hallway."

"I'm so sorry," Amanda said sweetly. "I left a bottle of Chanel Bois des Iles bubble bath in there, if you'd like to use it," she added.

Piggy eyes widening with greed, Mildred darted into the bathroom and slammed the door without so much as a thank-you, as though she was worried Amanda was going to change her mind.

Typical, Amanda thought, rushing down the dirty corridor toward her own bare room to dress. This boardinghouse stuff was for the dogs. Nosy neighbors peeping into her room at all hours, sniffing among her things for whatever they thought she wouldn't miss. Stern-faced Mrs. O'Malley with trailing rosaries and endless rules about curfews and gentleman callers and "being respectable"—ironic in a house in which every tenant, to Amanda's practiced eye, at least, either used to be a professional or was about to be. Having to wait in line for *everything*: the bathroom, the pay phone, the enormous morning vat of sludgy Irish oatmeal that qualified as the second half of room and board.

Oh well, Amanda thought, deftly zipping up the back of her black crepe Chanel dress (might as well match the bubble bath, she figured) and pinned her velvet hat into place. Mrs. O'Malley's was relatively clean, for what it was, and the price was right—at least, it would be once she was a little more . . . *liquid.*

And besides, it wouldn't be for much longer. She'd read in

Variety that Harry had just renegotiated his contract with the studio; he must be making a mint by now. Once they were back together, he'd bail her out. Even if they didn't move in together right away, he'd find her a better place to live, maybe even talk the studio into giving her a bungalow like they did Margo Sterling. Harry would take care of her. She was sure of it.

Parked on a crumbling corner next to a broken parking meter licked with rust, Amanda's gleaming dove-gray coupe looked as out of place as her Parisian hatboxes and monogrammed trunks piled on Mrs. O'Malley's uneven floor. Slipping behind the wheel, Amanda breathed in the rich scent of the burgundy leather seats, which still smelled new after almost two years. She ran her hand over the gold initials embossed on the highly polished door of the glove compartment:

α L F

Amanda Louise Farraday. A name—a *person*—she had invented all by herself, out of nothing. *If Harry and I get married, I'll have to change the monogram,* Amanda thought with a giggle. Another name, another identity to slip into as if it were one of her black silk gloves. She was sure it would fit her just as well.

Amanda drove. Slowly, the shabby buildings and crumbling streets gave way to neat little homes with orange trees in their well-kept yards, then gated mansions with sprawling emerald lawns dotted with palm trees, until the glittering paved expanse of Wilshire Boulevard stretched out before her. She pulled into the long circular driveway of Bullocks, enjoying the luxuriant crunch of the gravel beneath her tires. A uniformed valet jumped out to greet her. She dropped her keys into his outstretched hand and smiled graciously at the doormen as they ushered her through the glass-and-travertine doors into the lobby.

Maybe it was silly, but Amanda thought there was no place on earth that made her feel as safe as the Bullocks Wilshire department store. She loved the slippery floors of pale Italian marble, the immense art deco ceiling mural depicting planes, trains, and automobiles in a colorful paean to the steady thrum of optimistic American progress, the polished nickel columns and shining glass countertops in which one could catch a reassuring glimpse of oneself looking appropriately stylish and busy and important.

It was as if nothing bad could ever happen to you there, as though the cares and worries of the world were gone with a whisk of the revolving doors, like water past the rudder of a ship. A department store was beautiful and calm, filled with beautiful and calm people harvesting the beautiful fruits of their labor in the hushed reverent tones of visitors to an art museum.

With one important exception: in this art museum, *everything* was for sale.

"Miss Farraday!" the salesgirl exclaimed as Amanda stepped out of the polished mahogany elevator and into the designer salons of the fifth floor. "It's . . . it's you."

"Hello, Annette," Amanda said warmly. "How nice to see you. It's been a long time."

"It certainly has." Nervously, the girl's fingers flew to the ruffled collar of her starched white blouse. "Is there . . . is there something I can help you with?"

"There is." Amanda graced the girl with her best haughty, impersonal smile. Somehow, the expression made her think of Diana Chesterfield, although God—and Amanda—knew that Diana was no more to-the-manor-born than she was. "I'm looking for a new evening dress. Something rather spectacular, if you can swing it."

"Any special occasion?"

Amanda examined her nails with studied nonchalance. "Oh, only if you consider the Oscars something special."

"I . . . I see," Annette stammered. "In that case . . . I'd . . ."

"You'd what, Annette? Spit it out."

"I'd better get my manager," Annette said finally. "Just wait here."

Great. Amanda pursed her lips with impatience as the girl fluttered anxiously away. *This is going to be trickier than I thought.* Bracing herself, she tightened her grip around the packet of paper she clutched along with the slim patent-leather pocketbook in her left hand.

"Miss Farraday." Mr. Pierre, the designer department manager who seemed convinced that his sparse pencil mustache made him a dead ringer for Ronald Colman, strode across the plush velvet carpet, stroking the white carnation tucked in the buttonhole of his morning suit with long, manicured fingers. "A pleasure."

"And for me."

The manager let a terse smile play over this thin lips. "Annette tells me you're looking for something rather special."

"Isn't it silly?" Amanda clapped a small hand fetchingly to

74

her collarbone, letting out a silvery peal of laughter. The modest hand flutter to the décolletage was one of Olive Moore's patented maneuvers. *If only she could see me now.* "The Oscars are just days away, and I've just been so busy running around like a chicken with my head cut off that I've completely *forgotten* to do anything about a gown. I mean, I don't suppose you even have anything left, do you?"

"That depends." Mr. Pierre sniffed. "Is there anything in particular you had in mind?"

"Well, now that you ask"—Amanda looked up at him through her eyelashes—"there was a ruched green velvet Molyneux in this month's *Vogue* I thought might do the trick."

"Not black?"

"I thought it might be fun to branch out a little." Amanda let her smile deepen. "And besides, it's a *very* deep green."

"I see." Having stroked his boutonniere to the point of disintegration, Pierre moved onto his mustache. "Miss Farraday, much as it pains me to say this, there is the small matter of an outstanding bill."

Come on, Ginger, Amanda thought grimly. It had been ages since anyone had called her by the fake name she'd used when she was working for Olive Moore, and even longer since she'd thought of herself that way. But an occasion like this seemed to call for all the duplicity she could muster. *Show 'em what you're made of.*

"Oh!" she gasped prettily, letting her freshly moistened lips fall open the Olive-recommended one inch. Not so far as to spoil the shape of your mouth, and enough to keep your bottom teeth covered. *No one,* Olive said, *wants to see your bottom teeth.* "My goodness! Mr. Pierre, I can't tell you how mortified

I am. Like I said, I've just been so busy lately I've completely neglected my correspondence. I'll write you a check this instant for the *full* amount."

"Miss Farraday—"

"No, I insist! Just let me find my checkbook. . . ."

Carefully, Amanda deposited the newspaper on the nickel counter, careful to make sure the headline about her and Harry at the top of Louella Parsons's column was clearly visible as she made a big show of rooting around in her pocketbook. Mr. Pierre's beady eyes flickered toward it immediately, like a moth drawn to a flame. *Success!*

"Miss Farraday . . . ," he repeated, holding up his hand.

"Oh no!" Amanda wailed, like a woman who'd lost her best friend. *Careful, kiddo, don't overdo it.* "I can't believe it! I've left my checkbook at home. And this is the only day I have free until Oscar night." She let out a sigh, expertly strangulated, with just the barest threat of tears. "Oh well. I suppose I'll just have to wear an old gown, then. My escort will have seen it, of course, but maybe he won't remember."

Mr. Pierre's eyes were glued to the newspaper item. "And your escort is . . . Mr. Gordon, I presume?"

"Well." Amanda dropped her gaze demurely to the counter, lowering her voice to a shy hush. "I'm afraid I'm not quite at liberty to say. You understand. But let's just say I'm relieved he's not . . . *materialistic.* New York playwright and all that." She let one expertly shadowed eyelid fall in a slow wink.

That was all it took. "Miss Farraday, I believe we can help you."

"Really!" Amanda squealed with glee, clapping her pocketbook to her breastbone. "You will?"

"Certainly." Mr. Pierre let out a decisive grunt. "After all, you are one of our most valued customers. What's a few dollars and cents between friends?"

"Mr. Pierre, it's like you read my mind." Her voice was a feline purr.

"Good." The manager beamed. "Now, we do happen to have the green Molyneux you mentioned in stock, but if you have decided to consider color, there's a burgundy Mainbocher we've just got in that might be sublime. And of course, that's not to discount Madame Chanel, whose newest collection needs a lean silhouette. But of course, the Parisian designers don't come cheap—"

"Mr. Pierre," Amanda said happily. "I'm entirely in your hands."

The only thing that matters is that I look like a million bucks.

SEVEN

The eleventh annual Academy Awards had no official host.

It was the first time this had ever happened, and nobody was quite sure how. Some spoke in hushed tones of a bitter intra-Academy feud; smug insider types were spreading stories about individual studios pushing so hard for one of their stars to be named emcee that the Academy had finally thrown up its hands, King Solomon–like, and refused to choose anyone at all. Others, of the inveterate gossip variety, claimed the organizers had gone down a list of possibilities, each of which had proved too old, too boring, too unreliable, or too drunk to be trusted onstage.

Whatever the reason, it was abundantly clear that no one was steering the ship. The atmosphere in the ballroom of the Biltmore Hotel was practically anarchic. Whole categories were skipped. Confused—or tipsy—celebrities wandered across the stage, looking embarrassed and desperate, as though they'd gotten lost on their way to the bathroom. At least three times the proceedings came to a halt so that the next presenter (and in one case, the recipient) could be tracked down at the bar.

For Margo, the chaos simply seemed to add to the surrealism, the sense that the whole evening was like something out of a dream. She thought she'd been in Hollywood long enough not to get starstruck anymore, but no red-carpet premiere or Holmby Hills wrap party could have prepared her for *this*.

This was the *Oscars*.

Clark Gable and Carole Lombard were here, getting the stink eye from Joan Crawford, who was hanging on the arm of Franchot Tone. Katharine Hepburn was whispering something in Spencer Tracy's ear, much to Mrs. Tracy's visible chagrin. Leo Karp was sitting with Louis B. Mayer, who wasn't drinking, and Harry Cohn, who was. *Greta Garbo was there*. True, she wasn't actually *speaking* to anybody, but she was *there*.

"If the Germans dropped a bomb on the Biltmore right now, they could wipe out the whole movie business, just like that," Gabby whispered across the table, a mischievous gleam in her eyes.

Margo and Gabby hadn't been quite as close lately—the stunt Gabby had pulled last year making sure Margo caught her "boyfriend" Jimmy with his boyfriend in much more intimate circumstances than Margo had ever seen him made it a little hard to trust her—but Margo was glad she was there. She was glad they were all there, in their little Olympus enclave: Gabby and Jimmy; a preternaturally calm Larry Julius, his only concession to nerves the endless parade of smoldering cigarettes he kept inserting into the expressionless mask of his face; Dane, who was, of course, a shaking, trembling, nervous wreck; Gabby's mother, dressed to the nines in some sort of bizarre ensemble of ostrich feathers dyed a violent purple and—to Gabby's tremendous embarrassment—flirting outrageously with Larry's (ironically) ostrichlike assistant, Stan. Harry Gordon, although he looked markedly downcast, even before he lost, and his mother, a plump gray-haired lady with a European accent who every few minutes proclaimed she was about to faint with pride—but impressively, never did.

And what about my mother? What would she be like if she were here? Helen Frobisher's pale image swam unbidden into Margo's mind. The blond chignon with not a hair out of place, the icy blue eyes, the slim, manicured hands that were always cool, yet strangely comforting . . .

Her train of thought was interrupted by Dane's clammy hand squeezing hers. "You look beautiful," he muttered mechanically.

"So you told me."

"I did?"

"About a hundred times."

Poor Dane. His gaze looked almost haunted, fixed on something none of the rest of them could see. He'd barely even glanced at her when she'd floated down the stairs at the house in Malibu in the blue hydrangea dress two weeks of deprivation had finally let her squeeze into.

All that grapefruit for nothing, she'd thought. But it hadn't all come to naught. There'd been enough camera flashes in her vicinity to guarantee that, nominee or no, she'd have her picture in more than one newspaper tomorrow morning, and as for her effect on the players of Hollywood, Mr. Walt Disney himself had materialized before her, stroking his chin thoughtfully with an ink-stained finger and murmured: "Blue. Interesting. You look like a fairy."

"He's looking for inspiration," Gabby said. "Didn't you hear? He's notorious for it. Rex Mandalay practically had a fit when he saw *Snow White* and her dress looked exactly like one he designed for Olivia DeHavilland when he was at Warner Brothers. Rex wants to sue."

"Come on. You can't sue over a dress design on a cartoon."

"Oh please, Margo, this is Hollywood. You can sue someone who said they'd pay for lunch and then skipped out on the bill. You just have to decide if it's worth making a point. And the hell of it is, Rex would win too, if Karp would let him take it to court. But he won't. The dreaded negative publicity."

Gabby's eyes were unnaturally bright tonight. Clearly, she had decided chemical intervention was the only way her Oscar night was going to be quite as *peppy* as she wanted it, and she was putting the booze away at a pretty impressive rate too. *God help me*, Margo thought, *if she gets sick she's on her own. I'm not taking her to the ladies' room to wash the puke out of her dress. She's her mother's problem.*

"Besides," Gabby continued, the words tumbling out at an increasingly rapid pace, "as long as Rex Mandalay is under contract, every single sketch, every scrap of fabric, every goddamn thought in his head is the absolute property of Olympus Studios. Karp owns him, lock, stock, and barrel, just the same as he owns us. Rex just has a nicer dressing room."

"Oh, Gabs, come on," Jimmy said. "You don't really think that."

"Don't I? Why would I say it, then? And why would I be

performing tonight like a trained monkey with some overrated bandleader I've never even rehearsed with if I didn't have to jump whenever he said so?"

"Still," Jimmy said uneasily, "he's just doing his job. You make him out to be some kind of slave driver."

"Oh no," Gabby said sweetly. "That's not my intention at all. Mr. Karp is the slave *owner*. My mother is the slave driver."

Viola's head jerked up. "*Gabrielle*. Please."

"That's not my name," Gabby snapped back. "And what would you call someone who profits off the unpaid labor of another human being? I may not have been quite as good a student as Margo here—not that I ever had the chance—but it sure sounds an awful lot like slavery to me."

Viola's face, already rouged a bright red, turned purple. The table held its collective breath, braced for the shock of a mother's terrible wrath.

It was another mother who saved them.

"*Sha*, everybody, *sha*," Harry's mother interrupted, waving her hands in the air with unperturbed annoyance, as though Gabby and Viola were nothing but a couple of buzzing flies at an outdoor picnic. "Shut your mouths already and let an old lady hear what's going on, for once in her life. Spencer Tracy on the stage, can you believe it? That Sadie Gorenstein in her lifetime would see such a thing, who would have thought it was possible!"

Cracking his first smile of the night, Harry patted her hand. "Gordon, Ma, it's Gordon. You have to excuse my mother," he said, looking around the table. "She's not accustomed to drinking champagne."

Bette Davis was announced the winner of the Best Actress award, to no one's surprise. Watching the great star, dressed in black silk trimmed with an odd little stole of white feathers, march unsmilingly and determinedly across the stage to pick up the second statuette of her unsmiling, determined career, Margo felt herself relax at last. *So it was true.* Davis's Oscar was a fait accompli.

It made Margo realize what a long shot her hopes had been for this year, how many rungs she still had to climb. She hadn't lost anything or disappointed anyone; she was simply at the start of a very long road, a road most people would never even be able to find on a map. Somehow, this made her feel better— not just better, in fact, but *great*. For the first time since the nominations had been announced, she felt *free,* and she found herself on her feet, whistling and cheering with the others as Bette Davis finished thanking Jack Warner and took her final bows.

Spencer Tracy guided her toward the wings and stepped back to the microphone, tripping slightly over the cord as he did so. *Maybe he and Gabby will be sharing a bathroom stall later.*

"And now," the star announced, slurring his words slightly, "the Best Actor category."

Under the table, Dane's broad, slightly clammy hand found Margo's.

"To present the award," Spencer Tracy continued, mopping the sweat off his forehead with the palm of his hand, "we have a very special surprise . . . ah . . . presenter. Someone we all love very much, and who we haven't seen for a very long time. Ladies and gentlemen, may I introduce, or rather reacquaint you with, a wonderful actress and very dear friend . . . Miss Diana Chesterfield!"

Miss Diana Chesterfield.

It was like seeing a ghost.

Time seemed to stop. You could practically hear the sound of your own churning organs in the previously boisterous room as the great star floated toward the microphone, her expression serene. Her face was pale, but there was no trace of the mad, ruined girl Margo had seen ranting in a wheelchair at the sanatorium all those months ago. With her hair like spun gold, nodding regally in a white satin gown trimmed with snowy ermine, she looked like a storybook princess, like someone out of another time.

Then, suddenly, the crowd was on its feet. Gabby's jaw hung down somewhere around her ankles. Mr. Karp was weeping openly, accepting a monogrammed handkerchief from Louis B. Mayer, who, not to be outdone on the sentimentality front, was crying as well. From the corner of her eye, Margo saw Larry Julius's smug smile, a clear sign of pride at having pulled off such a coup.

Diana's curving rosebud lips mouthed her thanks, but Margo couldn't hear her. She couldn't hear her read the names of the nominees. She didn't hear the tearing of the envelope, or Diana's delighted squeal as she read Dane's name out loud.

All she saw was Dane Forrest leap to his feet without so much as a backward glance. She saw him rush the stage, gathering the golden statuette—*both golden statuettes*, she thought cruelly—into his arms. She saw him sweeping Diana into a lengthy, tearful embrace.

And she saw the gleeful photographers with their flashing bulbs, popping away at the glorious reunion of the dashing Dane Forrest and the gorgeous Diana Chesterfield, America's sweethearts, back in each other's arms at last.

Just like something out of the movies.

EIGHT

Typical. It was just so typical.

Just when all of Hollywood was *finally* going to devote their undivided attention to Gabby for a change.

She'd been so ready to perform. The dress the studio had "loaned" her was a sickly baby pink, as always, but was significantly lower cut than usual, which might actually convince the assembled moguls that the juvenile property known as Gabby Preston had cleavage that might be advantageously displayed on a more regular basis.

She'd come up with a way to deal with Eddie Sharp—whom she had still not met, let alone rehearsed with. She, Jimmy, and Walter Gould, the musical director of their production unit, had put together a list of songs she'd do and the keys in which she'd do them, and if Eddie gave her any trouble when she presented them to him, she'd say, "My way or the highway," just like James Cagney did in that old flick she'd watched in the Main Street cinema on the studio lot.

She'd never been in better voice; her low notes were rich, her high notes were soaring, and everything in between was pitch-perfect and full.

Best of all, the green pills for once were working the way they were supposed to. Mixed with the champagne, the little green darlings were giving her the feeling that she was invincible, that she could—and would—do anything she set her mind to.

And then Diana Chesterfield had to come back from the dead and steal the whole goddamn show.

God, look at her. It's like she's holding a press conference at her own table. The regal, ermine-caped star was barely visible through the scrum of press and well-wishers alike, not to mention the phalanx of slavering photographers gleefully shooting away, blinding anyone who had the bad luck to be seated nearby. *How the hell did they get here so fast?* Even from several feet away, Gabby could see that the heat from the flashbulbs was melting one of the giant marzipan Academy Awards covered in edible gold dust that served as centerpieces on every table at the ball.

"Poor Oscar," Gabby murmured to Jimmy. "His face is caving in. He looks like that painting you showed me in that book, the one you said was a portrait of Tully Toynbee."

At the mention of Tully, Jimmy groaned. He had always been fond of the dictatorial director whom Gabby had hated on sight. But when an errant exploding flash pot had badly burned the leg of a chorus girl on the set of their most recent picture and Tully had fired her on the spot when she'd asked to be taken to the doctor, even a trouper like Jimmy had to agree enough was enough. "You mean *The Scream*?"

"That's the one. Where do they keep it, Sweden?"

"Norway." Jimmy sighed, shaking his head. "Boy, you couldn't pay me a million dollars to be Margo Sterling right now."

"You already have a million dollars."

"You know what I mean. Just get a load of the mug on her. Poor kid looks like she just lost her best friend."

Squinting through the flashing light, Gabby spotted Margo, a shadowy blue figure sitting decidedly out of the camera's range, watching quietly as two men knelt reverently before Diana with a box of portable recording equipment.

"What do you think they're asking her?" Jimmy wondered.

"Probably where the hell she's been for the past goddamn year."

"Language, duchess, language."

"I thought Margo was duchess."

"You're right. I don't know what I was thinking. But look, I think both Your Highnesses are being usurped."

Bathed in the glow of the flashbulbs, Diana was saying something into the mike. Gabby couldn't hear what it was, but from the look on Margo's face, it was clear that the lovely Miss Sterling wasn't buying any of it.

There was one person who was, though, or at least appeared to be: newly minted Academy Award winner Dane Forrest, who was gazing at the coolly beautiful face of his long-lost paramour with undisguised rapture.

"Poor Margie," Gabby said. "I guess the clock had to strike midnight sometime."

"Oh, honey," Jimmy murmured, "I think it did that some time ago."

Suddenly, Gabby felt a sharp pang of sympathy for her friend. What must it feel like to see it all go up in a puff of smoke like that? Now that Diana Chesterfield was back—with a vengeance, it appeared—what was going to happen to Margo Sterling, the plucky, lucky girl who had swept in to replace her? Well, she could forget about whatever big classy property the studio had her set to star in this year; as far as Leo Karp was concerned, any qualities Margo Sterling might bring to a role would be wiped clean away by the box-office potential of Diana Chesterfield's glorious comeback. Margo would be demoted to what she looked like now: a glorified stand-in.

And as for her love life, well . . . if the look on Dane's face was any indication, Gabby would say the odds were a probable twelve to seven that Margo Sterling would be going home alone tonight.

Jimmy seemed to read her mind. "How long do you think they've got until Larry Julius decides a Dane and Diana reunion is just what the gossip columns ordered?"

"He wouldn't do that." Gabby sounded more convinced than she felt. "Not after everything that's happened."

"But we have no idea *what* happened, do we?" Jimmy mused. "The heck of it is, the kid's really nuts about him. First love and all that."

"And what about him?" Gabby asked. "Doesn't he love her? He's certainly made a big show of it."

"Sure he does, but not nearly as much as he loves being Dane Forrest. Believe me." A faraway look came into Jimmy's eyes. "I know the type."

Suddenly, Margo glanced toward them, as though she knew they were watching. Her miserable gaze met Gabby's for a long moment before she abruptly jerked it away. *She's embarrassed*, Gabby thought. "I should go talk to her."

"Oh no, you don't," Jimmy warned. "The last thing she needs right now is gloating."

"Give me a little credit," Gabby protested. "Who's gloating? I just don't think she should be sitting there all by herself, that's all."

She was starting toward Margo when she suddenly felt a hand on her elbow. She turned to find a man in the red uniform dinner jacket of the Biltmore Hotel. "Miss Preston," he said, "I'm so sorry, but I've been asked to fetch you. It seems you're needed immediately backstage."

"By who?" Gabby asked.

"By Mr. Sharp," the man said. "I can see you're busy, but I'm afraid I really must insist. He said it's most urgent."

"Don't worry," Jimmy said, grinning. "You go ahead. I'll find a handkerchief for Margo."

Yeah, Gabby thought crossly, *I just bet you will.*

Gesturing her through a side door, the man in the red jacket led her down a long corridor and a flight of stairs into the orchestra greenroom beneath the stage. A large, window-less room with a dirty linoleum floor, it bore a tableau virtually identical to the one in the rehearsal room at Olympus, sans the Viola-repelling gorilla at the front door. Musicians in matching midnight-blue tuxedos stood around smoking, noodling on their instruments, swearing cheerfully as they searched for matches and mouth reeds in untidy stacks of monogrammed instrument cases.

Across the room, she noticed Dexter Harrington jotting some notations down at a music stand. He nodded a quick greeting, and she smiled back, trying to hide her surprise at seeing him there. Integrated big bands might fly at some of the more sophisticated venues in the Northeast, but she'd never thought of the Governor's Ball as a bulwark of racial progressivism. Even if most of the people in the room *had* voted for Roosevelt.

A voice yelled over the din. "Preston! Over here!"

Following the voice, Gabby got her first look at the great bandleader Eddie Sharp.

It's the right name for him, she thought. The long, thin nose, the dark brilliantined hair scraped cleanly back, the square shoulders of his fitted jacket—everything about him seemed angular and exact, with two visible exceptions: the undone bow tie draped carelessly around his neck, and his full, sensual mouth.

A trumpet player's mouth, which turned down at the corners in a slight pout that seemed a little bit arrogant, a little bit mean . . . and *undeniably* sexy.

Get a grip, Gabby ordered herself. *So he's not terrible-looking. Big deal. You've got to keep it together. Show him who's boss.* "Mr. Sharp," she purred. "I hope that's not how you play."

It was a good opening line, one she'd thought of beforehand, and the twinkle in Eddie's eyes told her he knew it. "Only if you sing flat," he said.

He was holding in his hand a rubber ball with a kind of funnel-like spout sticking out the top. This he suddenly thrust up his nostril and squeezed, inhaling deeply.

"Amphetamine spray. You want some?"

"No, thank you."

"You sure? It opens the lungs and sinuses. Very good for singers."

"I'll pass."

"Suit yourself." Still squeezing the rubber ball, Eddie raked his shrewd black eyes over her, lingering, Gabby was pleased to note, on her décolletage. "Say, you look older than in your pictures."

"Funny," Gabby said smartly. "I don't remember ever seeing a picture of you at all."

Eddie laughed. "All right, kid. I got your number. Now, whaddya say we run through this sucker a time or two before they throw us to the lions?"

"Oh. So now you want to rehearse."

"I had somewhere else I needed to be that afternoon," Eddie retorted. "Someplace important. I don't need to be there to run through a simple song with a girl singer."

"Well, this girl singer doesn't run through so much as 'Mary Had a Little Lamb' without the bandleader."

Eddie gave his nose spray a thoughtful squeeze. "You know Ella Fitzgerald?"

Gabby smiled witheringly. "Rings a bell."

"Well, I just played a week with her up at the Savoy in Harlem." He smiled wistfully. "She was practicing all the time. Never joked around, never sat around with a flask drinking with the boys. You needed her, you had to go find her in a corner somewhere where she was running through scat, trying out changes, making up harmonies. Finally, I said to her, 'Ella,' I said, 'you're great. Better than great. You're a genius and you're going to be a big star. What do you need to practice so much

92

for?' She said to me, 'Eddie, it doesn't matter if I'm better than everybody else. I have to be better than *me*.'"

He looked at Gabby expectantly, as though he'd just said something deeply profound. Well, she wasn't going to give him the satisfaction. "What's that supposed to mean?"

"It means if you want to be great, you *never* give up a chance to rehearse. Even if it is only with the arranger. Who happens to be the best in the business, by the way."

"What arranger?"

"Dexter." Eddie nodded toward the scarred rehearsal piano, where the man in question was softly thumping out a vamp.

"He's the *arranger*?" Gabby gasped, looking at the tall figure hunched over the keyboard, a pencil clamped in his mouth. His eyes were half shut, and for the tiniest moment, Gabby noticed how his long eyelashes cast little shadows on the curve of his cheek. "I thought he was a side man."

Eddie shrugged. "He's both."

Gabby leaned forward, whispering. "And you think . . . you think the Biltmore is honestly going to let him play?"

Eddie gave her a challenging look. "Only if they want the rest of us to. Now, are we going to stand here all night or are we going to run through 'Ballin' the Jack'?"

Here we go. "Oh, we can run through it if you want," she said airily. "But we're not going to perform it."

"Really." Eddie's tone was carefully amused, but his face was not. "Don't tell me, you don't deign to learn music sent over by arrangers."

"Please," Gabby sneered. "I didn't have to learn it. I knew it, just like everyone else and their mother." *And I do mean mother,* she thought. That song had to be at least twenty years old. Viola knew it, for God's sake. "But I looked at your arrange-ment, and I'm telling you, it's not going to work."

"Is that right?" Eddie sneered right back. "Hey, Dex! C'mere for a second."

Reluctantly, the piano player tore himself away from the key-board. "What is it?"

"Little Miss Maestro here doesn't think your arrangement is going to work for her."

"Really?" Dexter's tone was cool, but Gabby thought she saw a flicker of what seemed like genuine concern in his dark eyes. "What's the matter with it?"

"Oh, it has nothing to do with the arrangement!" Gabby exclaimed. "The arranging is fine, musically."

Dexter raised his eyebrows. *"Fine?"*

"No, it's good," Gabby amended. "The problem is the song itself. 'Ballin' the Jack' is a dance number."

Eddie shrugged. "So let them dance."

"Don't you ever bother listening to the lyrics?" Gabby rolled her eyes about as far back in her head as they could go. These jazz guys might know an awful lot about musicianship and no-tation and all the things that made her practically throw up with boredom when Walter Gould went on and on about them, but none of them had the faintest idea what it took to put a song across. "It's not that kind of dance. It's a lyric dance for *me* to do. An . . . *instructional* lyric, if you know what I mean."

Eddie shook his head. *Oh brother,* Gabby thought. This was going to be even harder than she thought.

"Fine. I'll show you." Sighing, she pushed away the small area rug covering the ground where she stood and hiked up the skirt of her evening gown, tucking it firmly under each garter so her legs showed. "So the way you have it, it starts out instrumental," she said. "The easy opener. Very Tommy Dorsey. Nothing wrong with that. Go on," she commanded the musicians, who had begun to gather curiously around. "Play."

Dexter was the first at the piano. He was joined by an intrepid clarinetist and a bald guy with a trombone; the rest of them simply stood and stared. *And no wonder,* Gabby thought. *I probably look like I'm wearing a big pink diaper.* "Okay, good," she said. "So you keep up that vamp, maybe there's a little bit of a trumpet solo, if we're really going for the Dorsey." She gestured encouragingly to a cornet player, who, with a glance at Eddie, hesitantly joined in. "Then it's quiet, and then I come up front and sing. *First you put your two knees close up tight . . . then you swing 'em to the left and you swing 'em to the right . . .*"

It wasn't really such a bad song, she thought as she sang. The melody wasn't anything to write home about, but her voice felt clear and powerful and so supple that when the second chorus came, she ignored the insipid lyrics entirely and let go with a torrent of hot scat that seemed to take on a life of its own, ending on a big belted high note. *Not bad.*

"Then the trumpet takes over again," Gabby continued hastily, gesturing again to the cornet player, "and picks up where he left off. The piano comes in, maybe the trombone—that's up to you guys. You get faster, but how much of this can you listen to, I mean, really? And you know it too, because then you put in this piano vamp"—she pointed at Dexter—"which is the natural place for me to come in with the time step."

On the downbeat, Gabby started to tap. Nice and slow at first—what Jimmy liked to call leisurely—throwing in a couple of extra little changes and syncopation to keep it interesting to herself, then faster, then double time. The musicians followed the rhythm of her feet, racing to keep up. The sound was filling out; more musicians were joining in. They reached the last instrumental crescendo. *I need a big finish*, Gabby thought. Wildly, she flung herself into four devilishly difficult butterfly turns, the acrobatic backward rotating leaps so beloved by Tully Toynbee (and the reason Gabby no longer had any cartilage in her left ankle), took a last deep breath, and belted out the last line of the song, her voice ringing from the rafters: *"And that's what I call Ballin' the Jack!"* The horn section blared as she held the last note, arms outstretched, falling to her knees like Al Jolson, waiting for an ovation.

No applause came. Eddie stared at her, his mouth half open. The rubber ball of nasal spray fell to the ground with a forlorn little bounce or two before it came to rest by the leg of the piano.

"Well?" Gabby panted. "Say something."

"That . . . that was incredible," he stammered finally. "Why can't you just do *that*?"

Crabbily, Gabby tugged her unruly skirts back down over her newly sweat-dampened thighs. "One, because solo tap numbers look ridiculous from anyone who isn't Fred Astaire. Two, I don't have any tap shoes or a short dress. Three, even if I was willing to go out there with my skirt bunched up and dance around looking like some kind of swami who just dropped a load in his pants, the stage is about eight inches too high for anyone to see what I'm doing. Four—and finally—that song won't do anything for either one of us."

"What do you mean?" Eddie asked.

"I mean, I can sell a cutesy dance number, sure. You can take some tired novelty number, jazz it up, and make it hip. And Leo Karp knows it."

"Of course he does," Eddie said smugly. "That's probably why he signed me to a seven-year contract."

"With a six-month option, right?" Gabby was getting irritated. "Olympus has five thousand people on the payroll. It's no skin off Karp's nose to pick a few extra horn players for what . . . one fifty a week?" Looking around the room, Gabby saw from the men's faces that it was probably a whole lot less than that. "For all you know, he signed you just to make sure nobody else did. And then in six months, maybe a year, he'll drop you again, and there won't be any more contracts, or any more magazine covers, or any more checks waiting at the studio post office. Unless you show him you can do whatever Artie Shaw or Glenn Miller or Tommy Dorsey can do—or do it better."

Eddie snorted. "I was asked to give a performance, and that's what I'm going to do. I'm all through auditioning."

"Oh, give me a break." Gabby was getting mad. "Of course you're auditioning. You're never done auditioning. Never. I'm auditioning. You're auditioning. Everybody upstairs who just lost one of those little gold men is auditioning to get one next time, and everyone who won one is auditioning for the part that will get them another. For God's sake, even the studio bosses—*even Leo Karp* is auditioning."

"Oh yeah? For who?"

"For the money guys in New York who could pull the plug on the whole operation at any minute!" Gabby was shouting now. "For Jock Whitney and Nick Schenck and Hunter Payne. For the new talent they need to attract, and the old talent they need to stay. You want to be in the picture business, you better get used to auditioning every day. *Every single day.* Until you die, or you're the last man on earth, whichever comes first. Otherwise, you can pack up your horns and go back to the Savoy to back whatever girl singer is coming up next."

The room was silent. The only sound Gabby could hear was her own short breath. Eddie Sharp stared at her, his face hard, his lips white. Defiantly, she brushed a sweaty chestnut curl off her forehead and stared right back. *Go ahead*, she thought furiously. *Walk out. You know I'm right.*

It was Dexter who spoke first. "What do you think we should do?" he asked quietly.

It's now or never. "Do you know 'I Cried for You'?"

"The Billie Holiday song?" Dexter said, stealing a glance at a stony-faced Eddie. "Sure."

"Well," Gabby said quickly, "it's actually the Arthur Freed song. He wrote it. Arthur Freed, who is sitting out in the audience tonight. Arthur Freed, who has just been tapped to head up a new musical unit at MGM."

Eddie frowned. "But we're at Olympus."

"Do I have to explain everything? These guys are only interested in having what they think somebody else wants. It's the first rule of Hollywood! Why the hell do you think people get divorced so much out here?"

A couple of the musicians looked like they were about to laugh, which somehow just made Gabby madder.

"I'm serious!" she shouted. "If Karp thinks Mayer might have a use for us, he'll do anything to keep us. The sky's the limit!"

Eddie Sharp wasn't laughing. "How would you arrange it, Dex?"

"You open it slow," Gabby blurted out before Dexter could answer. "Show them we can do a good old-fashioned torch song." She sang a couple of bars a cappella to demonstrate. "Then, just when everybody's so heartbroken they're practically killing themselves, we suddenly bring it up tempo. Just like that. Remind them there's something worth living for. They're going to go crazy."

"Torch, then swing," Eddie gave her a wry smile. "Like Judy Garland's doing with 'Zing! Went the Strings of My Heart'?"

"No," said Gabby, lifting her chin. "Like Gabby Preston doing 'I Cried for You.'"

Eddie looked thoughtful for a moment.

"Okay," he said finally, with a decisive nod. "Let's do it."

"Really?" Gabby squealed.

"We'll run through it a couple of times first. A-flat, right?"

She nodded, speechless.

"Thought so. It needs an instrumental solo in the intro. Trombone."

"I was thinking clarinet, actually."

"Clarinet." Eddie snapped his fingers. "Better." He turned to the waiting crowd. "All right, fellas, you heard the lady. 'I Cried for You' in A-flat. Make *me* cry."

It's all happening, Gabby thought jubilantly, watching as the musicians scrambled to their places around her. *I won.* Somebody actually *listened* to her for a change. It was a thrilling sensation.

Also new, and even more thrilling, was the way Eddie Sharp was looking at her. Not just with desire, the way she'd seen men look at other girls and longed for them to look at her that way. There was something else in his admiring expression, something even better. *He's looking at me with respect.*

"Gabby!"

Oh no.

At the friendly trill of that familiar voice, Gabby's heart sank like a stone. Standing in the doorway, as though conjured from midair by some vengeful fairy godmother, was Amanda Farraday, looking . . . well, pretty much looking the way Amanda always looked, only more so. She was wearing a dark green velvet gown that clung to every dangerous curve, cut low to expose a generous swath of décolletage. Her red hair, shining like satin, tumbled loosely over her creamy shoulders in a way that somehow seemed positively indecent outside of the boudoir.

Oh no, oh no, oh no.

"Jimmy said you were down here," Amanda said breathily. She seemed not to hear the low wolf whistles coming from the horn section. If you looked like Amanda, Gabby thought, after a while you probably just stopped noticing. "I just wanted to tell you to break a leg."

"Thank you," Gabby said stiffly. "I didn't know you were going to be here."

"Oh, it was sort of a spur-of-the-moment thing," Amanda replied. In her flushed face, her eyes looked uncharacteristically, almost unnaturally bright. Something was lighting her up inside. *If I didn't know better, I'd think she'd been at the green pills.* "Say, you haven't seen Harry anywhere, have you?"

Gabby shrugged. "Not since the ceremony."

"Oh." Amanda's face fell, which somehow made her look even more gorgeous. *Like some kind of tragic heroine,* Gabby thought. *God, I hate her sometimes.*

"Well, I didn't mean to interrupt," Amanda continued. "I just wanted to say hi, and that I hope you knock 'em dead out

100

here. And, um . . ." She leaned forward slightly, giving everyone a nice view. "If you *do* happen to see Harry, don't tell him I asked about him, okay?"

The men seemed transported as she turned and walked away. *So predictable.*

"Friend of yours?" Eddie asked when everybody's tongues were safely back in their mouths.

"Why? You want me to call her back in here?"

"That depends." A small smile played across Eddie's beautiful mouth. "Can she sing?"

"Not a note."

"In that case, tell her never to interrupt rehearsal again. Now come on, boys. Let's take it from the top."

NINE

Amanda knew Gabby Preston about as well as anyone could. After living—or rather, existing—in her spare room for months with a ringside seat to the rages and tantrums and equally frequent fits of wild jubilation that most people experienced only at moments of life and death but that for Gabby were just another day. Amanda didn't think there was much her mercurial friend could do to surprise her.

But she'd never seen Gabby the way she was onstage tonight. She was absolutely on fire.

It wasn't that she was doing anything particularly special— Amanda had heard "I Cried for You" sung dozens of times, sometimes even by Gabby herself. It was something about the *way* she was singing it. The lyrics were addressed to a faithless lover, telling him that the singer was over him, thank you very much; she'd found somebody else, and now it was his turn to cry. But Gabby's rendition—the velvety throb of her voice haunting yet powerful, her huge dark eyes glistening with un-shed tears—made it all seem like a lie. Like she was putting on a defiant front while she was falling apart inside. The wounded bravery made it all the more heartbreaking, so much so that when she suddenly gave a little stamp of her foot and the band broke into a joyful up-tempo Dixieland swing, the audience gasped with relief. Maybe her heart was broken, but she was going to be okay. And if she was lying about how happy she was, at least she was doing it with style. It was the kind of lie Hollywood could appreciate.

Gabby belted the final, glorious note, and the audience leapt to its feet, roaring its appreciation. Cheering along with the others, Amanda looked reflexively toward Mr. Karp's table, to see if he was paying attention to her friend's triumph, and caught a glimpse of a familiar figure leaning against the door-way. His hands in his pockets, a thoughtful expression on his face. The person she'd been searching for since she came in.

Harry.

Feeling her gaze on him, he looked up, and their eyes locked. Amanda's heart stopped, just as it had that afternoon at the Brown Derby that had filled her with such desperate hope. She gave him a small smile, lifting her hand in the tiniest of greetings.

Harry turned and fled.

I have to go after him, Amanda thought. *I have to talk to him.*

It was the whole reason she'd come here, to this party where she didn't quite belong, in this dress she definitely couldn't af-ford. She couldn't let him slip away. Not this time. Not like this.

Wildly, she searched the room, trying to see if anyone had

noticed the silent scene between them, but all eyes seemed fixed on Gabby, who was basking in the attention with the graceful delight of a great star. For once in Amanda Farraday's life, no one was looking at her. It couldn't have happened at a better time.

Gathering up her skirt, she bolted through the door and down the hall. The black flap of a slightly too-large tailcoat disappeared around the corner.

"Harry!"

If he was trying to get away from her, he wasn't doing a very good job of it. The hallway he had chosen came to an abrupt dead end. Harry stood against the wall, scratching his head and staring at an enormous potted rubber plant with such a quizzical expression that Amanda had to laugh.

"What are you going to do? Hide in that plant?"

Harry studied the dark green leaves, as though he expected them to spring to life and give him instruction. "I don't know. Maybe."

"Well, don't. You'll get dirt all over your tailcoat and the rental place will charge you extra."

At the mention of his legendary frugality, even Harry had to smile.

"You're right," he said quietly, looking at her for the first time. "Hello, Amanda."

"Hello."

"Hello."

They laughed again and stood staring at each other, unsure of what to say next. "Wasn't Gabby terrific?" Amanda tried, feeling awkward.

Harry scratched his nose. "I only caught the very end.

I was . . ." He pushed his glasses back up. "I was putting my mother to bed upstairs."

"Your mother," Amanda said. "I thought that must be her."

How many times had Amanda dreamed of being introduced to Harry's mother? Of Harry ushering her into the cramped but fastidiously clean Brooklyn sitting room he had always described in such vivid detail? Of him saying, "Ma, this is my girlfriend, Amanda. This is Amanda, my fiancée. This is Amanda, the girl I love"? In these fantasies, Amanda always imagined Harry's mother—a squat black-and-white blur, from what she'd seen in photos—wrapping her plump arms around her in a lilac- or lily-of-the-valley-scented embrace before pulling out the cracked leather photo albums of Harry as a baby. Together, as allies, they'd laugh over his tightness with a dollar, his irrational hatred of mushrooms, the way, like Hansel and Gretel with the breadcrumbs, he seemed to leave a trail of crumbled tobacco and crushed potato chips wherever he went.

"And have you noticed," Amanda would say, "how when he's nervous, he plays solitaire, only without any cards?"

"While whistling 'God Bless America' over and over again?" Mrs. Gordon would say. "Absolutely!"

"I flew her in," Harry said now, not without a modicum of pride. "She wanted to see the ceremony."

"Did she have a good time?"

Harry grinned. "You can say that again. Little old Jewish ladies are not exactly accustomed to unlimited champagne. God knows what she would have been like if I'd won."

"You will," Amanda said fervently. "Someday."

"We'll see." They looked at each other for a long time. "So," Harry said finally. "Diana Chesterfield has resurfaced."

"I saw," Amanda said. "I hope you gave her quite a hard time for disappearing off your picture."

"Aw, it didn't turn out so bad in the end."

"Even so." Amanda shook her head. "Did she have any explanation for where the hell she's been the past year?"

Harry shrugged. "Something about falling madly in love with some English duke she met on an Atlantic crossing whose family refused to accept her, so she was shut up in some castle until a handsome male secretary helped her escape to Paris to lick her wounds, so to speak. Kind of a cross between Wallis Simpson and Countess Olenska. Undoubtedly inspired by just those two."

"You don't believe her?"

"Believe her?" Harry shrugged again. "What does it matter if I believe her or not? I'll tell you one thing though, there's no way Dane Forrest can dump poor little Margo Sterling and take her back. I mean, how could he? After she's admitted to being with all those other men."

Ah. Amanda thought of that line from some Shakespeare play Harry was always quoting. *There's the rub.*

"Harry," she said, "we need to talk."

He looked back down at the leaves. "Do we?"

"You know we do."

Harry knitted his eyebrows doubtfully. "I don't know if that's such a good idea."

Desperate times call for desperate measures, Amanda thought. She took a step toward him, strategically leaning slightly forward so that even with his head bent he would catch the fullest glimpse of her creamy cleavage.

"Please? Isn't there someplace we can go?"

Behind Harry's thick glasses, his eyes took on a narcotic glaze. "I . . . The studio got me a room upstairs. We could go there for a couple of minutes, I guess."

"And your mother?"

Harry grinned. "She's down the hall."

God, Amanda thought. *If I were as good with money as I am with men, I'd be running the whole damn studio.*

Harry's junior suite at the Biltmore was the hotel-room version of an Olympus writer: small, dark, and overpriced.

"'Why can't the actors just make it up as they go along?'" Harry said. "That's something my producer said to me. 'You just come up with the story and let them act it out in their own words.' He actually said that."

He turned toward the small, sparsely equipped bar cart to fix them a couple of drinks. He'd been chattering nervously like this since they got on the elevator.

"Like it doesn't matter. Like it's a silent picture where they can be talking about their pets and what they're going to eat for dinner, because they're going to put a title card over it in post anyway." Shaking his head, he handed Amanda a glass of lukewarm scotch. "No wonder Scott Fitzgerald and William Faulkner and Dorothy Parker—you know, real writers—are drinking themselves to death out here. Sorry," he added, "I don't have any ice. If you want, I can call for some."

"It's all right." Amanda took a steadying sip of the amber liquid. "At least you don't have to worry about them forgetting their lines," she said, taking another sip. "If they're making them up themselves, I mean."

"Yeah. And you know, the hell of it is, it comes straight from the top. If Karp gave a damn about writers, then the rest of them would have to. But frankly, I'm not sure the man can even read, let alone appreciate good writing. As far as he's concerned, we're bottom feeders. A bunch of faceless insects scuttling across the ocean floor, scavenging whatever scraps we can." He took a sip of his drink and made a face. "God, I miss New York. The weather's lousy and the subway smells like pee, but at least the people there appreciate the written word."

Amanda smiled. Listening to Harry's familiar, unchanging litany of grievances, she could almost pretend the last six horrible months had never happened.

"Is this really what you want to talk about?" she asked.

"I guess not." Harry looked sheepish. "Anyway, you were the one who wanted to talk."

"I know." Amanda's heart was pounding. Desperately, she searched her mind for all the coquettish things she'd thought of to say when and if this moment came, but the only thing that sprang to her lips was the truth. "Oh, Harry. Everything has been so awful since . . . since you left. I can't tell you how . . ." She swallowed hard. "If you had only let me tell you about . . . about the past. I wanted to. I wrote you letters. Hundreds and hundreds. Trying to . . . I don't know . . . to *explain*."

Harry frowned. "I never got any letters."

"I was too afraid to send them." Amanda looked down at her hands, fighting back tears. "But the important thing—the thing that you *have* to know—is that all of that, it was all over before I met you. Before I ever knew there was going to be a you."

"I know," Harry said quietly.

108

His face was close to hers. She looked deep into his dark eyes, breathing in the familiar smell of him, of cigarettes and ink and the fancy lime-scented English soap that was the only expensive thing he allowed himself to buy. "Oh, Harry," she gasped. "I miss you so much." The tears she had been struggling to hold back suddenly burst from her eyes, falling thick and fast over her powdered cheeks.

"Amanda, no," Harry murmured. "Don't cry. Please. Don't cry."

But she couldn't help it. He put out his arms to comfort her, cautiously at first, but at the familiar touch their bodies fell together, fitting as perfectly as they always had. "Don't cry," he whispered again, "don't cry." She lifted her face and his lips met hers. They were kissing now, the tears still streaming down her face, their lips wordlessly saying all the things that had been left unspoken for the past six months.

If it had been a scene from a picture, this would have been the part when it faded to black.

But sometimes, Amanda thought happily as she guided Harry's warm hands toward the zipper of her gown, *sometimes real life is even better than the movies.*

TEN

God. She's so beautiful.

Seeing her bright hair spread in a silky fan across the pillow, her long eyelashes casting soft shadows on her pale cheek, Harry thought, as he often had, that looking at a sleeping Amanda was like being somehow transported into some undiscovered pre-Raphaelite painting. Like being with one of the ethereal, half-magical beauties in the Arthurian legends he had loved to read as a little boy. It was as if the enchantress Morgan le Fay or the Lady of the Lake had materialized in the bed to bestow her favors upon some lucky bastard of a mortal peasant, and the lucky bastard was Harry.

He'd never felt worse in his entire life.

Amanda's eyes fluttered open. "Good morning."

"Good morning."

"What are you doing dressed so early?" she murmured. A

lazy feline smile spread across her face as she wrapped her arms around his waist.

"It's not that early. Anyway, I have to go to the studio."

Her smile faded. "Today? Who's going to be there?"

"Everyone who wasn't there last night." Harry extricated himself from her grasp, turning his head away. He couldn't look at her, not right now. "Besides, I get the most done when it's quiet. Fewer people around to bother me."

"Harry." Amanda sat up. "If this is about not winning last night . . ."

"It has nothing to do with that," he snapped. "I'm on a deadline, that's all. Production schedules don't change just because somebody else went home with an Oscar."

"Oh." She cast her eyes downward, pulling the sheet around herself protectively. "Of course. I understand."

Harry felt a sudden stab of remorse. "Do you . . . do you need a ride home or anything?"

She shook her head. "I have my own car."

"Then, listen, stay as long as you want. And order breakfast— hell, order anything. Champagne, caviar, anything."

"For breakfast?"

"Why not?" He shrugged. "Listen, Amanda . . . I'm really sorry about this."

"What do you mean, 'this'?"

He looked down, unable to meet her eye. "About having to run off to the studio," he said finally.

"Oh." The relief in her voice was palpable. "Don't worry about it, darling, I understand."

Darling. He placed a swift, dry kiss on her expectant lips. "I'll call you, okay?"

God, could I be any more of a heel? Harry thought as he scurried out the door. *I might as well have left fifty bucks on the dresser.*

His head pounded with the ache of last night's Scotch as he rapped his knuckles on the door at the far end of the hall.

"Who is it?" came a fearful voice.

"Ma, it's me. Open up."

"Harry!" There was a symphony of jangling and clicking as Sadie Gorenstein labored to open the collection of locks and latches on the door. From the sound of things, Harry wouldn't have been surprised if she'd brought some of them with her especially from New York. "Where have you been? I've been up for hours. It's still dark and there I am already wide awake, staring at the ceiling."

"It's the jet lag, Ma." He kissed her cheek. "Remember, I told you how California is three hours earlier than New York."

"Sure, I remember, but I don't understand. To me, time is time." She ran her hands self-consciously down the front of her flowered dress. "I'm embarrassed, I don't have anything to offer you."

"It's okay."

She gestured helplessly around the room. "If only you could have found me a place with a kitchen, I could have prepared you something. Made you eggs with belly lox and lots of onions, just the way you like."

"I have to go to the studio this morning anyway," Harry said. "Some rewrites that have to be in by the end of the day, or else." He'd already lied to Amanda; why not lie to his mother too? "Besides, Ma, you don't make breakfast in a place like this, you order it. Just pick up the phone and tell them to bring you eggs or toast or anything you want, and to charge it to the room."

112

"A cooked breakfast?" Sadie made a face. "It won't be kosher."

"It wasn't kosher last night, and you ate."

"That was different. With all those people around, I didn't want to be rude. Besides, with a cooked breakfast, they'll put bacon with it."

Harry sighed. "So have the fruit plate."

"Fruit plate? Here?"

"Yes, here. California has the best produce in the whole world. Believe me, there'll be such fruit on the plate you never even knew it existed." *Jesus*, Harry thought. *Five minutes with my mother and already I'm talking like a character from* The Jazz Singer. "And after breakfast, go down to the lobby and the driver will take you anywhere you want to go. Shopping, anything."

"The driver?" Another face. "You want your mama should be alone in a car with a strange colored man?"

"His name is Arthur, Ma," Harry said. "He's from the studio, and he's a very nice man. You'll like him, he's from the Bronx. And I'll be back here around six to take you to dinner."

"Dinner? Where dinner?"

"I thought we'd go to the Vendome on the Sunset Strip. It's a French restaurant, and they've got card games in the back, like Pop used to play on Hester Street."

"You want I should eat with a bunch of gamblers?"

"Gamblers know how to eat. It's one of the best places in town."

"But all your fancy-schmancy friends already saw me in my dress."

"So buy another one." Harry kissed her cheek again. "I'll see you at six. Try to have fun."

In the lobby, Harry was suddenly somehow seized by the wild notion of going back and asking Amanda to look after his mother for the day. Why not throw the two inescapable women in his life together and see who made it out alive? But the flames of that idea were soon doused by the ice bucket of reality. He could never introduce his mother to Amanda, not in a hundred years, and certainly not as his *girlfriend*.

It wasn't just because she was a Gentile. Harry assumed that Sadie Gorenstein, like hundreds of other mothers who had lost their bright Jewish boys to the lights of Hollywood, had long ago made her uneasy peace with the fact that it was very likely the girl her darling son brought back to Brooklyn would not arrive equipped with her own gefilte fish recipe. She would be a Gentile, with no *people,* no family, no place. Whatever world had spawned the primordial Amanda, there was, as Gertrude Stein would say, no *there* there. It was almost laughable, thought Harry, without even a hint of a chuckle, how little he actually knew about the girl who had vacuumed up every speck of his mental and emotional energy since almost the moment he met her. He imagined the two of them sitting stiffly on the enormous antimacassar laid protectively over the velveteen sofa in his mother's *tchotchke*-cluttered living room in Flatbush: "Ma, this is Amanda. I don't know her real name or how old she is. I think she's from Oklahoma but I'm not sure, I don't know if she has any brothers and sisters or what her father did for a living, or if he is still living, or if he ever existed at all. I don't even know where she lives, but by God, I think I want to marry her."

No. Harry shook his head. *That wouldn't go over well at all.* And that was before you even took into account the one incontrovertible factual thing he knew about Amanda, regarding what she used to do for a living—what she used to be and, as far as he knew, what she still *was*. Sure, she denied it, but that didn't explain how she'd looked like a million bucks every time he'd seen her recently. Something—or more likely, *someone*—was keeping her in Paris fashions and French perfume, and it sure as hell wasn't a contract player's fifty bucks a week.

Well, Harry thought, letting himself into his new corner office in the Writers' Building on the Olympus lot, *she's not going to make a fool of me this time*.

He still loved her, or at least, he still *wanted* her, that was clear. Which was why he couldn't trust himself around her. Last night had been incredible as always, but afterward, as they'd lain in bed, her head nestled against his chest, her smooth arms wrapped around his neck, Harry had started conjuring horrible pictures of Amanda looking the same way at other men, saying the same things, *doing* the same things, to the point that he'd disentangled himself from her sleeping embrace in disgust. Even now, they swam into his mind unbidden; the harder he tried not to think about it, the more explicit and intense the images became. They'd never go away, he was sure of it. Maybe it was his problem. Maybe he was just too old-fashioned, too chauvinistic. It didn't matter. That was the way it was.

And yet, if she materialized right now in his office, her lips parted, her arms outstretched, looking at him the way she always did—as though Harry, shy little Harry Gorenstein with the kinky hair and the crooked nose and clothes that were always just a little bit too big and a little bit too wrinkled, was the only man in the world—he knew he would be unable to resist. And then he would hate her for it. And she would hate him for hating her. And so it would go, on and on, a vicious cycle that would drive both of them crazy and destroy their lives. Unless he put a stop to it.

Jean, his new secretary, had carefully cleared off and dusted a spot on his end table for the Oscar statuette that just yesterday they had all been so sure was going to be his. The bare polished wood gleamed up at him reproachfully. *Told ya so.*

Sighing, Harry reached into his desk drawer for some papers to cover it up and came up with a fistful of typewritten pages with a familiar title:

```
                An American Girl
                By Harry Gordon
```

An American Girl. His masterpiece. The script he had written for Amanda. The movie that was supposed to make her a star and declare his undying love for her at the same time. Currently languishing in development hell, without an actress, without a director, without a chance of being made.

Harry could never keep his fingers off a sore. With an appetite for pain that was almost perverse, he turned the first page and began to read.

God, it was good. Heartfelt and gripping, so different from all the anemic little efforts he'd been making since. *Too good to sit gathering dust in a drawer,* Harry thought. But what to do with it? When the studio first commissioned the screenplay from him, they had intended it to be a musical vehicle for Gabby Preston. Was that still possible? After her incredible performance last night at the Governor's Ball—a performance that had, quite frankly, shocked Harry, who had always thought of her as no more than a bratty little kid—the producers were certain to be looking for a project for her, and fast. But the best scenes of the script didn't seem to lend themselves to big production numbers. They were intimate scenes between characters who talked passionately about their hopes, their dreams, their ideas about the world, their plans for the future.

Just a few people in a small room.

Suddenly, Harry had an idea. An idea that, if executed properly, could solve *everything.* He lunged for the phone and dialed the switchboard.

"Operator, I need to place a long-distance call to New York City. Right away."

There was a brief pause as the operator hesitated. "I don't know if I'm authorized to place long-distance calls from Mr. Gordon's office."

"Dammit, this *is* Mr. Gordon."

"Oh, Mr. Gordon, of course! I do apologize. What's the number?"

Harry flipped frantically through his address book. "Gramercy 5-7349." He rubbed his thumb excitedly over the gilt edges of its pages as he waited for her to connect the call.

"Group Theater, Harold Clurman's office. How can I help you?"

"I need to speak to Har—Mr. Clurman, please. Right away."

"I'm afraid Mr. Clurman's in a meeting, sir. May I ask whose calling?"

"This is Harry Gordon, in Los Angeles."

"Oh!" The secretary's little gasp gratified him more than was perhaps seemly. "I see. Shall I . . . shall I go and get him?"

"No need." Harry grinned to himself. "Just go in and tell

117

him I have a play for him. Then come back and tell me what he says."

"Yes . . . yes, sir. Right away."

There was a rustle of static as she hurried away. Harry slid a stale cigarette from the crumpled pack on his desk and inserted it into his mouth unlit, chewing on the filter until she came back.

"Mr. Gordon?"

"Yes?"

"He asks how soon he can see it."

Harry pumped his fist in triumph. "Tell him he can have it, and me, by the end of the week."

"You?" The secretary sounded shocked. "But aren't you in Hollywood?"

"Not for long I'm not."

Now there was only his agent to call. For this one, he actually needed to light the cigarette.

"Harry, baby," came the familiar garrulous voice over the phone. "What can I do for you?"

"I'm going back east for a while, Myron," Harry said matter-of-factly. "You're the first to know. I need you to take care of my affairs while I'm away."

"Now, sweetheart, come on." A note of concern, or more likely, panic, crept into the agent's voice. "If this is about last night, believe me, it's no big deal. It sounds like a cliché, but it really is an honor just to be nominated. We'll pick it up one of these years, you'll see."

"It's not that. It has nothing to do with that. It's business."

"And may I ask what business?"

"Of a personal nature," Harry said coolly. "Don't worry,

118

Myron, I'll be back. It's only for a few months. *The Glass Key* can go into production without me. I'll send any rewrites they need through the wires. In the meantime, please see that all my other correspondence gets forwarded to the Waldorf Astoria."

"Anything else?"

"Only one thing." Harry blew a smoke ring. It quivered nervously near the tip of his nose before dissipating into the air. "It doesn't matter how you do it, but it's very, very important, and it needs to be done by the time I get back."

"Anything," the agent said. "Just tell me what it is."

Harry crushed the glowing ember of his cigarette against the desk.

"By the time I get back, I want you to have fixed it that I never bump into Amanda Farraday again."

ELEVEN

All of Hollywood Is Asking: Who Is Diana's Duke?

The large storybook letters of the *Picture Palace* headline swirled and twined in and around each other, like something out of a medieval illuminated manuscript. They'd even gone so far as to top the purple W with a delicate engraving of a crown last seen during the coronation of George VI two years before.

Olive Moore took a long, restorative sip of sherry from her Waterford crystal glass. Then she smoothed the pages back against the dark leather blotter on her desk and began to read.

In case you've been living under a rock in the two weeks since the Oscars—or, like sore-loser screenwriter Harry Gordon, just boo-hoo-hooed yourself all the way back to Broadway—here's the big scoop on the lips of all the usually nonspeaking Tinseltownspeople: Diana Chesterfield is back! That's right, America's Number One Female Box-Office Star, mysteriously missing from our screens and hearts these past twelve months without so much as a postcard to her forlorn fans, has made her triumphant return to the Hollywood stratosphere, and in a fashion appropriate to a thespienne of her caliber:

Thespienne. Olive had to smile at that.

---

a dramatic surprise entrance to present the Academy Award for Best Actor to her frequent costar and erstwhile paramour Dane Forrest. Spectators worried the tongue-tied Mr. Forrest was about to double over from the double shock (believe us, we didn't expect him to win either!) as he stammered his way through a much-abbreviated acceptance speech in which he failed to thank anyone, most conspicuously his (conspicuously) unnominated and current paramour, Miss Margo Sterling, who may have been swathed in peacock blue but looked like she was all in lemon. Had just swallowed one, that is.

But the real question is just where has our darling Diana been? Speculation has been ripe among Hollywood's cognoscenti, and by that, we mean the people who think they know everything about everyone. But there's only one place that knows the truth, dearest reader, and that's your own humble *Picture Palace,* which has the most exclusive of exclusive interviews with the dazzling Miss Chesterfield herself! Turn to page 14 for the whole scoop!

With an impatient sigh, Olive flicked through the pages, past ads for lipstick, hand cream, and a bizarre kind of vibrating belt that promised to reduce the waistline through the magic of electricity; until she found the page with a silvery black-and-white photograph of Diana in full evening dress, lounging incongruously beside an outdoor pool, with an accompanying wall of text. She skimmed the first few paragraphs, which summarized Diana's beauty, achievements, and all-around star quality, until she found an actual quote.

"I suppose it sounds terribly silly," says Diana shame-facedly, a blush creeping into her usually porcelain-pale cheeks. "But I really thought I was going to quit the movie business for good, and for the oldest and best reason there is. For love."

But let's begin at the beginning, shall we? It seems the madcap Miss Chesterfield decided to take a spon-taneous holiday to the Continent just days before she was due to start shooting *The Nine Days' Queen,* the hit picture that would eventually star her alleged on-screen successor (and romantic rival?), Margo Sterling.

"I had to see about some gowns in Paris," she mur-murs demurely. After all, what's Olympus Studios when Coco Chanel is waiting?

It was on the Atlantic crossing, however, that she

met a dashing English duke lingering just outside the door of her lavish first-class cabin. "He was quite certain it was his, you see," Diana says, "and perplexed by how his key didn't seem to fit in the lock. I think he'd had rather a lot of whiskey just before the dressing gong rang." When the screen's most luminous goddess emerged from her chamber to see what all the fuss was about, the tipsy toff thought she was something out of a dream. He insisted on escorting her to dinner, of course. . . .

"Of course." Olive sniffed, refilling her brandy glass.

One thing led to another, and by the end of the evening, he declared his intention to make Diana Chesterfield his duchess. "He said he'd throw himself overboard if I refused," Diana says. "He actually had one foot over the railing. How could I say no?" Madly in love, she disembarked with his lordship in Southampton and in a matter of days was ensconced in his magnificent family seat, ready to begin a new life among the crème de la crème of society . . . with one condition: that they keep news of their engagement absolutely secret.

Her caution proved to be prophetic. Still reeling in the wake of Mrs. Simpson and the abdication, British society has in recent years become unfairly hostile to plucky young American girls, and pressure from the duke's family (ever a lady, Diana discreetly refuses to name names) made marriage between these star-crossed lovers out of the question.

So why didn't the heartbroken Diana come home to lick her wounds? She casts her lovely eyes down toward the white hands trembling in her lap. "To tell the truth, I was too embarrassed. You see, I'm an old-fashioned girl at heart. All I've ever wanted is a home and a family of my own. I've always said I'd give up the pictures in a second for love, and that's just what I meant to do. And when it didn't work out"—she glances up, her sapphire eyes brimming with tears— "well, I suppose I was just too ashamed at what a silly little fool I'd been."

And what of Margo Sterling, the new blonde on the block, who slotted so neatly into her place, both on- and offscreen? Don't look for a catfight here. "I truly admire her work in her pictures very much," Diana says sincerely, "and I'm so pleased to have the chance to get to know her better. I'm just sure we'll be the best of friends."

"Olive?"

Startled, Olive lunged for her open ledger book and covered the magazine with it.

It's so silly, she thought, but she didn't want any of her girls seeing her read this kind of frivolous picture trash. It might make them think their boss was just like them.

"Yes, Lucy," she said, beckoning the bottle-blonde standing slouched in the doorway with a brisk wave of her hand. "What is it?"

"I just wanted to know if I'm working tonight. Else I thought I'd go out to the pictures. There's that new picture with Irene

Dunne and Charles Boyer playing at the Egyptian. Mitzi saw it last night and said it was just dreamy."

Olive flipped through her alligator-skin appointment book. "As a matter of fact, you have got a date. It's that fellow who calls himself Mr. Peterson."

"Oh no!" Lucy cried. "Not him. Not again."

"I'm afraid it can't be helped, dear. He called up and asked for you personally."

"But his breath is always so terrible. Honestly, he smells like he swallowed a dead rat." Lucy's narrow shoulders shuddered. "And he gets so drunk at dinner, and then he gets *mean*."

Olive sighed. "Try to bring him back here, then, dear. Or have him take you to the Roosevelt. The bellboys know enough to keep an eye out for you there, and you can always call Raymond at the front desk if you get into a jam."

"Just once, I'd like to be pleasantly surprised. One of these guys calls up with a fake name and it turns out he's Charles Boyer." She smiled wistfully. "I bet Ginger's met Charles Boyer, don't you think so?"

Olive's head snapped back up sharply. "Ginger?"

"On account of her being in the picture business now," Lucy said. "I bet she's met all kinds of stars."

"I don't know what you're talking about. Now get dressed, and tell the maid to bring up another bottle of sherry. The decanter was barely half full. Go on."

Nodding, the girl did as she was told. Olive leaned back in her chair and pulled the magazine back out from underneath the ledger book.

It was a good story, all right. Not a word of it was true, obviously, but she had to hand it to Larry Julius and the Olympus press office for constructing something so deliciously sophisticated and romantic, so dizzyingly daffy—indeed, rather like the plot of a Diana Chesterfield picture. In fact, Olive wouldn't be a bit surprised to see a Diana Chesterfield picture just like it very soon. Olympus had even fixed it so Diana wouldn't have to go back to Dane Forrest and their sham of a romance. Olive was happy about that, at least. She knew what a strain it had been on them all those years, having to pretend. Now Dane, at least, could have some happiness.

But the woman he'd chosen to have his happiness with was going to pose a problem.

Margo Sterling.

"I truly admire her work in her pictures very much, and I'm so pleased to have the chance to get to know her better. I'm just sure we'll be the best of friends."

If that wasn't a warning shot over the bow, Olive didn't know what was.

Instinctively, her hand flew up to the collar of her blouse, where she used to wear her gold-and-pearl pin, the one she'd parted with all those months ago.

At last, it was time.

"Oh, my little Margaret," Olive murmured, reaching for the last of the sherry. "You're going to need me more than ever now."

"Oh, give me a *break,*" Margo groaned, hurling the latest issue of *Picture Palace* off the side of the bed. "I've never read a bigger load of garbage in all my life."

"Margo, I can't hear you. Come in here if you want to talk to me."

With another groan, Margo gathered up the rumpled magazine and carried it into the bathroom, where Dane stood shaving in front of the mirror. "It's about Diana."

"There's a surprise."

"Just read it," Margo insisted as Dane shaved. "I mean, are you kidding me? An English *duke*. And they couldn't get married because his family didn't approve? That doesn't even make any sense! There's no title higher than a duke except a royal prince, and they're all already married. If he's supposed to be a duke, he would have already inherited and he could marry whomever he wanted. It just doesn't add up."

"It doesn't add up," Dane said, "because it's a lie."

"Right, but they could at least have gotten the story straight. Made him a viscount or something. This is just so easy to disprove, it's ridiculous."

Dane wiped his face with a towel. "Luckily, I don't think most of *Photoplay*'s audience is familiar with the exact pecking order of the British peerage."

"It's in *Picture Palace*." Margo pouted. "And some of them will. British people."

"Honey," Dane sighed. "I don't know what you're getting so worked up about."

"I'm not."

"You are." He turned away from the mirror to face her. "Believe me, Larry Julius has thought this out better than you ever could. And frankly, you should be grateful to Diana for going along with it and selling it as well as she did. It's good for her, it's good for the studio, and most of all, it's good for us."

"I don't see how."

Dane gave her a hard look. "Please don't do this."

Margo looked down at the wet floor. She knew what Dane meant. By having Diana so publicly repudiate their "romance," Larry had set it up so that Dane could hardly ever be expected to "take her back." Their romantic lives, constantly rearranged at the whim of the studio as if they were chess pieces on a board, would remain as is for now. "She 'can't wait' to get to know me better," she muttered. "What the hell is that supposed to mean?"

"Maybe exactly what it says," Dane said. "She is my sister, after all. Even—maybe even especially—if we're the only ones who know it. It's not out of the realm of possibility that she might want to be your friend."

"Yeah," Margo said. "Such a friend she stepped right in and took my part."

Dane let out a sigh. "What part?"

"In the *Madame Bovary* picture Raoul Kurtzman is doing."

Dane frowned. "I thought they were borrowing Claudette Colbert from Paramount for that."

"They were, but she and Zukor asked for some ridiculous salary, and I was next in the running." *At least, I was hoping I was.*

Dane's eyes lit up. "But they gave it to Diana?"

"You don't seem very disappointed for me."

"Margo." Dane's voice carried a note of warning. "Come on. You're too young. It's a perfect role for Diana, with everything she's been through. Are they really giving it to her? Where'd you hear that, anyway?"

"Where else? From Gabby." Scowling, Margo snatched a washcloth from the side of the tub and began to wipe up Dane's stubbly little hairs from the lip of the sink. It was his bathroom, but still, it drove her crazy how he just *left* them there like that. "She seems to know everything lately."

"Anything else interesting?"

"Not really. Mostly she just goes on and on about that bandleader. Eddie Sharp. The one she sang with at the Governor's Ball. Sounds like she's crazy about him."

Dane snorted. "That'll end well."

"I don't know," Margo said. "It sounds different this time. Like he really respects her . . . I don't know . . . her *talent*. She thinks he's going to offer her a contract to record with him." She picked up Dane's comb, still oily with Brylcreem, from the ledge in front of the mirror and ran her fingers absently over the teeth. "What do you suppose that's like?"

"To be respected for one's talent?"

"No, to be under contract to just one person like that. Like Paulette Goddard was with Charlie Chaplin. Or all those girls who sign with Howard Hughes."

Dane rolled his eyes. "I don't know. I suppose it's rather stifling. Like a kind of marriage."

"And what's *that* supposed to mean?"

"Margo, please. I don't have time for this. I'm due on set in an hour. The car will be here any minute, and I haven't even gone over my lines yet. Look." His tone softened as he reached for her hand. "Why don't you get dressed and ride along? You haven't been to the studio in weeks. You can drop in on Raoul Kurtzman, maybe a couple of the writers. Have lunch with Gabby." He grinned. "Hell, maybe you'll bump into Jimmy Molloy and figure out some way to try to make me jealous. That always cheers you up."

Dane meant well, Margo knew, but there was such self-satisfaction in his tone, such condescending, knowing *smugness*, that she couldn't stem the swell of anger bubbling up inside her, any more than a kettle on the stove could keep from boiling over. "And who are you planning to make me jealous with? Some extra behind the backdrop? Or should I be prepared for a cozy photo op with darling sister herself?"

"Stop it." Dane seized her by the shoulders, his face dark as a thundercloud. "That is enough. I swear, Margo, say one more word about Diana, just one, and I'll—"

"You'll what?" Margo shouted.

The doorbell rang before he could answer her. Dane had it rigged to sound through the telephone in every room of the house. Now it echoed through the walls of the bedroom, high and shrill as an ambulance siren, seeming to echo the alarm Margo felt.

"Goddammit," Dane muttered, releasing her. "George! Answer the door! *George!*"

"He's probably in the guesthouse, listening to the radio and drinking Coca-Cola," Margo said bitterly. "That's all he ever does these days."

Pushing her aside, snatching his shirt from the back of the chair, Dane rushed toward the front door.

With a stab of real fear, Margo followed close on his heels. She couldn't let him leave like this. Not after a fight. Not when he was off to a studio full of girls. Bored dancing girls parading around in no more than a few scraps of net and a couple of spangles; ambitious chorus girls who would do anything to see their name in the papers; vulnerable, starstruck girls who would trail him around like a puppy for so much as a friendly word. Girls not so very different from how Margo had been when Dane had first laid eyes on her, slouched on the bench outside soundstage 14 and weeping as though her heart would break.

Never mind the fight, Margo thought suddenly. *I may never let him go to the studio without me ever again.*

"Dane, wait," she pleaded helplessly as he opened the door. "I'm sorry. Darling, I'm so sorry. I want to come with you, I do. Tell Arthur to wait just a minute and I'll get dressed right away."

Only it wasn't Arthur standing on the front porch, chauffeur's cap in hand.

It was Larry Julius. Dane and Margo gasped in unison, as cleanly as if they'd been cued.

"Hello, Dane." Larry smiled pleasantly, his ever-present cigarette dangling from his lips. If he was at all surprised by the state they were in—Dane's disheveled hair and unbuttoned shirt, the freshly tearstained Margo in her lace peignoir with nothing underneath—he certainly didn't look it. "And darling Margo. Well, well. How convenient to find you here. Two birds with one stone."

"Larry." Dane found his voice. "What are you doing here?"

"Studio business, what else?" Larry said cheerfully. "I've got orders to bring you both straight to Mr. Karp."

Dane and Margo exchanged a look, instantly back on the same side. As Gabby Preston always said, at Olympus, there were only two reasons for a summons from Mr. Karp: Oscar or firing squad.

And the Oscars were over.

"Can't . . . can't it wait?" Margo squeaked.

"Do you think I'd have schlepped all the way out to Malibu if it could? And wipe that look off your face, duchess," he added. "It's not like I'm the Gestapo. From what I understand, the Gestapo gives you five minutes to get dressed and come quietly." Larry grinned. "I'll give you three."

TWELVE

Gabby Preston's heart was pounding, and for once, it wasn't the pills.

It had been like this ever since the crashing ovation that had greeted her after her performance at the Governor's Ball had lifted her higher than any pill ever had. A steady thrum, a quick succession of triplets, like a waltz you were dancing too fast. Only instead of its usual panicky reproach—"go faster" or "not enough"—it beat out a new and infinitely more delicious phrase:

Eddie Sharp. Eddie Sharp.

Barely a day had passed since their mutual onstage triumph before a huge pink stuffed cat had appeared on the front porch of the house on Fountain Avenue, with a note attached to the ribbon collar around its neck. Viola had automatically reached for it, but Gabby had jealously snatched the note out of her mother's reach and carefully read it herself, her lips moving silently, patiently sounding out the words until she was sure she'd gotten them right: *Hey, Kitty Cat: Here's hoping we make more beautiful music together soon. Eddie.*

Truth be told, Gabby might have preferred a more grown-up gift, like jewelry or perfume, but she was hardly going to complain. In all their weeks—months?—of fake dates, that cheapskate Jimmy Molloy had never given her anything the studio hadn't picked out and paid for, and she knew it had been the same when he was fake-dating Margo. And yes, maybe it would have been a teensy-tiny bit more flattering if he'd written *Love, Eddie* or *Yours, Eddie* or even "Anything" *Eddie*, but what did it matter? Boys probably didn't think about things like that anyway.

She put the note away carefully in the blue velvet pouch she'd inherited from Viola, with the ripped-up pieces of her sister Frankie's goodbye letter and her father's old pipe. When she called Eddie to thank him, his secretary told her that Mr. Sharp had gone to Palm Springs for the week.

For a wild moment, she wondered: what if she drove out there and *surprised* him? Wouldn't that be a hoot! It was a simple-enough operation to throw some clothes in her old cardboard suitcase, still littered with stickers and stamps from the vaudeville days, and sneak the keys to the Cadillac out of a napping Viola's handbag.

She only made it as far as the driveway when her hands started to shake. It wasn't that she couldn't *drive*, Gabby told herself, but taking the car to the market or even the studio was one thing; driving to the middle of the desert a hundred miles away without being sure where she was going was quite another. She thought she'd just go back to the house and have a drink to calm her nerves and get her courage up before setting out, maybe with a map.

But one drink turned into three, and eventually she gave up altogether. Sometimes the green pills made Gabby want to do things that weren't necessarily the *smartest* when she thought about them later on. Even if she did make it to Palm Springs in one piece, maybe it wasn't the best idea, *strategically*, to just drop in on Eddie like that, unannounced. When Amanda had been staying with the Prestons, on the rare occasions she could be roused from her Harry Gordon–induced catatonia to offer the advice about boys that Gabby craved, she had mentioned that men liked it when you played hard to get.

So Gabby was playing hard to get. She'd waited a week, until she was sure Eddie would be back, and then she managed to hold out another three days. And it was worth it. When at last she broke down and telephoned that morning, she finally—*finally*—got something she could use.

"Oh, no, Mr. Sharp isn't in. He's recording on the Olympus lot today."

It was like music to Gabby's ears—beautiful music, the kind Eddie wanted to make together.

She hung up the phone, called the studio, and asked them to send a car for her, and an hour later, here she was strolling nonchalantly across the Olympus lot as though she'd planned to be here all along. *Easy as pie. And if Eddie has been thinking about me even one-sixteenth as much as I've been thinking about him,* Gabby told herself, *he's going to be pretty damn happy to see me.*

The recording studios at Olympus were clustered behind the grand compound housing the administrative offices of Mr.

Karp—supposedly because he liked to throw open his windows to listen to the beautiful music that came from them, but in reality, this was just a story the publicity department had fed to the movie magazines, designed to make the gullible public feel as if the second-most-highly-paid man in America were a fan just like them. Every last studio was completely soundproof.

Gabby took the shortcut around the garden of tropical flowers decorated with Greek-style statues depicting the twelve Olympian gods and goddesses in a rather more modest state of dress than was strictly classical (the prudish Mr. Karp refused to have them any other way).

A gleaming studio limo pulled up in front of the grand building, and Gabby crouched behind an enormous magenta azalea bush to see who was getting out. It was Margo Sterling and Dane Forrest, accompanied by Larry Julius, looking so serious he could have been a prison guard walking them to the gallows. *Jesus*, Gabby thought. *I wonder what they're in for.*

She didn't have much time to ponder this delightfully fascinating problem before she saw a familiar black-clad, bright-haired figure in dark glasses trudging slowly down the cobblestone road. "Yoo-hoo!" Gabby called. "Amanda."

"Gabby," Amanda replied, stiffly returning her friend's proffered embrace. "Hello."

"Did you get a load of those two?" Gabby asked, gesturing to the limo still idling by the curb.

"Who?"

"Who do you think? Our own Romeo and Juliet. Walking into Karp's office like they were going to their own funeral."

Amanda's lips were strangely white. She pressed them together tightly in a grim approximation of a smile. "I'm afraid I might be doing the same thing."

"You've got a meeting with *Karp*?"

"No, of course not. You think I've ever even met Mr. Karp? They've got me in with some underling."

Gabby gulped. "It's not about your contract, is it?"

"I don't know. They didn't tell me."

"What does your agent say?"

Amanda gave a short bark of a laugh. "He's either very busy or very busy pretending to be. I couldn't get him on the phone."

"I'm sure it's fine," Gabby said kindly. "He probably is just awfully busy. You know how they are. And you've still got *weeks* left on your contract. They're probably just checking in. You haven't exactly been out and about as much as you used to be. They haven't seen you in person in a while. Maybe they've got a picture they want to put you on and just want to make sure you didn't get fat or something."

"Maybe," Amanda said, but she didn't look convinced.

"Sure. And even if it . . ." Gabby paused. Everyone in Hollywood was superstitious. Saying certain unthinkable things out loud seemed to invite bad luck on the speaker and listener alike. ". . . if it isn't *good news*," she said finally, "there are plenty of other places to go. MGM needs new faces."

"MGM." Amanda snorted. "Yeah, right. Why don't I just apply to be the Queen of England, while I'm at it?"

"Columbia, then. Or you could sign with one of the independents. David Selznick is doing awfully swell things with those girls he keeps importing from Europe. Howard Hughes might take you on. Or Oscar Zellman, he's always been fond of you."

Amanda's gaze darted toward the neat row of stucco buildings at the end of the row, as though desperate to think about anything other than what an exclusive contract with Oscar Zellman might entail. "Are you recording today?"

Gabby shrugged. "I'm not sure yet. Maybe."

"With Eddie Sharp? You sounded marvelous together the other night."

"Do you really think so?" Gabby's heart leapt in her chest.

"Oh yes. It was the best thing I've heard in ages."

"I'm so glad! I wasn't sure you'd heard it. I didn't see you afterward." Gabby grinned mischievously. "Come to think of it, I didn't see Harry afterward either." Suddenly, she felt a painful stab of envy. Margo, living in Dane Forrest's house, sleeping in his bed, just like they were husband and wife; Amanda, off somewhere in the dark with Harry Gordon. *Everyone's doing it but me*, Gabby thought miserably. *I'm just some stupid virgin singing "Zing Went the Strings of My Heart"; in the meantime, everyone else knows what it feels like.* "I don't suppose you found him, did you?"

Amanda shut her eyes. "I have to go. I'm late."

I said the wrong thing, Gabby thought. "Amanda, I—"

"It's all right. I just really have to go."

"Okay, okay." Gabby gave her friend an apologetic smile. "I'll probably be in the commissary later, if you feel like coming by. We'll pig out on ice cream, if they'll let us."

A terse nod was all Amanda could manage before she scurried away.

Pushing back her guilt—*Why, why do I always say the wrong thing?*—Gabby focused her attention on the task at hand. She knew Eddie Sharp's orchestra was in one of those studios. Nothing more than a wall of stucco (and fiberglass, and a special state-of-the-art soundproofing rubber that the studio had discreetly ordered—at great expense to Mr. Karp's pocketbook and morality—from some scientists in Nazi Germany) separated her from Eddie. Just the thought of it was enough to make a shiver of excitement run down her spine.

But which one was it? She couldn't very well go barging into every studio. Interrupting the wrong recording session could cost Olympus hundreds of dollars, dollars that would be deducted from her paycheck, if the conductor was surly enough to tell someone about it. And then she could kiss any semblance of a life goodbye for the next hundred years. Maybe two.

There was a little stone bench nestled against Mr. Karp's trellis wall. Mostly hidden from the street, it provided a good view of the side entrances of the recording studios. *I'll just sit right there*, Gabby thought, *and wait. If anyone asks me what I'm doing, I'll just say I was looking for a quiet place to learn some lyrics or something.*

The sun was hot, and the sweet, waxy smell of oranges drifting from the little grove in front of the commissary was strong and soothing. It had been days since Gabby had slept of her own accord, but suddenly, her eyelids began to droop. She saw Eddie's face looming before her, his eyes sparkling, felt the warmth of his breath as his beautiful lips came slowly toward hers. In the distance, an odd scraping sound, faint at first, grew louder and louder.

Funny, she thought, *that was how it sounded when the old vaudeville guys used to do the soft shoe.* But there was no vaudeville anymore. It had to be something else: the papery scratch of a nail file, Viola's old willow broom sweeping the dust from the front porch, a scared little ghost crab scuttling across sand . . .

"Gabby?"

Groggily, she opened her eyes, blinking against the bright light. Silhouetted against the sky, blocking out half the sun like a partial eclipse, was the blurry face of Dexter Harrington, a thin stream of cigarette smoke curling from his amused mouth.

"Dammit," Gabby said, "why does everyone think I'm so goddamn funny?"

Dexter laughed out loud. "Are you always so cheerful in the mornings?"

She coughed in reply, pointing at his cigarette.

He took another drag. "What are you doing here?"

"Learning my lines." She scowled at him.

"You looked asleep to me."

"Haven't you ever heard of hypnosis?" she asked crossly. "It's supposed to help with the memorization process. Ask anyone."

"Don't you worry that if you sit here long enough, old Mr. Karp is going to look out that fancy window of his and wonder what he's paying you for?"

"Funny," Gabby said coolly, "I could ask you the same thing."

"Me?" Dexter dropped his cigarette butt on the ground and stubbed it out with the tip of his shoe. "I'm hard at work laying down a track."

"Oh?" Gabby arranged her features in a convincing look of surprise. "What are you recording?"

"It's supposed to be some background jazz for a movie, but things have gotten a little off track. You know Eddie."

I don't, but I want to. "Mind if I tag along?"

140

"Well, well, well, look what the cat dragged in." Eddie stopped yelling at his horn section long enough to rake his eyes over Gabby. "What's shakin', toots?"

In a polo shirt with the sleeves rolled up over his muscular arms and a porkpie hat pulled low over his eyes, which only served to call extra attention to his incredible mouth, Eddie looked like about the hottest guy Gabby had ever seen. Even if she hadn't been struggling to swallow the handful of green wake-up pills she'd surreptitiously fished out of her pocket and jammed into her mouth as she followed Dexter into the building—it wouldn't do to be sleepy in front of Eddie—Gabby would have been tongue-tied at the sight of him.

To her relief, Dexter answered. "I found her catching forty winks on the bench outside."

"Lazy bum." Eddie grinned. "What say we put you to work before you get picked up for vagrancy?"

The pills had dissolved in the back of her throat, but still Gabby could barely speak. "What . . . what do you mean?"

"I want a female vocal on this track we're laying down. 'Little Girl Blue.' Rodgers and Hart. I'm trying to fill in with clarinet, but it just doesn't work structurally without the sung melody for reference. Once through, and one pickup at the bridge. You know the song?"

"Sure. Oh, and speaking of cats . . ."

"Yeah, yeah. Later. So, we'll do it in A-flat, over the playback. That should be fine for you, no?"

"Wait!" Gabby cried. This was all happening so fast. Not so much as a how-do-you-do and he was already putting her

141

to work. What should she do? More importantly, what would *Amanda* do? *Play hard to get. Keep your head. Don't give him something he wants until he gives you something you want.* "Wait just a second. You don't expect me to just sing for you for *free*, do you?"

Eddie's mouth twitched. "I was thinking of it more as a favor between friends."

Oh God, is he mad? I made him mad! Quickly, she tried to cover with a joke. "Sure, friends is great," she said in her best impression of one of the Dead End kids, miming as though she had a cigar clenched between her teeth. "Friends ain't gonna keep me off the streets and out of the joint, you know what I mean?"

Eddie laughed. "All right, kid, whaddya want from me?"

What did Gabby want? The answer flew into her head, clear as crystal. *I want to be alone someplace with Eddie.* "Well," she said shyly, "remember how the other night you told me you'd take me out sometime to hear some *real* music? 'Not all this treacly studio crap,' you said. *Real* jazz."

"And that's what you want?"

"That's what I want."

Eddie looked thoughtful. *Pensive*, even. It was a word she'd heard Margo use, and she liked the sound of it. "All right. It's a date."

"Really?" Gabby's squeal probably didn't fall under the banner of hard to get, but she couldn't help it. "Tonight?"

"When else? Meet me in the studio commissary at eight. I'll take you someplace that'll knock the socks right off your feet. Now get your cute little caboose in front of that microphone and make me a happy man."

Beaming ear to ear, Gabby did as she was told. Who cared about leers on the faces of some of the men, or the flicker of hangdog disapproval on Dexter's? They could whisper and stare all they wanted. It didn't make any difference to her. She was going on a date, a real date, with Eddie Sharp! He'd said so right in front of everybody! It was too, too wonderful for words.

But it was only when Eddie was in the booth and she had the headphones on that she realized how wonderful it was.

"Oh, and Gabby, one more thing," he murmured, in a low, sexy voice he knew only she could hear. "Make sure you don't bring your mother."

It was then, and absolutely then, staring through the glass of the recording booth into his dark, twinkling eyes, that Gabby was surer of one thing than she'd ever been about anything in her entire life. She didn't care what it took. She didn't care how it happened.

Gabby Preston was *going* to lose her virginity to Eddie Sharp.

And as far as she was concerned, it couldn't happen soon enough.

THIRTEEN

"Children!"

Leo Karp clapped his small, square hands together in delight as Margo and Dane were ushered into his office. His palms gave off a thick, dull echo, like the sound of a baseball landing hard against the pocket of a leather mitt. "I couldn't be happier to see you both. Dane, my boy," he said, playfully cuffing the crook of the younger man's arm. It was about the only part of him the famously diminutive Mr. Karp could easily reach. "I don't think I have to tell you how proud we are of you. And, Margo, my dear." He took her hand in both of his and raised it to his lips theatrically. "You look absolutely radiant. Keeping your weight under control, I'm glad to see. I wish more of our girls had your kind of discipline."

Margo blushed furiously, running her gloved hands down the skirt of her silk flowered dress. *That's Leo Karp, all right,* she

144

thought. *You can't gain or lose an ounce in this place without him hearing about it, and he wants to make sure you know it.*

"Good to see you too, Leo," Dane said firmly, settling himself into one of the white leather chairs. *Since when does he call Mr. Karp by his first name?*

If Mr. Karp was taken aback by this sudden informality, he didn't show it. "And for you to come—both of you—to see me just like this, on such short notice, with your busy schedules, well . . ." He beamed. "It just warms my heart."

For the first time since Larry Julius had materialized on the doorstep, Margo felt a stab of real terror. Thankfully, her mandatory summonses to Leo Karp's pristine, all-white office fortress had been seldom, but in her limited experience, the more extravagantly and lovingly the studio chief humbled himself before you, the more impossible and painful his demands were about to be. The day he'd commanded her, on pain of firing and subsequent homelessness, to give up any thought of Dane and to embark upon a completely fake public relationship with Jimmy Molloy (who frankly couldn't have been less interested in women in general and Margo in particular), he'd practically driven himself to tears begging her to think of him as her own father.

Dane produced a cigarette from his engraved gold case and lit it with painstaking slowness. It was a well-known fact that Leo Karp hated cigarette smoking. Normally, the only person who got away with it in his presence was Larry Julius, who, sure enough, was already puffing away from his usual chair beneath the enormous white lacquer cage that housed Nelson and Cleopatra, Mr. Karp's pair of matched white cockatoos.

It's a power play, Margo thought suddenly. *He's trying to show Mr. Karp that he's not scared of him.*

"I'm sure it's our pleasure, Leo," Dane said with studied calmness, exhaling lavish curlicues of smoke through his mouth and nose. "Now, are you going to tell us what this is all about, or do you not want to spoil the suspense?"

"Suspense? Who do I look like, Alfred Hitchcock? I just wanted to have a chat with my two favorite stars, that's all. Shouldn't a proud papa get to have a nice visit with his children?" Mr. Karp was still beaming, his tone terrifyingly light. "After all, so much has happened since I've last seen you. Diana Chesterfield, for instance. You must be so relieved to see she's back safe and sound."

Here it comes, Margo thought, feeling the color drain from her face. *He's going to tell Dane he has to go back with Diana and we're all through.*

She felt a sudden urge to fling her body over Dane's, as though she were a bodyguard throwing herself in front of an oncoming bullet. Yet a glance at Dane, suddenly gone as still and inexpressive as a wax figure, told her that such a dramatic gesture would be unwelcome. Apparently, stiff upper lips were the order of the day.

Margo straightened her spine, trying to coax her body into the regally fatalistic posture she had assumed when she approached the execution block in the final scene of *The Nine Days' Queen.* What was it Raoul Kurtzman had whispered in his tortuous English into her ear before the cameras rolled? *Cutting off your head, you can't stop them. But you can stop them from the satisfaction of seeing you afraid.*

"Of course," Dane said quietly. "It's a great relief."

"And such a surprise!" Mr. Karp crowed. "If I hadn't known about it already, we wouldn't be having this conversation. I would have dropped dead of a heart attack right there."

"Diana's always known how to make an entrance."

"That she has." Mr. Karp smiled benevolently. "Now, Dane, I want you to know, I appreciate what she's put you through."

"What she's—"

"She's quite contrite, believe me, and eager to befriend you both. I told her to give it time. But I hope you'll soon be able to forgive her." He looked at them both with pleading eyes. "For the sake of the Olympus family. A father wants all his children to get along."

Who, exactly, Margo wondered, *is this performance for?* Surely Mr. Karp was aware that everyone in the room knew that the story Diana had parroted to the magazines was a total fiction, concocted by none other than Larry Julius himself. Surely he knew, and knew that they knew, where Diana had been all along, that until recently the role she'd been playing had not been so much "prisoner of love" as "inmate at the asylum."

And while he might not exactly have known the extent of the bargain with the devil Dane and Diana had made in their joint thirst for stardom—Dane was sure that nobody, not even Larry Julius, knew that—he must have suspected that behind closed doors, their relationship may not have been quite what it seemed.

Yet once an official studio version of a story had come over the wires, you could put Mr. Karp to the rack and he would never admit it was anything less than absolutely, one hundred percent true. Nobody had any choice but to play along with the script he had provided. Not for the first time, Margo wondered whether of all the great actors who had passed through Olympus's gates, Leo F. Karp wasn't the greatest of them all.

"Still, just to make sure we don't have any"—Mr. Karp paused to think of a suitably neutral, and therefore meaningless, phrase—"any unnecessary *misunderstandings,* I've put her straight back to work on the new Raoul Kurtzman picture. *Madame Bovary,* written by some French fellow. It's a closed set, and as you know, Kurtzman's a real taskmaster when he wants to be. You're not likely to see her in the commissary or out on the town for a while. When it makes sense to get the three of you together, Mr. Julius will orchestrate it as he sees fit, isn't that right, Larry?"

Larry coughed. "You bet, boss."

"So you see." Mr. Karp gave a satisfied nod. "It's the best thing for everyone."

The best thing for everyone. Diana in Madame Bovary. So the rumors were true. Margo had expected as much, but still, hearing it straight from the horse's mouth felt so terribly final. She stared at her lap, willing herself not to cry.

It was as if Mr. Karp could read her thoughts. "Margo, dear, I know you're disappointed," he said, his tone gentle. "If it makes you feel any better, Kurtzman did mention you for the part. But in the end, it wasn't his decision to make, and in time, you'll see I was right. A part like this, playing this kind of woman, this Emma Bovary, an unfaithful woman, an impure woman"—he moved his hand through the air as though waving away a particularly bad smell—"that isn't for you. Especially not under the circumstances."

Under the circumstances?

148

"What circumstances?" Margo finally found her voice. "What are you talking about?"

Mr. Karp nodded solemnly at Larry Julius, who produced a briefcase from behind his chair. From this he took several pieces of paper and placed them carefully on Mr. Karp's desk. They were magazine pages, or rather, they were the mock-ups magazines made of their pages, showing how things should be laid out before they were sent to the printer. Margo recognized the familiar typeface of *Picture Palace* in the headline that marched across the top:

Is There No Decency?
Yet Another "Wholesome" Hollywood Couple Discovered Living in Scandalous Sin!

And then beneath it all, there were pictures of Dane and Margo. Not the usual film or publicity stills the magazines usually ran, but a grainy photograph that looked like something you'd get from a private investigator. Margo leaving the house in Malibu in the early-morning light; Dane bare-chested under his dressing gown, watching her go. The two of them half dressed, caught in an intimate moment on the small strip of sand behind that house that was supposed to be Dane's beach.

Dane's *private* beach.

Margo's head was spinning. Wildly, she scanned the close-set type, but the smudged letters seemed to swirl together in a crazy jumble. All she could make out were a few phrases:

Malibu love nest . . . Hotbed of immorality . . . What must her parents think?

"Oh no," Margo gasped. "Oh no, oh no, oh no."

Mr. Karp was shaking his head. "Personally, I don't understand why the public wants to see this trash. In the old days, the magazines kept out of the gutter. All of a sudden, it's a race to the bottom, ever since that disgraceful story in *Photoplay* last year."

"Hollywood's Unmarried Husbands and Wives." Already it was one of the most notorious articles ever to hit the movie colony. A roundup of virtually every major player living illicitly—or even more scandalously, *extramaritally*—with a lover, it had ruined careers, angered the Hays Office (the Hollywood censors who took it upon themselves to make sure stars stayed pure enough for Middle America, on- *and* off-screen), inspired "moral" boycotts all over the country, and destroyed more than one marriage to a formerly pliant partner who had been more than happy to look the other way, as long as affairs weren't made public. *It's the knowing that's the problem*, Margo thought. Look at Vivien Leigh. She'd been living for ages with Laurence Olivier, and nobody minded a bit, even though they were both married to other people. Then David O. Selznick picked her to play Scarlett O'Hara, the tabloids started sniffing around, and all of a sudden, Olivier got shipped off to New York to do a play and poor Vivien had a twenty-four-hour armed guard posted around her house, just in case he should somehow manage to slip away. *Everything's fine as long as no one knows who you are.*

Margo looked back down at the pictures of her and Dane. Of their life, their most private, most intimate life splashed across the pages for millions of strangers to pore over, leer at, disapprove of. Suddenly, for the first time in a long time, she thought of that horrible night at Doris's coming-out party all those months ago, of Phipps McKendrick pushing her down on the lawn, of his fury and confusion when she tried to fight him off, as if he thought she was supposed to be there for him to do with whatever he wanted. As if she had no right to any feelings or desires of her own.

As if I were a thing.

Margo felt like she was going to be sick.

Dane, however, was all business, his voice urgent and low. "What's to be done?"

"There's only one thing to do in a situation like this."

Larry Julius seemed to have taken over, and in a way, Margo was relieved. Larry could give her the bad news straight, without couching it in a lot of meaningless sentimentality or guilt about how disappointed he was that she hadn't turned out to be such a nice girl after all. Larry Julius didn't think anyone was a nice girl. "Thanks to my guy on the inside, we have a week before this is due to go to press. Plenty of time to change the story."

Margo braced herself. *No tearful scenes. No special pleading.* He'd tell her she'd have to give Dane up, and she'd take it like a man. They both would.

Larry smiled. "Congratulations, you two. You're getting married."

"Married?"

It was so different, so totally, utterly, *wonderfully* different from what she'd been expecting that Margo couldn't help but scream. "We're getting married?"

"Sure, duchess." Larry laughed. "What'd you think? We haven't had a big studio wedding in a long time, and there's no time like the present. It'll be a gas to plan. And we'll have the press along every step of the way: the ring, the bridesmaids, the dress, and of course the ceremony. We'll have to throw it all together in a hurry, but nobody can do it like we can. Shouldn't take more than about six weeks."

Six weeks! Margo's heart leapt in her chest. True, it wasn't exactly the proposal of her dreams, but what did that matter? The familiar images she hadn't even dared to think of over the last several months started rushing into her mind. Banks and banks of gorgeous flowers, all in shades of lavender . . . no, palest pink would look better in the photos. An audience full of the most glamorous movie stars in the world—maybe even a world leader or two!—staring at her in awe and admiration as she floated down the aisle in a diamond tiara and gorgeous white gown, clutching her father's reassuring arm . . . and Dane Forrest, still the most handsome man Margo had ever seen, whose picture had once hung above her bed in the olden days in Pasadena, waiting for her at the altar, the light of love shining in his eyes.

"Oh, Dane," she murmured, gazing up at him in adoration.

And suddenly it hit her like a ton of bricks.

It only lasted a moment, the slack look of horror that she saw there. A split second before his face regained its practiced equanimity. That amused nonchalance that set racing the hearts of women all over the world.

But a split second was enough.

He doesn't want to marry me. And he never has.

152

Larry Julius was opening a bottle of champagne he'd mysteriously produced out of nowhere. "Congratulations, you crazy kids."

"Mazel tov." Leo Karp was beaming. "And let me be the first to kiss the bride."

FOURTEEN

There was plenty of stuff to do at Olympus when you had an afternoon to kill. In fact, the whole place had been designed specifically—and rather creepily, if you really thought about it—so that you *never* had to leave.

After Amanda failed to turn up for lunch in the commissary, which was either a very good sign regarding the redhead's future prospects at the studio or a very bad one, Gabby had wandered for a while around the studio's Main Street, looking at the penny postcards for sale in the specially zoned Olympus post office and leafing through the magazines at the newsstand. She ducked into the movie theater and caught the beginning of the old print of *An Affair of the Heart* they were screening in honor of Diana Chesterfield's triumphant return. After a while, she noticed Margo Sterling sitting in the back.

At least, Gabby *thought* it was Margo. It was hard to tell in the dark, with the heavily veiled hat she was wearing. Whoever it was, she was all alone and, from the sound of the faint sobs welling up from behind the veil, seemed about as eager for company as Greta Garbo, so Gabby beat a hasty retreat through the side door, which handily deposited her on the sidewalk right in front of her favorite place on the whole studio lot: Dr. Lipkin's office.

After she'd gotten all her prescriptions refilled—and scarfed down some of her medicinal bounty right there in the waiting room—she felt so good she thought she'd walk all the way up to the hills behind the back lot and visit the horses. But the stables were closed on account of some Western they were shooting that day, so she scrapped that plan and stopped by the little yellow schoolhouse in the orange grove where Olympus's younger stars had their mandatory three hours of schooling every day. When Gabby had first arrived at Olympus she had sat in the classroom for three afternoons before Viola had managed to produce some official-looking and almost certainly one hundred percent fake paperwork stating Gabby was sixteen and therefore exempt.

But Gabby had liked it in there: the smell of the chalk, the neat white strokes of the cursive alphabet marching across the tops of the blackboards. It was a pleasant place to sit and listen for a while—at least, until Miss Higgins started asking people to read out loud and Gabby fled in the humiliating and very real terror that she might be called on next. Another couple of pills, along with a healthy swig or two from one of the bottles Jimmy Molloy kept in his unlocked bungalow, soon restored her equilibrium.

But nothing could compare with the sight of Eddie Sharp

leaning over the car door and the knowledge that he had come for her.

Nothing, Gabby thought, *nothing could make me feel better than this.*

"Yoo-hoo, Eddie! Over here!"

He waved at her, frowning slightly. "Is that what you're wearing?"

Gabby ran her hands anxiously over the sides of her dress. A tight-fighting burgundy crepe with a white lace Peter Pan collar, it was the same one she'd been wearing all day, although she had added a pair of white kid gloves and a little velvet evening jacket with a fox collar she'd smuggled out of the wardrobe department that afternoon when Sadie's back was turned.

"What's the matter? Isn't it smart enough?"

"Smart enough?" Eddie laughed. "Honey, where we're going, you're going to look like Eleanor Roosevelt."

"Oh. I didn't know."

"It doesn't matter. We can stop by your place if you want to change. Or something."

His tone was casual enough, but there was a twinkle in his eye—a twinkle that seemed to say that Gabby Preston changing clothes was something he might very much like to see. Gabby was tempted to say yes. She imagined Eddie sitting on the canopied bed in her pink bedroom, watching as she unzipped her dress, slowly stepped out of her slip . . .

Quickly, she pushed the thought aside. They couldn't run the risk of going to her house. Viola would probably be there, and if she was, Gabby would never get out again. That was the reason she hadn't gone home to change in the first place. "It's out of the way," she said quickly.

"You don't even know where we're going."

"Well, I know what traffic is like," Gabby insisted. "And besides, I'd rather be overdressed." She struck a dramatic pose, her hand to her forehead like a silent film actress. "Remember, I'm supposed to be a movie star."

Eddie laughed. "That you are, peanut. Well, suit yourself. Now come on." He opened the passenger-side door and patted the seat. "Get in."

Gabby slid across the smooth leather, feeling the knot in her stomach tighten painfully and deliciously as Eddie's lips carelessly brushed her cheek in greeting.

This is it. My first real date. Tonight there would be no hairdresser tying up her corkscrew curls with little-girl hair ribbons, no packs of photographers or sour-faced studio chaperones or flacks murmuring instructions into her ear: "Smile, Gabby. Now look surprised. Now hold his hand, now kiss his cheek." Tonight, she was just a regular girl going out with a boy for the simple reason that she *wanted* to.

And, she thought, as she inched closer to him on the seat, just until she could feel the warmth of his thigh kiss her own, *because he wants to go out with me.*

Eddie lit a cigarette and offered her a drag. Gabby usually didn't smoke, since Viola was sure it would damage her voice, but this time she eagerly accepted.

He must want to kiss me, she thought excitedly, *or at least, the thought doesn't totally disgust him. That's what it means when a boy offers you something his lips have touched.* To be honest, she wasn't completely sure this was a hard and fast rule, but she liked the sound of it. It seemed like something Amanda would say.

"Thanks," she said, suppressing a cough as she handed the cigarette back to him. "I needed that."

Eddie looked amused as he turned the key in the ignition. "Glad I could help."

They drove down through the hills. The scenery was changing now. The Hollywood Gabby knew, with its palm-lined boulevards and pale stucco palazzos, was falling away. The houses were smaller here, crammed together like cans on a grocery store shelf, the carefully irrigated and manicured green lawns replaced by arid patches of gravel and cement. Then the houses disappeared completely and they were suddenly driving slowly down a bustling city street alight with neon signs and flashing lights. People spilled out the doors and onto the sidewalks as though they'd been pushed, the men in baggy suits, the brightly dressed women laughing loudly as they teetered on too-high heels.

"Oh my God," Gabby marveled, looking around at the crowded vibrancy that surrounded them, so different from Southern California's usual outwardly placid sprawl. "Is this still Los Angeles? I feel like we're in an actual *city*!"

Eddie grinned. "Welcome to Central Avenue, sweetheart."

He pulled up outside a large brick building on the corner. The sidewalk was swarming with people. Gabby tried to read the large sign dangling over their heads, willing the letters to stay put instead of flipping around in backward circles in her head the way they usually did.

D, she thought firmly, remembering her sister Frankie's patient voice in her head: "You can always remember *D*, Gabby, because it looks like a sail and it rhymes with *sea*."

D-U-N-

"The Dunbar Hotel," Eddie said before Gabby could finish. He seemed to have mistaken her concentration for speechless wonder. *Thank God.* "You ever been here?"

"No."

Thrillingly, Eddie slipped a proprietary arm around her waist as he led her through the door. "You're going to love it. It's like the Cotton Club of the West Coast."

Gabby had never been to the Cotton Club either—the most she'd seen of Manhattan was a glimpse of the skyline over the Hudson River the time that sleazy booking agent with the bright red mustache and what seemed like about eight hands every time he touched you had booked the Preston Sisters into the Palace Hotel, Newark. But from the way she'd heard sophisticated New York types talk in hushed tones about what *fun* it was on 125th Street, she expected it to be, well, *naughtier*. Red lighting, people reclining on brocade couches smoking opium pipes, scantily clad long-limbed beauties writhing hypnotically on the stage, like that picture she'd seen in one of Viola's magazines of Josephine Baker in Paris wearing a skirt made of bananas and nothing else.

The Dunbar, on the other hand, seemed like a standard-issue supper club. Sure, the stage was a little shabbier, the tables a little closer together, the dress code not quite so strict—although Gabby, spying quite a few evening gowns and even a white dinner jacket or two in the crowd, couldn't quite understand why Eddie has made such a fuss over her dress. Otherwise, it was pretty much like the Cocoanut Grove or the Trocadero or any other place she'd been stuffed in a stupid pink tulle dress and sent with Viola and Jimmy and a phalanx of Olympus operatives to make sure she was seen by the right people and laughed at the right jokes and didn't have too much cleavage showing in any of the photographs. It had the same hum of ambient noise and clouds of cigarette smoke, the same uniformed waiters balancing precarious trays of drinks, the same candles sunk into the same glasses casting the same shadows on the same white tablecloths.

But there was one difference. *One very, very big difference.*

"They're all Negroes," Gabby whispered across the table to Eddie. A furtive glance around the room confirmed it. From the lowliest busboy to the corner table of elegantly attired grandees sitting behind a velvet rope, she and Eddie were the only white people in the place. "Everybody here. Every last one!"

Eddie lit a cigarette. "I wondered how long it would take you to notice. It's not a problem, is it?"

"No, of course not," Gabby said, although she had never been around so many black people before. There was that nice Arthur, of course, and some of the other studio drivers; the odd session musician; a handful of Olympus contract players who played domestics and kept to themselves on the lot, although most of them were currently on loan to Selznick for *Gone with the Wind*. Back in her vaudeville days, she'd once shared a bill with a torch singer whom she'd found changing into a sequined Madame Vionnet evening gown in the middle of a frozen, garbage-strewn alley behind the theater. Gabby had asked her why on earth she was doing such a ridiculous thing, and the singer had replied that she wasn't allowed to use the same dressing room as the white acts. Gabby had been appalled at the time, but otherwise, she had never given the matter of race much thought one way or another. Suddenly, she found herself thinking of Dexter Harrington. Maybe he was here somewhere, blending in with the crowd, while she was the one sticking out like a sore thumb. "It's just that, I mean . . . are we even allowed to be here?"

"Fortunately, they're pretty fair-minded about things down here. If you can pay your check, you can stay." Eddie grinned. "And lucky for you, I'm paying." He signaled for the waiter. "Rusty! Over here!"

The red-jacketed waiter made his way smoothly toward the table and clapped his hand into Eddie's outstretched one. "Eddie. How you doing, man?"

"Not bad, not bad. Just here to catch the show."

"Well, you won't be disappointed. It's going to be a hot one."

"That's what I hear." Eddie smiled. "Oh, Rusty, I want you to meet a good friend of mine from the studio. Gabby Preston."

A good friend. It didn't quite have the ring of *girlfriend*, but it was better than nothing. *Give it time.*

"Oh, sure." Rusty nodded easily. "I've heard you on the radio. Nice set of pipes. Can I get you something to drink?"

"Scotch," Gabby replied, too quickly, and immediately flushed. Why did she have to do things like that? Margo Sterling would never do something like that. Margo Sterling would daintily sip a single glass of champagne, and even then, only if her date positively insisted. *Eddie's going to think I'm some kind of drunk.*

But Eddie just laughed. "I guess you'd better bring us a bottle of J and B. And ice?" Gabby nodded. "And a bucket of ice for the lady."

"Got it. You hungry?"

Gabby shook her head, her magical little green appetite suppressant already in her hand. Maybe she'd blown it with the drink order, but she wasn't going to make things worse by stuffing her face in front of Eddie. On this point, sources as diverse as Amanda, Viola, and Scarlett O'Hara's Mammy were absolutely agreed: you were never, never, *never* supposed to eat in front of a man.

"Well, I'm starving," Eddie said. "I think you'd better bring us a basket of fried chicken. One of the big ones, with waffles. Mashed potatoes and collard greens with ham hocks on the side. And for dessert . . . sweet potato pie."

"You sure? We got coconut cream tonight too."

"What the hell, bring us one of each." Eddie turned to Gabby. "Promise me you'll at least try everything. You won't be sorry. They've got the best soul food here outside of the South."

Gabby nodded, having taken the distraction of Rusty's departure to surreptitiously shove the green pill in her mouth. "Whatever you say," she said, once a couple of practiced gulps had forced the dry tablet down her throat. "You're the bandleader."

"That's what I like to hear. Now," Eddie said, stubbing out his cigarette. "What was that thing you just took?"

"What?" Gabby felt a sudden stab of panic. "What are you talking about?"

"Whatever you just swallowed. It looked like some kind of pill."

"It's just something from the studio," Gabby said quickly. "To give me energy. It's mostly just vitamins."

"Oh, believe me, I know all about those kind of vitamins. Everybody takes them on the road."

"Even you?"

"Are you kidding me? How else are you supposed to play four

shows a night, seven days a week? Only thing is, though, they make you awful jumpy."

Gabby shrugged. "I don't mind."

"Maybe you don't, but some of us need our beauty sleep. So then you've got to find something else, something stronger to calm you down."

"I guess that's what Scotch is for," Gabby said.

Eddie raised his eyebrows. "I guess so. Among other things."

He looked like he was about to say something else, but then the lights dimmed and the band came onstage.

The band. This, Gabby thought, was the real way the Dunbar was different from all the other places. She had never heard anything like the music that was coming out of the horn of the tenor saxophonist.

It started out as "Body and Soul," a song she'd heard hundreds of times, but after the first four bars, the familiar tune fell away as the saxophone played around it, taking the music through twists and turns she'd never imagined. And yet, somehow she still heard the melody through it all, haunting and clear, and she realized it was all in her mind. *The saxophone's making harmony in my head,* Gabby thought. It was like . . .

"Magic," she whispered.

"You like it?" Eddie asked when the music stopped.

"Oh yes." Gabby's eyes shone with tears. "It's just . . . I don't even know what to say."

"Good." Eddie grinned. "I knew you had taste. They'll take a break now. Come on, let's go backstage. I want to see if they'll let me sit in on the next set."

"You?"

"Yes, me. I do happen to play a little trumpet, or have you

163

forgotten? Besides"—he shrugged—"how else am I going to figure out how to copy what he's doing in my session tomorrow?"

Gabby frowned. "Eddie, you can't . . . you wouldn't . . . *borrow* someone else's music, would you?"

"Borrow?" Eddie snorted. "Certainly not. Good artists borrow. *Great* artists steal. And I'm the greatest thief there is."

He held out his hand to her. A little shiver went up Gabby's spine at his touch. Obediently, she followed as he pulled her through the crowded room and out into the crush of people hanging out on the sidewalk. Eddie steered her expertly around the corner and through a side door, into a kind of anteroom cluttered with the usual musicians' detritus: the stacks of instrument cases, the discarded reeds. At the far end was another door, half open, through which Gabby caught a glimpse of the miraculous saxophone player and a couple of his side men sitting around mopping their foreheads with their rolled-up shirtsleeves.

"Wait here," Eddie said, suddenly all business. "I'll just be a minute."

He disappeared behind the door, closing it tightly behind him.

Alone, Gabby felt awkward and out of place. *This is why people smoke,* she thought, slouching against the wall, trying to make herself as small as possible. *So they always look like they have something to do.*

"Gabby?"

"Dexter. Hi."

"I thought that was you." Wherever Eddie was, it seemed Dexter couldn't be far behind. He looked at her with a quizzical expression. A slightly battered cornet dangled from his hand. "What are you doing on Central Avenue?"

"I came to see the show. With *Eddie*," she added importantly. "He asked me this morning, at the studio, remember?"

"Oh, that's right." Dexter looked amused. "I don't know how I could have forgotten."

Frankly, Gabby didn't either. Eddie's invitation—even if she *had* had to give him just the teeniest little nudge—had been such a momentous occasion she could hardly believe that even Dexter Harrington would fail to understand its import. "Have you been here the whole time?"

"Me?" Dexter looked puzzled.

"Yes. Did you just get here, or did you see that band?"

"See the band?" Dexter began to laugh. "Gabby, I was *in* the band."

"You were?" Gabby's eyes widened in surprise. "That wasn't you on sax. And I didn't see a piano."

"I was on trumpet." Shaking his head, he snapped open an instrument case and carefully laid the horn against the worn velvet lining. "It's okay. I guess I don't stand out as much here as on the Olympus lot, huh?"

"It's not that, it's just . . ." Gabby hunted desperately for some way to feasibly change the subject. "I just mostly noticed the saxophone player," she said finally. *Lame, but not untrue.*

Dexter's eyes shone. "He's something else, isn't he? He's just moved back from Paris. I met him over there when he was playing with Benny Carter and Django Reinhardt."

"Jango what?"

"Django Reinhardt. He's a Belgian gypsy with two fingers,

and the greatest guitar player in the history of the world. It's surprising you haven't heard of him."

"Not really." Hollywood was an insular place. Gabby listened to records the studio gave her, watched the movies they told her to see. She could name every Broadway play a producer had optioned over the past eighteen months and reel off the vital statistics of any up-and-comer who might challenge her for a part, but the outside world was a lot of noise, consigned to a few blurry black-and-white minutes of newsreel sandwiched between a double feature. Until embarrassingly recently, Gabby had thought Benito Mussolini was just the latest baritone in MGM's long search for a continental replacement for Nelson Eddy. "I haven't heard of a lot of things. What's the sax player's name, anyway?" she asked.

Dexter looked at her strangely. "Didn't they announce it?"

"Yes, but it was too noisy to hear. I didn't hear your name either, remember?"

Dexter pulled a crumpled leaflet out of his pocket. "Here's the program. You can read all about everything here."

Gabby looked down hopelessly at the smeared text marching mercilessly across the creased paper. Maybe it was the pills she had swallowed or all the Scotch she had drunk, but the letters seemed to be jumping around more than ever, swarming and multiplying hideously, like a colony of ants on a clean kitchen floor. She squinted, willing them to stay put, making out a C here, an X there, but it was no use. She might as well have been staring into a black hole.

"It doesn't matter," she said quickly. "I was just asking to be polite. I'd better go and find Eddie now anyway."

Dexter was looking at her intently. "You know, Gabby," he

said quietly, "if you have trouble reading, just say so. I can help you. Nobody else needs to know."

"I don't *need* any help," Gabby hissed, shoving the program back at his chest. "Especially not from someone . . . someone like *you*."

She regretted the words the moment they came out of her mouth, but it was too late now. She'd been assigned to this script, and she was sticking to it. Ignoring Dexter's look of hurt and confusion, she pushed past him imperiously, flinging open the door that had swallowed Eddie.

"Gabby." The doorway belched forward a cloud of thick, pungent smoke. Eddie choked out her name in a dry, froglike croak, gazing at her with placid, red-rimmed eyes. "What are you doing back here?"

"Looking for you," Gabby retorted. "Didn't anyone ever tell you it's bad manners to leave your date waiting?"

"No." Eddie burst out laughing, smoke streaming from his mouth. "I don't think I've gotten to that part yet in my, whaddyacallit, my *etiquette course*."

Now they were all laughing, all the musicians crammed in the small smoky space. Gabby wasn't the least intimidated anymore, just angry with all these grown men hiding away in a closet like children sneaking cookies from the pantry before supper.

"Well, it is," she said, tapping her foot impatiently. "And it's even worse manners to have some of that and not offer her so much as a single puff."

There, she thought. *That'll show 'em.* And Dexter, whom she could still feel behind her, staring at her back with those wounded puppy-dog eyes.

"Oh, honey," Eddie chuckled. "See, this here isn't a cigarette, sweetheart."

"I know *exactly* what it is," Gabby said impatiently, "and believe me, it's *exactly* what I need right now."

A chorus of hoots went up from the stoned musicians.

"Damn," one of them said. "Looks like you hooked a live one."

"Watch out, Sharpie," said another, "that chick of yours is viper mad."

Eddie lowered his voice. "You really want some? You sure?"

Gabby wasn't sure, not exactly, but the gauntlet had been thrown down. "Of course," she said firmly. "I'm dying for it."

"All right." A little smile played over Eddie's lips. "Benny, pass her the joint."

Benny, the guy who had called her viper mad—Gabby thought he was the trombone player—dutifully handed over the little smoldering bundle. Gabby held it gingerly between her thumb and forefinger, examining it. Shorter and flatter than a regular cigarette, it looked like one of the tobacco roll-ups the camera crews were always smoking on set.

"Wrap your chops round that stick of tea," somebody sang softly. Another couple of people joined in. *"Blow that gage, and get high with me. . . ."*

"All right, Gabby," Eddie said. "It's simple. Just suck it slowly. Breathe in deep and don't exhale until I tell you to, okay?"

It felt like swallowing a lit match. Her throat, then her lungs felt like they were on fire. *I'm suffocating,* Gabby thought. *I'm going to die.*

"Ready to exhale?" Eddie asked. "Okay. One, two . . ."

And suddenly, his hot, open mouth was on hers, greedily

sucking in the vapor that erupted from Gabby's mouth. *This is happening*, she thought wildly. *Eddie Sharp's lips are touching mine.* They lingered just a moment, just long enough to inhale every last bit of her smoke, before he pulled away again, grinning at her.

"Not bad for your first time," he murmured.

It was not quite a kiss. Not quite.

But sometimes, Gabby thought as everything around her dissolved into a warm, happy haze, *sometimes not quite is more than enough.*

FIFTEEN

When Leo Karp told Margo she'd better start sleeping at her studio bungalow from now on, Dane Forrest had to summon every last bit of his acting prowess to hide his relief.

It wasn't that he wouldn't miss her while she was playing the role of a lifetime as Olympus's virgin bride. But Leo Karp had just thrown him a curveball that would make Lefty Grove weep with envy, and he needed some time on his own.

To think. I just need to think.

His first impulse was to go straight to Diana's house and pour his heart out to her, but he quickly thought better of it. It might be late at night, but the photographers surrounding his sister's very slightly decrepit Beverly Hills mansion observed no division between night and day. Even now, they were probably out there, huddled in the bushes out back by the pool, hanging from the treetops in the pitch-darkness like a pack of bats.

Vampires, more like. All he needed was a single blurry photograph of him, a newly engaged man, entering or leaving the home of his "former paramour" at a suspicious hour to leak to the press and they'd be on him like flies on a carcass.

Poor Margo. She'd looked so hopeful, so pathetically *happy* when Mr. Karp had started talking about wedding gowns and diamond rings. Did she have any idea what she was getting into? Their marriage would be one long nightmare of damage control, scarcely begun before people started waiting for it to end. It wasn't a shotgun wedding, it was a snapshot one. Was that what Margo wanted? If it wasn't, he ought to save her by breaking her heart. Be cruel to be kind. Send her back to Pasadena to lick her wounds, find a nice boy to marry, have a family and a real life.

And if it is what she wants? Then she wasn't the girl Dane thought he might love. She was a girl he didn't know at all— and yet knew all too well. *Just like every girl in this godforsaken desert town.*

What he needed was a good, stiff drink. Schwab's was too crowded with lower-level studio types, the kind who, having heard whispers around the lot, would be full of questions he'd rather not answer, and he wasn't dressed for any of his regular haunts on the strip.

Instead, he found himself pulling over outside at Barney's Beanery. Even a coffee shop had to keep a bottle of something stronger behind the counter, he reasoned, and it was so near to closing time, the place had to be almost empty. *Safe.*

The only car in the parking lot was a little dove-gray coupe with a black silk scarf draped over the dashboard, a trace of familiar perfume wafting out the open window.

Why not? Dane thought. He had to be with someone tonight.

She was sitting in a booth in the back, an untouched pot of coffee in front of her. Her hair was copper; her face was white.

"Amanda." Dane felt alive with possibility. "Fancy seeing you here."

"Oh, Ernie." She looked up at him with eyes that melted his soul. "From now on you'd better just call me Ginger."

SIXTEEN

The impending Sterling/Forrest nuptials took over Hollywood, just like they were supposed to. All anyone could talk about was the Wedding of the Year.

The breathless details, filtered carefully to the magazines by the publicity office, were on everybody's lips, everywhere from the opulent gambling tables in the back room of the Clover Club to the bare-bones lobby of the Central Casting office: Margo's four-carat emerald-cut diamond engagement ring, custom-ordered from Cartier in the same style as the (admittedly much bigger) one the former Edward VIII had given to Mrs. Simpson. Dane's absurdly romantic proposal, which apparently involved about a thousand pale pink tea roses and a moonlit ride on Abraham and Sophie, the two Olympus horses devoted Sterling/Forrest watchers knew the couple had been astride when they'd had their first reported lovers' spat during the filming of *The Nine Days' Queen*, now under limited re-release as *The Picture Where It All Began*. The planned honeymoon trip to Paris, paid for personally by none other than Mr. Karp, where the stunning Mrs. Forrest would first come face to face with her specially made haute couture trousseau, also—it was reported—courtesy of Uncle Leo.

"A Fairy-Tale Wedding for a Fairy-Tale Bride," said *Photoplay*.

"Lucky in Life, Lucky Love," advertised *Modern Screen*.

Picture Palace took a longer view: "Margo Sterling Is Living the Dream of Every Girl in America."

Still, this was a town whose principle industry was the manufacture of illusion. The citizens of Hollywood were all too aware that things were not always what they seemed. There were always plenty of cynics eager to burst even the prettiest bubble. Rumors abounded that the dashing Dane—who frankly had a bit of a reputation around the gin joints of Sunset Strip—was perhaps not dashing quite as . . . *eagerly* to the altar as the Olympus publicity machine might have you believe. The most tenacious know-it-alls were already eagerly examining Margo Sterling's enviably slender waist for the telltale thickening that must have sealed the deal.

Some of the lesser—and less studio-friendly—gossip rags were running a story with the sensational headline "Inside Margo Sterling's Dark Past," which used as its main source a Mrs. Phipps McKendrick, née Evelyn Gamble, a "young Pasadena society matron" who relayed "in the strictest of confidence" how Margo, in a former life, "had always been a troublemaker, terribly fast with boys" and how Mrs. McKendrick hoped marriage might reform her old friend and at last provide some relief to her poor parents, who had been "just heartbroken since she callously abandoned them to pursue a life of hedonistic pleasure on the silver screen."

"Can you believe this?" Margo had hissed to Dane as she pulled the smudged clipping from her purse on one of their rare nights together since the studio had laid down the law about just the level of blameless chastity they expected from their blushing bride. "Abandoned *them*? Is that what they call being disowned these days?"

"I don't know what you're getting so upset about," Dane said, downing his martini in one gulp. He'd been drinking a lot lately. "Just forget about it. I don't know why you even look at that stuff in the first place."

"She's always hated me," Margo fumed. "She married Phipps, she's got everything she ever wanted, and still she's trying to ruin me."

"Who?" Dane looked confused.

"Evelyn *Gamble*. From Pasadena. The one I told you about, who used to be so appalling to me at school? She was there that awful night, the one when I ran into you late at Schwab's?" Margo shuddered, unwilling to go on. Dane gave her a blank look. "Forget about it," she said finally, disgusted.

Then there was the matter of the other story floating around, one made all the more unpleasant by the fact that it was probably true: that on the night Dane Forrest was supposedly proposing on horseback to the swooning Margo Sterling, making all of her dreams come true, he had actually been spotted in a back booth at Barney's Beanery (not a very sexy alliteration, true, but there you have it) with an ethereally beautiful if grimly white-faced Amanda Farraday.

Was he giving his mistress the brush-off? Simply continuing

something that had been going on the whole time? Or—tantalizingly—starting something up? All speculation—and like everything, it depended on who you asked—but it was generally agreed that they had looked awfully cozy working their way through the better part of a bottle of Scotch.

The gossip about Amanda's nocturnal activities had reached the lady in question by way of the loathsome Mildred, the down-the-hall tenant at the boardinghouse, who seemed finally to have figured out just who her glamorous neighbor was. Gleefully, she recounted all the different hypotheses "you know, going around the inside circles."

"Well, I guess now I know why you got all these fancy outfits," Mildred chortled. "But if you're screwing some big movie star, what the hell are you doing in a dump like this? Guess you ain't very good at it. Send him over to me when he's sick of you, will ya? I'll show him a thing or two."

For her part, Amanda had been sufficiently horrified by the story to call Margo immediately—if you could call it "immediate" when you had to wait in line for half an hour to get a crack at the phone.

"We just happened to run into each other and had a drink," Amanda said when she finally reached Margo after eleven tries and enough nickels to keep her in coffee and milk for a week. "I'd had a hard day, and Dane was kind enough to listen. I swear nothing more happened than a handshake goodbye before we climbed into our separate cars. There's nothing more to it than that." *She's got to believe me*, Amanda thought. *And even if she doesn't, at least it's the truth.*

But Margo was dismissive. "There's no need to explain or apologize. In fact, I'm glad you called," she continued. "I've got something to ask you, but I wasn't sure how to reach you." She paused for a moment, almost as though she were reading from a script. "I wondered if you'd like to be one of my bridesmaids."

"Jeepers," Amanda said, temporarily transformed back into Norma Mae Gustafson, Oklahoma hick, from the shock. "Are you sure?"

"Positive. The studio thinks it's a good idea."

"But do you?"

Margo sighed. "Why would it possibly matter what I think?"

Larry Julius's hands are all over this. It was, Amanda had to admit, a brilliant strategy. What better way to explain away a late-night meeting with another woman than for that woman to be publicly affirmed as an extra-special super-close best-best friend of the bride? They could have been huddled in that booth planning a surprise for Margo, or better yet, celebrating the fact that the proposal they'd dreamed up together had gone off without a hitch. It was the perfect cover, so perfect that Amanda knew her participation in what was fast becoming the Wedding of the *Decade* was absolutely nonnegotiable.

Joining Amanda in the highly visible bridal party was Gabby Preston, an obvious choice given her previously established—if privately rocky—friendship with Margo, and the fact that her star was undoubtedly *finally* on the rise. Ever since her performance after the Oscars last month, Gabby was nearly as ubiquitous in the Hollywood press as the frenzied speculation over the contents of Margo Sterling's wedding registry. Reams of paper and whole segments of radio shows were devoted to wondering what Gabby would do next. Would she make a picture? Release an album? Both?

And just what was the nature of her relationship with that

fast-talking, fast-living bandleader Eddie Sharp, with whom she'd been running around town suspiciously often of late?

Eddie Sharp's girl. Quite a leap for someone who just two short months ago had been barely allowed to be seen in public without sausage curls and a sailor suit.

Rex Mandalay was designing the wedding gown, of course. As for the Paris trousseau, it was currently being fitted to the headless dressmaker's dummy marked "Margo Sterling" in the costume department of Olympus—a shrewd customer like Leo Karp was hardly going to shell out thousands of dollars for haute couture when he could have the seamstresses already on his payroll knock off reasonable approximations of whatever was in *Vogue* that month.

But Larry Julius's surveys of the public showed that the "average American woman," whoever she might be, would like at least one aspect of the "royal wedding"—as onlookers were beginning to call it, only somewhat facetiously—that she could "relate to"; therefore, it had been decided that the bridesmaids' gowns would be selected off the rack in a splashy shopping trip cum photo shoot that would be the latest installment in the breathlessly chronicled journey to the altar. Margo and her Doting Bridesmaids. Laughing, gushing, pink-cheeked, and full of hope. Just like any other group of girlfriends in America with an unlimited budget and access to the most exclusive by-appointment-only bridal boutique in Beverly Hills.

"Look at us," Gabby crowed. She and Amanda were crowded into the dressing room of Madame Nicole's Salon Parisienne, the two of them swathed in enough pink tulle to outfit a corps de ballet of obese ballerinas. "More likely than not, they'll build a whole picture around us. A brunette, a redhead, and Margo's blonde. One of each. Believe me, around these parts, that's what passes for a great idea."

Oh, please, Amanda thought. *Please let Gabby be right.* Anything to stay an employee of Olympus Studios for just a few months longer, get a few more paychecks, have a few more precious weeks before they came to haul her off to debtor's prison. *Do they even still have those?*

Outside the door, a crew of burly photographers were laying waste to the shop, moving whatever they had to to get the right shot. Madame Nicole's anguished cries came through the slatted door. "*Mais non, mais non!* Not zee Louis Quatorze armoire!"

"Lady, it's blocking the sight line," came the gruff reply. "We'll put it back when we're done."

"But eet eez *très* delicate! Please be careful! Zat armoire eez worth more zan all of you put togezzaire!"

"*Togezzaire,*" Gabby snorted, mocking the distraught woman's heavy French accent. "You know she's from Cleveland, right?"

"Not really?"

"That's what Rex Mandalay says. He used to know her back when she worked the men's counter at the old Hamburger's Department Store. Salon Parisienne." Gabby sniffed. "The closest she ever got to Paris is selling a necktie to Maurice Chevalier." She maneuvered around Amanda, examining her reflection critically in the three-way mirror. "Get a load of this. Can you believe the size of this thing?"

Amanda reached behind to pat the huge bow at the back

of her own dress, its stiffened wings reaching inches past the confines of her waist. "It *is* going to make it kind of hard to sit down."

"Sit down? Are you kidding me? We look like we could set sail."

There was a sharp rap on the door. "Girls! Are you ready in there?"

Normally, a specialist operation such as this would require a senior-level flack such as Stan, Viola Preston's on-again off-again beau with the unpronounceable last name, or even Larry Julius himself. But the aggressive femininity of Madame Nicole's domain had proved too much even for seasoned pros such as they, and instead, they had Florence Pendergast running the show. A spare, thin-faced woman constantly exhaling cigarette smoke through the veil of her hat, making her look like some sort of horror-movie special effect, the ambitious Miss Pendergast was one of the few women in the Olympus press office and was determined to make a success of the awesome responsibility with which she had been entrusted if it meant keeping them up all night and smashing Madame Nicole's shop to smithereens.

"I don't know. Are we?"

"Very funny, Gabby. The lights are all set up and boy, are they hot. We've got to get the shot before they set the curtains on fire."

"*Zut alors!*" Madame Nicole made a strange whinnying sound.

"Now, we want to get a shot of you two coming out of the dressing room, when Margo sees you for the first time. Kind of a play on the first time the groom sees the bride. We're using that as an image reference."

Gabby rolled her eyes.

"So whenever you're ready," Miss Pendergast continued, "just come out the door and we'll snap away. Side by side. Big smiles, please. Make it dreamy. As though you're imagining what it'll be like for you one day, when it's your turn to walk down the aisle."

Amanda looked doubtfully down at her enormous skirt, as wide and unyielding as a basketball cut in half. "I don't think we can both fit through the door."

"One at a time, then. Come on. Hurry, please."

Gabby sighed. "Well," she said, "I guess we can't stay in here forever."

Grimacing, the girls maneuvered themselves one by one out of the dressing room and into the blinding light of cameras, the metallic popping of the flashbulbs punctuated by Madame Nicole's small shrieks as the shower of heated glass fell on her cream velvet carpet. Margo Sterling, looking fresh as a daisy in a lemon-yellow silk dress and a chic Marlene Dietrich beret, sat on a pale peau de soie tuffet, a teacup poised daintily on the way to her lips.

"Well?" Margo asked when the photographers stopped to reload. Miss Pendergast had set about comforting the now-hysterical Madame Nicole. "What do you think of the dresses?"

Amanda bit her lip, half trying to think of something nice to say, half trying to stave off the sudden wave of nausea. She'd been feeling sick to her stomach an awful lot lately.

Gabby, as usual, was not so reticent. "Margie, you can't seriously be . . . *serious.*"

Margo's face fell. "What . . . what do you mean?"

"They're huge, for starters. You saw, we could barely fit

181

through that door. How are we going to walk down the aisle? We'll put someone's eye out with these bows. It's like we're wearing wings. And the skirt? It's so big a family of four could camp out in it. For all I know, they are. There's so much room under here I'd never know they were there."

Amanda stifled a laugh. Gabby was right. *I could rent out space under here,* she thought. *Make a buck or two as a landlady.*

Margo scowled. "They're *supposed* to be big." A hard edge had crept into her voice. "They're modeled after the gowns Walter Plunkett is designing for *Gone with the Wind.* Madame Nicole says hoopskirts are going to be all the rage next year, after the movie comes out, and I'm going to be the first to have them in my wedding."

"Well, hoop-de-doo," Gabby said. "You're not the one walking around wearing an open umbrella, Margie."

Margo stiffened, preparing her response. Amanda watched the two of them anxiously. Normally, this was the point in any verbal disagreement when Gabby's eyes would begin to shine with the unnatural brightness that meant she had taken one too many green pills and was spoiling for a fight, but today, her expression was glazed, her voice strangely calm. *What the hell is she on?* Amanda wondered. *And can I get some?*

"Amanda?" Margo said coolly, her eyes never leaving Gabby's. She seemed as perplexed as Amanda by Gabby's mellow expression. "Do you feel the same way?"

"Oh, I don't mind," Amanda lied. "Whatever you want, it's your wedding. Only . . ." She trailed off, hesitating.

"Only what?"

". . . only I just wondered if maybe they came in another color?"

A muscle jumped in Margo's jaw. "I already ordered pink flowers. And the studio likes Gabby in pink."

Gabby groaned. "Tell me about it."

"I know, I know that. I just wondered . . . if there was anything else you were maybe considering . . ."

"I'm not letting you wear black," Margo said shortly. "It's a wedding, not a funeral."

"Of course, I know that. I just thought, maybe a lovely soft gray—"

"What, so you can match your car?"

"Blue, then. I thought you loved blue."

"No good." Margo shook her head. "The pictures in the newspapers will be black-and-white, and blue photographs as white. Didn't you see Wallis Simpson's dress? She was wearing that gorgeous dress in robin's-egg blue, and then *Life* didn't tint the pictures and everyone who saw it made fun of her for trying to pass herself off as some sort of virgin bride."

"You're wearing white, aren't you?" Gabby said meanly.

Margo's jaw took on a funny set. "*I've* never been married before."

Amanda sighed. "Look, it's your big day, Margo. What you say goes." All three of them knew what a load of bull that was, but it seemed like the thing to say. "Maybe Gabby could wear this color, and I could do a soft lavender or something? It'd look the same in pictures. Pink is just such . . ." She paused, searching for the right words. "Such a difficult color for redheads."

"You've worn it before," Margo said crossly. "You showed up at Mr. Karp's wrap party for *The Nine Days' Queen* in that pink gown."

That pink gown. Amanda felt a fist tighten around her heart

183

at the memory. Harry had given her that dress, had chosen it himself to surprise her. She still remembered the sweet, scared look on his face as he presented it to her, eager for her to like it, hoping she'd understand what it meant.

"That was Mainbocher," she muttered, unable to look up for fear of crying.

"Well, these aren't. But they're pretty damn close," Margo said, gesturing for one of Madame Nicole's frantic assistants to take her demitasse away. "Don't worry, though. They're going to give you both a really good price."

"Price?" Amanda gasped.

Margo leaned forward, beaming as though she were about to give them a wonderful surprise. "Well, normally one of these dresses costs about four hundred dollars. But because of all the publicity we're going to give them, Madame Nicole has agreed to give them to us for two."

"Two . . . two hundred dollars?" Amanda stammered.

"Each," Margo added. "Don't worry. The studio will advance it. They'll just deduct five or ten bucks out of your paycheck every week until it's paid off."

Now I am going to be sick. Granted, this had hardly been an unusual feeling over the last couple of weeks, but this time, it felt serious. *I wonder if Madame Nicole has ever had someone throw up all over her fancy velvet carpet.*

"Well, just you wait until it's my turn," Gabby said, tugging at her enormous bow. "I'm going to get you back for this, Margo, and good."

Margo snorted. "I'm not holding my breath."

"You never know." Gabby smiled a mysterious smile Amanda

knew she was copying from Barbara Stanwyck in *The Mad Miss Manton*. "It could be sooner than you think."

"Really?" Margo perked up, suddenly interested. "Things have gotten that serious with Eddie Sharp already?"

"Well," Gabby said, "we've been seeing an awful lot of each other. The magazines don't even know the half of it. Three times this week alone. He's been taking me everywhere. I've met all his friends. And not just on the Strip." She grinned. "Downtown. Central Avenue."

"Down*town*?" Margo looked at Amanda worriedly, as though searching for help. "Gabby, I don't know. Isn't it awfully dangerous down there? I mean, it's full of—"

"Negroes?" Gabby said sharply, her chin tilted pugnaciously.

There she is, Amanda thought. *There's the Gabby we know and love.*

"I was going to say *drugs*," Margo said. "Drug dens and dope fiends."

"Well, I can't speak to that," Gabby said. "The most I've seen Eddie and his friends do is blow a stick or two of gage."

"Gage?" Margo's mouth dropped open. "Gabby, are you talking about *marijuana*?"

"I believe that's another name for it."

"Don't tell me you've *tried* it?"

"Oh"—Gabby waved her hands in the air, as though batting away a fly—"I've done way more than try."

"Gabby!" Margo's eyes darted around the room, as though a fleet of policemen were going to arrive any minute. "How can you? People go crazy from that. Reefer madness is a real thing, you know. You could lose your mind!"

185

"You're assuming I have one to lose."

"And then it just leads to all kinds of other things," Margo continued. "All sorts of pills and needles and powders . . ."

"Oh, Margie, please. Don't be such a square," Gabby said. "You think that's anything I haven't done before? What do you think the things the doctor gives you are? When Viola was a kid, you could buy cocaine by the gram right at the counter of the pharmacy, and she says those little green pills make you feel exactly the same. And opium? Morphine? Heroin? What the hell do you think is in those sleeping pills Dr. Lipkin hands out like candy? You want to see dope fiends, take a look around the Olympus commissary sometime. Reefer is kid stuff compared to that. All it does is make you feel kind of happy and silly and calm, same as having a couple of drinks does. And it makes you feel so sexy." Gabby lowered her voice to a naughty whisper. "Apparently, it makes things *dynamite* in the sack."

Now Amanda was interested. Gabby had been going on and on about losing her virginity since Amanda had known her, but Amanda had always assumed she'd spill everything the minute it happened. "Gabby, are you and Eddie *sleeping* together?"

"Not yet," Gabby said. "But it's just a matter of waiting for the right moment. He's made it clear he's *interested*, if you know what I mean. And don't give me that look, Margo," she added crossly. "I don't expect him to get down on one knee and propose first. But he'll want to. When it happens, it's going to be so incredible he'll never want to let me go. I'm going to knock his socks off, believe me. I've been studying all the pictures in those dirty books Viola keeps in her underwear drawer for ages.

I'm going to show him things he's never even dreamed of. God knows I've been waiting long enough."

"But, Gabby," Margo said, her tone more plaintive than nagging, "what if you get into trouble?"

"Well, then I'll call Larry Julius," Gabby said. "That's what he's there for, isn't it?"

"Girls!" Florence Pendergast's smoke-belching cry brought them to attention. "We're almost ready with the next setup. Now, for this one, Madame Nicole and her attendants"—she gestured to a couple of small women in white smocks, who looked absolutely terrified at the prospect of being photographed—"are going to attempt to show you some other options, but you're going to act as though you love these dresses so much you couldn't bear to consider wearing anything else. All right?"

"They don't call it acting for nothing," Gabby whispered to Amanda.

"I heard that. Now come on, girls, this is for the magazines." The photographers raised their cameras as Gabby and Amanda smiled. "One, two, three . . ."

"Yoo-hoo! I'm here!"

The famous voice, sultry and strong, was unmistakable. Every jaw in the room dropped to the glass-covered floor.

Diana Chesterfield. In the flesh.

She strode regally across the room, smiling graciously, as though surrounded by a coterie of adoring fans swooning over her every move. Amanda didn't know whether it was because she was currently encased in a wearable cupcake or because Bullock's Wilshire had *finally* cut off her last existing line of credit, but she found herself eyeing the movie star's up-to-the-minute clothing hungrily: the white raw-silk suit with the built-up shoulders and nipped waist that *Harper's Bazaar* had deemed "the silhouette of the new decade"; the broad-brimmed flying saucer of a hat; the enormous diamond brooch in the shape of a panther, its single emerald eye winking brightly from its onyx-spotted face.

Cartier. Wonder who that came from.

"There's my blushing bride," Diana cooed, swooping down to kiss the air on either side of the astonished Margo's cheeks. "Darling Margo. A million apologies, I'm so sorry I'm late, traffic was such a *bore,* as usual. Now tell me honestly, how *are* you?" ;

"Diana!" Margo gawped. "Surprised, I guess."

Diana let out a silvery peal of laughter. "Isn't she a doll?" she asked no one in particular. "She's going to be the most charming bride. Being in love suits her, don't you think? And, Gabby Preston, you brilliant thing." She clasped one of Gabby's small, sticky hands in both of her gloved ones. "I am just in awe of you. Absolutely in awe. The voice of Ella Fitzgerald in the body of Clara Bow. You're an absolute angel, that's what you are, sent by God to let us all hear a little of heaven."

"Golly whiz, Miss Chesterfield," Gabby said, for once in her life seeming at a loss for words. "Thank you so much."

"Please, call me Diana," the star replied, smiling warmly. "Now, I know you'll forgive me, because things have been so busy since I got back, but ever since that glorious night at the Oscars, I've been meaning to ask you to lunch and talk it all over."

"Really?" Gabby squeaked.

Diana nodded seriously. "Absolutely. Now, are they banging down your door with offers? Do you know what your next picture is going to be?"

Gabby shrugged nervously. "No. . . . I mean, I know there's some stuff on the table. . . ."

"Well, think about it carefully. I don't know who you've got advising you"—Margo and Amanda both knew the answer to this, which was no one, followed at some distance by Viola—"but you've got to be prudent. You've got heat right now, heat that could take you all the way to the top, but not with the wrong picture. It has to be quality." Diana paused, pouting thoughtfully. "There's a play opening in New York that might be a good fit. *An American Girl*, I think it's called. They've just started rehearsals, but the writer is Harry Gordon, so I'm sure they'll be negotiating the picture rights any minute."

"Harry Gordon! In New York?"

The words were out before Amanda could stop them, so seized was she with an irrational, wild mixture of joy and fear. On the one hand, his office hadn't been lying, and he hadn't been avoiding her; he really was away. On the other, if Harry was opening a play on Broadway, he'd be gone for months. *When will I see him again? Will he even come back at all?*

Diana turned slowly toward Amanda, looking the redhead up and down as though seeing her for the first time. If there was a flicker of recognition in her ice-blue eyes, it was quickly replaced by a look of impersonal appraisal. "I don't believe we've met," she said coolly.

So that's how she wants to play it, Amanda thought. *Well, let her.*

"Amanda Farraday," she said, lifting her chin defiantly. *This may be Diana's show, but I can play my part my own way. She's the star, not the director.*

"What a lovely name," Diana murmured. "Sometime you must tell me how you thought of it."

"Diana." Margo had finally found her voice. "I don't mean to be rude, but . . . what are you doing here?"

"Oh my God!" Diana's hands sprang to her cheeks in a gesture of exaggerated surprise that had the bonus effect of advantageously displaying a diamond ring at least twice the size of Margo's. "Didn't Dane tell you?"

Margo stiffened. "Tell me what?"

"That I've been asked to join the bridal party. Groom's side, of course." She smiled sweetly. "You see, Dane dined at my place last night, and I'm afraid I was being such a terrible *bore* about just how terribly thrilled I am for the both of you and how I wished I could do something to help that he asked me to stand up for him, just to get me to stop flapping my mouth. And for old times' sake, I suppose," she added thoughtfully. "Now, don't worry, darling. I may be the best man, so to speak, but I'm not going to show up in a tuxedo. I mean, really, after Marlene, what's the point?" She flicked a lazy hand across the tulle of Amanda's skirt. "I suppose this . . . is one of the *options* we're looking at?"

Speechless, Margo nodded.

"Well, this won't do at all, will it? The guests will mistake us for the wedding cake, and we can't have that." Diana poured herself a cup of tea and draped her body languorously across a velvet chaise. "Nicole," she called, "let's see something in blue. Something akin to that glorious Mainbocher Wallis Simpson was married in, don't you think? And bring some champagne.

190

This is a festive occasion, after all." She let out a merry peal of laughter. "Just look at the three of us. Me, Gabby, and Amanda. A blonde, a brunette, and a redhead." She struck a pose, the kind that silently invited the flashbulbs to pop away. "Oh my *goodness*. We're going to have such *fun*."

Seventeen

"Unbelievable." Margo tore into her steak. She ripped off a huge hunk with her fork and shoved it into her mouth. The bloody juice dripped down her chin. "Absolutely unbelievable." With a grunt, she hacked off another bite.

"Would you prefer a meat cleaver?" Dane asked over his glass of Scotch. "They don't usually put them out on the tables at the Polo Lounge, but perhaps they could fetch us one from the kitchen."

"I mean, the nerve," Margo went on, as though she hadn't heard. It was funny, she thought. She used to hang on Dane's every word, hardly daring to believe that *Dane Forrest*, her erstwhile idol, was addressing her. But familiarity had bred if not quite contempt, then a decided lack of awe. It was getting easier and easier to ignore her fiancé. *Especially when he's been drinking like this.* "The way she walked into the place? Giving orders to the salesgirls? Shoving herself into the front of every picture? Telling the cameramen how she wanted to be lit? I mean, my God."

Dane laughed. "Diana's been a star for a long time. She doesn't exactly understand what it is to play the second fiddle."

"Well, she better start learning. I'm the bride, and what I say is supposed to go. As far as this wedding goes, I'm Laurence Olivier. The star and the director. I'm in charge."

"Darling." Dane drained his glass and motioned to the waiter for another one. "If you were in charge, there wouldn't be any wedding."

Margo dropped her fork and knife on her half-empty plate with a clatter, her heart dropping into her stomach. "What's *that* supposed to mean?" she demanded.

"Oh, come on, Margo." Dane rolled his eyes. "Relax. All I meant was that left to our own devices, we might have done things differently. We would have had more time to plan, for starters. Would have waited a little longer. Gotten to know each other a bit better."

"We know each other pretty well, if you ask me," Margo retorted. *What is he talking about?* Back in Pasadena, girls eagerly accepted proposals from boys with whom they'd shared no more than a handful of waltzes at a debutante ball, whereas Margo had been with Dane for months. *What else could he possibly want to know?* "Besides," she added crossly, "if we don't know each other well enough, it's not my fault. You're the one who's been keeping things from me."

"Like what?"

"Like *Diana*, for instance," Margo insisted. "Why didn't you tell me you asked her to be in the bridal party?"

193

At least Dane had the decency to look guilty at that. *Finally.* "I was going to."

"When? The wedding is only two weeks away!"

"I know, I'm sorry." Dane looked around anxiously for his drink. "But it just happened. We had dinner, and it seemed to mean so much to her, and I owe her. . . ."

"You might have at least *asked* me first," Margo said. "I mean, how do you think it will look to have the woman everyone thinks is your great lost love standing there with us at the altar? It's humiliating! You're going to look like a bigamist, and I'm going to look like a fool."

Dane's drink arrived at last and he took a long, grateful sip. "Well, Larry Julius thinks it's a good idea."

"Larry Julius?" Margo cried. "You told *Larry Julius* before you told *me?*"

"Margo, please. The naïveté is no longer charming or convincing. And actually, it was Diana who called him. But he was quite impressed with the idea. Thinks it will send a good message to the public that things are really over between Diana and me, that she's giving her blessing for them to abandon any reservations they might have about you and me. 'A stroke of genius' is the phrase I believe he used. And personally," he continued, after taking another long slug of Scotch, "I think it's all rather stylish. Wickedly urbane, like something out of a Noel Coward play. Usually that sort of thing appeals to you."

"Right, except the separated couple always gets back together in Noel Coward plays," Margo pointed out. "And the new wife is always some ghastly, undereducated twit her husband can't wait to be rid of. Is that what you think of me?"

"Margo." Dane leaned forward urgently, both palms flat

on the table. His green eyes, lately dull with liquor, burned with their old fire. "Diana is my *sister*. I thought at least one of us should have some family at the wedding. *Real* family, that is."

Family. It was a word the two of them normally avoided like the plague, and yet here it was, unavoidable, the elephant in the Polo Lounge. As far as Margo knew, the girls Friday in the press office had mailed an invitation to the Pasadena address she had nervously provided just as soon as the thick, cream-colored, gold-lettered cards had come back from the engravers, but as yet there had been no response. *Maybe they're just not coming*. Maybe her disowning, which in her more honest moments she had to admit had not been without convenience in the past year, was truly permanent. Maybe they really were never going to forgive her for disobeying their wishes and coming to Hollywood.

Or maybe, Margo thought, staring down at the blood congealing on her plate, *maybe they just don't care*.

Dane seemed to sense just how deep his remark had cut. "Margo, I'm sorry."

"Never mind."

"No, that was wrong. I shouldn't have said that."

"It's fine. I don't want to talk about it."

"Still. I'm sure you'll hear from them soon."

Margo jerked away from his hands as he reached toward her. "I *said*, I don't want to talk about it!"

"Fine, then don't. That'll be a change." Dane sat back, averting his eyes from her as he flipped open his gold cigarette case inlaid with dark jade that matched his eyes. *The one Diana gave him*. "Finish your steak. It's getting cold."

Obediently, Margo picked up her knife and fork. "Aren't you going to order something to eat?" she asked.

"Actually, I've got to run. I'm supposed to meet Clark Gable at the Clover Club in half an hour to play cards with some of the fellows."

"Gable!" Margo exclaimed, her mouth full of steak. "Isn't he on his honeymoon?"

Dane gave her a watery smile. "Honeymoon? Don't make me laugh. He married Carole in Arizona on a weekend, and Selznick had him back on the *Wind* set Monday morning."

"But I thought we were supposed to have the whole night together." Margo pouted. "Can't I come with you?"

"I'm afraid it's a bit of a boys' night. Belated bachelor party, really."

"You might have told me."

"When? You've been ranting about Diana since the moment we sat down. I didn't think it was gentlemanly to interrupt." If his grin was supposed to show he wasn't annoyed, it wasn't working.

"But I haven't seen you in days," she protested. "We've got so much still to talk about."

"Like what?"

"Like where we're going to live after the wedding, for one."

"I thought we were going on some sort of romantic Parisian sojourn. Just you, me, and a small battalion of Olympus flacks."

"After that," Margo said impatiently, "we need to find a house."

Dane looked puzzled. "What's wrong with my house in Malibu?"

196

"Malibu?" Margo almost laughed. Sometimes she didn't know if Dane was making fun of her or if he was really that clueless. "It's a million miles away, for a start. From the studio, from the city, from all of our friends—"

"I know. That's why I like it."

"And besides," she continued, pretending not to hear him, "it's totally unsuitable for our needs. After we're married, we're going to be expected to properly set up house, to have parties and dinners and things. The place in Malibu barely has a dining room, let alone rooms for entertaining, or for staff. Or a nursery."

"A nursery?" Dane bolted upright in his chair. "Now I'm really getting out of here."

"Please, Dane," Margo begged. "Please say you'll at least go and see a few places with me this week. Mr. Karp's realtor has a new house in Bel Air he thinks might be just perfect for us, and there are some things in Holmby Hills. . . ."

"I'll think about it." Dane tossed off the rest of his Scotch and stood up. "Now I've got to go. I'll leave the car here and take a taxi, okay?" He kissed her forehead. "Be a good girl and I'll call you in the morning."

Margo watched him go.

He didn't even tell me he loves me.

She looked around the room at the small groups of glamorously dressed luminaries ensconced in the Polo Lounge's famous dark green booths, slurping down plates of the famous spaghetti Bolognese, shouting remotely at unfortunate underlings on one of the famous tableside telephones. *Everything in Hollywood is famous*, Margo thought, *even if nobody's ever heard of it before*. There was a time when she would have been thrilled at the scene, and a bit later on, thrilled at how little it thrilled her.

Now she just felt nothing.

Maybe it was the stress of the wedding. It had all happened so fast, and from the proposal on, nothing had been at all the way she had imagined it would be. Despite their differences, no matter what had happened between them, she had always expected her mother to be by her side as she puzzled over all the delicious little decisions she had always daydreamed about making: the pink flowers versus the white, the lamb chops versus the lobster. Whatever maternal failings Helen Frobisher might have had, you could count on her knowing precisely the way things ought to be done. She'd have known just how to handle Diana Chesterfield that afternoon at the bridal shop, matched her icy stare for icy stare, withering put-down for withering put-down. "Wallis Simpson?" her mother would have thundered. "Do you really propose to appear at my daughter's wedding in the raiment of a known adulteress?" *And a knockoff, at that.* Poor Florence Pendergast would have melted in a puddle on the floor. Gabby and Amanda would have been lucky to escape with their lives.

So absorbed was Margo in imagining this amusing scene that she hardly noticed Perdita Pendleton, the most senior and consequently the most feared gossip columnist in town, sweep down upon her table. She wore a vivid orange turban with a single dyed feather affixed to the front, making her look like a particularly frivolous bird of prey.

"If it isn't the gorgeous Margo Sterling!" she exclaimed.

"Hollywood's favorite blushing bride." Perdita spoke as she wrote, in captions.

"Perdita," Margo said. "Hello."

"Don't tell me I just saw the divine Dane dash out on you? Not a lovers' quarrel, I hope?" Her beady eyes glittered in anticipation of a scoop.

"Not at all," Margo cooed. "He simply had to run. He's playing cards with Clark Gable tonight at the Clover Club."

"Without you? The beast."

"Not really. I'm relieved, honestly." Margo tried to laugh gaily. "You know what those boys can get up to."

"I certainly do." Perdita nodded sagely. "Well, I'm here dining with Gary Cooper. William Powell is supposed to meet us. Still licking his wounds over the Gable-Lombard union, poor thing." Her lipsticked mouth stretched in the customary wide smile that somehow never seemed to reach her eyes. "You're welcome to join us."

"That's ever so sweet of you," Margo said, "but I've just finished, and anyway, I really must go."

"Of course. You need your beauty sleep, after all. Have a good night, dear. We're all looking forward to next week. Imagine, a real Pasadena society girl marrying one of our gypsy breed." The smile widened into a grimace. "Your lovely parents must be so proud."

"They are," Margo said firmly. "Bursting."

The white stretch limo was idling by the curb, waiting for her. *Say what you will about stardom,* Margo thought, sliding across the rich leather seat as the uniformed chauffeur closed the door smartly behind her, *it certainly does have its perks.*

"Going back to the studio, Miss Sterling?" the driver asked.

"Actually, no," Margo replied. Her heart was pounding from the thought of what she was about to do. "I need you to take me to Pasadena."

In the rearview mirror, she could see his eyes go big with surprise. "Pasadena, miss?"

"Yes. Forty-Six Twenty-One Orange Grove Boulevard. Just go east and I'll show the way."

"Very good, miss."

God, she was nervous. She had to have something to help her calm down or she was going to be sick. If only she'd ordered a Scotch of her own before she left. "You're new, aren't you?" she called out to the driver, her voice trembling slightly. "What's your name?"

"Saunders, Miss. And yes, just started driving for the studio about a week ago."

Saunders. Margo smiled to herself. *Leave it to Dane to snag a proper English chauffeur for himself.* "Did Mr. Forrest leave anything to drink in the car, Saunders?"

"Try the bar, miss. He likes to keep it stocked."

"The bar?"

"Under the divider, by the floor. It's a hidden panel."

Margo ran her hands over the highly polished wooden panel in front of her. The baseboard sprang open at her touch, revealing a neat row of cut-crystal decanters filled with liquids of varying shades of brown. She picked up the one that looked like brandy, poured a generous amount into a heavy tumbler etched with the Olympus logo, the thunderbolt encircled by a wreath of laurel leaves, and took a steadying sip.

"Find it all right, Miss Sterling?" Saunders called.

"Yes, thank you. It's quite cleverly hidden, isn't it?"

"This is an old car, miss. Mr. Julius had it fitted with the bar back during Prohibition. Designed it himself."

Of course he did, Margo thought. *Nobody can hide something better than Larry.* "Well, he did an awfully good job. I never would've guessed it was there if you hadn't told me."

"Apparently—or so Mr. Forrest tells me—there used to be a special button to press that could dump the whole thing out onto the road at a moment's notice, decanters and all. But that's since been removed, of course."

"Yes, I can see how that would be impractical."

Margo drank the rest of her brandy in one gulp and reached forward to pour herself another very small one. She was beginning to feel better. Settling back in her seat, she peered out the tinted windows at the familiar landscape. The lights of Hollywood receded as the limo began the slow climb into the hills. Margo had made this trip only once since she'd first come to Hollywood for good, and yet it felt so familiar, so inescapable, the way the first day back at school used to feel.

Like the summer never happened, Margo thought. *Like you'd never been gone at all.*

They were beginning to make their way downhill again, back toward a world of green lawns and palm trees. *It looks so much like Beverly Hills*, Margo thought, yet the two towns might as well be separated by an ocean, for all the people had in common. "Stay left," she told Saunders. "This road will turn into Orange Grove, and then you just keep going straight."

"Yes, miss."

It was too dark to see past the tinted glass now. Margo rolled down the window to watch the familiar houses. The

Pierreponts' sedate redbrick colonial. The big California Tudor where Timmy Mulvaney, the little boy she used to babysit, lived. The Winthrops' Spanish-style mansion with the red tile roof, where she and Doris used to creep out on clear nights to look at the stars.

Doris. Margo felt a little pang in her heart at the thought of her former friend. Whenever she'd fantasized about planning her wedding with her mother, in her heart of hearts she'd always imagined that Doris would be there too. Doris, her maid of honor, the sister Margo, a lonesome only child, had never had.

But Doris and all the others were gone now. Margo Sterling had never met them. They were just a bunch of people Margaret Frobisher used to know.

Saunders pulled up at the curb of a large white house half hidden by a pair of wildly flowering jacaranda trees. "Is this it, miss?"

"Yes."

"Would you like me to wait outside?"

"Actually, would you mind terribly circling around for a bit?" A white stretch limo was terribly conspicuous. She didn't want to run the risk of anyone noticing it out front.

"Very good, miss."

Margo climbed out of the car. The night air was chilly for April. The fresh outdoor scent she had always associated with her childhood, of orange blossom and freesia and something else, something indefinable and grassy, flooded her nose. Anxiously, she looked at the walkway to the house, wondering what to do next. Should she walk straight up to the front door and knock?

Better not, she thought. Her father had a tendency to answer the door himself on his nights in, and she couldn't handle him slamming it in her face.

Slipping out of her shoes, she crept silently around the side of the house, ducking behind the hedges and flowering trees to be sure she was out of sight. When she was safely at the back of the house, she rapped on the kitchen door, tentatively at first, then louder, until she rattled the blinds that hung down over the panes of latticed glass.

"All right, all right," a familiar voice called. "I'm coming, I'm coming."

"Emmeline," Margo whispered, holding her arms out tentatively, half to protect herself, half longing for an embrace.

"Miss Margaret." The housekeeper had turned white as a sheet. "What on earth are you doing here?"

"I wanted to see you." Margo gulped, blinking back tears. The mere fact of Emmeline's presence, the sight of the broad face, the strong hands that she had watched so many times iron dresses and pull cakes from the oven and wipe away tears, was almost too much for her to bear. "And I need to talk to my parents."

"I'm afraid they're out tonight, Miss Margaret. At Mr. and Mrs. McKendricks' house—Miss Gamble, what was. They're having some supper party, on account of their housewarming."

"Oh. I see."

A gust of wind blew through the yard. Margo, who had left the Polo Lounge in too much of a hurry to claim her coat, shivered.

"It's freezing," Emmeline said. "Hurry, hurry. You'd best come in before you catch your death of cold."

The kitchen was the same as ever—same black and white linoleum tiles forming a checkerboard pattern on the floor; same collection of heavy copper-bottomed pots hanging above the oven, as though waiting for a single blow to send them clanging—yet Margo found that her eye was drawn to the tiny things that had changed since the last time she'd seen it: Geraniums sticking out of the blue willow pitcher instead of hydrangeas. The yellow dish towels swapped out for white. The remains of a chicken on a serving tray instead of the bones from a roast. She blinked several times, as though her eyes were the lens of a camera, capturing a memory.

"You want a glass of milk?" Emmeline asked, wiping her hands on her apron.

"No, thank you. But I'd take a cup of coffee if you have some on."

"When do I not?"

Emmeline had bustled over to the stove, flicking switches, fetching cups, filling jugs with milk and sugar with impossible speed. In less than a minute she managed to get the whole mess, along with a plate of freshly baked shortbread rounds, onto a wooden tray. Margo watched her with the same fascination she held for unusually adept dancers who could learn a whole routine after watching it once. It was wonderful to watch someone at the top of their game, and Emmeline was no less a master of her domain than they were. *How did I never notice it before? Why did I always take her for granted?*

"Thank you." Margo picked up the warm cup.

"Can I get you anything else? I've got one of my special lemon meringue pies in the icebox."

Emmeline's lemon meringue pie. It had been one of Margaret

204

Frobisher's favorite things in the world, the surefire remedy for any hurt. It was under a plated slice of lemon meringue pie that Emmeline had secreted Larry Julius's salvaged business card, after Mrs. Frobisher had ripped it to pieces in a rage. *The business card that changed my life,* Margo thought. *All this is because of Emmeline.*

"I'd better not," she whispered, her voice choked with the threat of tears.

"Just as well," Emmeline said. A sharp note had crept into her already anxious voice. "I'm afraid you can't stay long, anyway. They could be back any minute."

Margo barked a short laugh. "Oh, please. Mother's finally invited to one of Evelyn Gamble's parties and she comes home early? I don't think so."

Emmeline shook her head, pushing a gray curl back over her forehead with a roughened hand. "With the way your father has been lately, who knows?"

The coffee cup seemed to jump in Margo's hand. "He's not been ill, has he?"

"Just some stomach misery when he eats rich food and drinks too much. It's nothing serious, Miss Margaret," Emmeline said in a voice that was thoroughly unconvincing. "Nothing to worry yourself about."

They're not getting any younger, Margo thought. *They aren't going to be around forever.* This knowledge, which at various points in her life might have seemed like a kind of relief, hardened her resolve about what she'd come to do. "Emmeline," she began, setting down her coffee cup firmly, "I have something to tell you."

"That you're getting married?" Emmeline was suddenly very

busy pouring coffee into her own cup and stirring with a small tin spoon.

"You knew?"

"She won't allow picture magazines and the like in the house, but I look at them sometimes while I'm waiting on line at the drugstore. So I've seen a headline here and there. I've got to keep an eye on my Margaret, you see." She glanced up from her coffee, looking almost shy. "I guess that's the ring."

"Yes." Margo held out her left hand for the housekeeper to see.

"Well," Emmeline said, giving the glittering diamond a little tap with her callused thumb. "Isn't that something. May it bring you real happiness, baby."

"Thank you." Margo was feeling bolder now. "They were supposed to send an invitation here."

"Oh?" Emmeline was busy with her coffee again.

"Yes," Margo said firmly. "I gave them the address myself. We haven't heard anything back."

"I can't speak to that. Your mother handles her own correspondence."

"Emmeline, please." Margo grabbed the housekeeper's hand and squeezed it roughly. The cold, heavy band of her engagement ring dug painfully into her finger. "Did it arrive? Did she see it?"

Emmeline sighed, pulling her hand away. "I put it on the tray with all the other mail, just like I always do, and brought it to her in the morning room. When I came to take the tray away again, it was still there."

"It was."

"Yes, miss. All the other post was gone except that one envelope. She just left it sitting there, all alone."

"She didn't even open it?"

Emmeline busily began to tidy up the coffee things, her answer implied by her silence.

"She didn't," Margo said dumbly, shaking her head. "She didn't open the invitation to my wedding." She didn't know whether to laugh or cry.

"Now, Miss Margaret." Emmeline turned back to her with a look of concern. "You've got to understand. Maybe it's no comfort to you, and Lord knows, I'm not saying it's right, but your mother has her own reasons for feeling the way she does."

"What?" The word came out in a wounded howl, startling even Margo with the force of its anger. "What possible reasons could she have?"

"That's not my place to say," Emmeline said, her voice wobbling but holding. "That's for her to tell you, whenever she feels the time is right."

Margo wanted to scream. When? What the hell has she been waiting for all these years? Instead, she took a deep breath. "Emmeline, if I left a letter for her, could you figure out some way to make sure she reads it?"

"And let them know you were here? That I let you in? I'll lose my job."

"Then give her a message for me. Tell her I called. Tell her I called and called and wouldn't stop calling until you agreed to tell her what I had to say. Tell her my wedding is next week and I need to see her. She doesn't have to tell Father. She doesn't have to tell anyone. But I've simply got to talk to her. I can't

207

get married unless my parents are there. It just wouldn't feel right. It would be all wrong." As Margo said these words, she was shocked at the intensity with which she felt them. "Please, Emmeline. Say you'll tell her."

Emmeline was still for a long moment. Finally, she sighed. "Is there someplace you want to meet her? She'll want it to be somewhere she won't see anyone she knows."

Margo thought fast. "Schwab's Drug Store." *That's where all the trouble between us started,* she thought, *and that's where it should all be laid to rest.* "In Hollywood. Tell her I'll be there every day this week at five o'clock. I'll stay there as long as I can. She can come and meet me and still be home in time for dinner, with no one the wiser."

"All right." Emmeline set her mouth in a grave line. "All right, I'll tell her."

"Promise me."

"I promise. Now you've got to go. It's getting late. They'll be home any minute, whether the master's feeling poorly or not." Emmeline bit her lip. "But let me ask you something, Miss Margaret."

"Anything."

"Why does it matter so much to you? After everything that's happened between you, why do you still care?"

That's a good question, Margo thought. *I should ask myself that.* "I don't know," she said simply. "I guess, no matter what, she's still my mother."

Emmeline stood very still, looking off into the distance with an expression Margo couldn't define and didn't care to. Finally, Emmeline gave a brisk nod. "I'm going to pack some things for you," she barked. "I don't like the idea of you on the long drive back with nothing to eat."

It's not that far, Margo wanted to say, but she knew better than anyone that while physical distances may be short, psychic ones can seem insurmountable. She watched, in awe once more, as Emmeline moved swiftly around the kitchen, fixing sandwiches, wrapping up pie, pouring the rest of the coffee into a metal thermos and packing it all, along with a couple of oranges, into one of the white string bags Margo remembered her using a lifetime ago to deliver lunch to the gardeners working outside.

"Thank you," Margo said, accepting it at the door. It seemed like a woefully inadequate phrase for everything Emmeline had given her, but she could think of nothing else to say.

"You're welcome, Miss Margaret," the housekeeper said formally.

She opened her mouth as though she was about to say something else; then, suddenly, she threw her arms around Margo in a rib-cracking embrace. "I'll be at that wedding, honey child," Emmeline whispered fiercely in her ear. "Let the devil himself try and stop me."

EIGHTEEN

Sucking in her stomach as far as it could go, Gabby tugged at the zipper of the dress, wincing a little as the sharp metal dug into her fingers. She let out a little gasp of triumph as she felt it close. *Finally!*

She took an experimental breath or two and smoothed the material over her hips before she took a step away from her bedroom mirror, frowning at her reflection. *It zips, but does it work?* On Amanda, the satin-faced black crepe with the low sweetheart neckline looked dramatic and impossibly chic, offsetting her creamy skin and copper hair to perfection.

Gabby, on the other hand, looked like she was going to a funeral.

She sighed with disappointment. It just wasn't fair. After all that dieting, all those pills, she finally had a waistline tiny enough to fit into the corseted Mainbocher Amanda had seemed to slip into so effortlessly. *And still,* Gabby thought glumly, *still I look like the world's best-dressed Sicilian widow.*

Snatching up the short length of drinking straw she'd taken from the Olympus malt shop and trimmed with a pair of nail scissors, Gabby leaned over one of the neat lines of greenish powder she'd laid out carefully on the polished surface of her dressing table. A single sharp inhale and the powder disappeared up her nose. She'd been crushing up her pills and snorting them since she noticed some musician friends of Eddie taking cocaine that way in the dressing room at the Club Alabam a couple of weeks ago. It took a little time to crush the powder fine enough not to burn, but it made them work so much faster. Already her heart was racing as she leaned over to snort the second line.

Gabby wiped her nose and looked back at her reflection. *I just need a little more color, that's all.* Swiftly, she snapped up the little pot of blush from its place on her dressing table and brushed the bright pink powder over the apples of her cheeks and into her hairline, like Viola had taught her to do years ago to keep herself from being washed out by the footlights.

Lipstick was next, a rich scarlet carefully applied to accentuate the deep cupid's bow of her upper lip. Her big expressive eyes were her best feature—even the Olympus makeup artists, who were not exactly shy about expressing their distaste for her various other perceived facial deficiencies, regularly marveled at how they hardly had to do anything to make them pop—but Gabby spat on a cake of mascara anyway and rubbed it onto her lashes with a little brush. *It can't hurt,* she thought, diligently working the dark powder all around her lash line. *Every little bit helps.*

Leaning back from the mirror, Gabby inspected her handiwork. *Not bad.* Her bright cheeks and spidery lashes looked *painted,* true, but *vivid,* a little like a china doll. Her eyes dropped to the neckline of her dress—or more accurately, to the two empty pouches just beneath it. *It's not that they aren't there. They just aren't quite in the right place.*

She opened her top dresser drawer and took out a pair of thick woolen socks. Carefully, she folded each sock into a kind of pad and stuffed them into the cups of her bra. *Much better,* she thought, admiring the way her new cleavage strained against the fabric. But what if tonight was the night? What if Eddie Sharp finally reached in there and came up with two handfuls of slightly sweaty wool?

"I'd die," Gabby said aloud to her reflection. "I'd die of embarrassment."

She glanced at her watch. *Six-fifteen.* As was their custom, Jimmy Molloy was supposed to pick her up at seven and take her back to his bungalow at the Chateau Marmont, where Eddie would be waiting to take her out again. It was the ruse they'd been playing for weeks, and it worked like a dream. Jimmy and Gabby always made sure to have their picture taken in the bar before Eddie showed up, and she and Eddie never went anywhere they were likely to be photographed. But it required coordination. Even if she could have convinced Viola to drive her down to Wilshire for an emergency shopping trip, there was no time now. Besides, she'd want to know why Gabby needed a new dress just to go to the movies with Jimmy, and that would give the whole game away.

Reluctantly, Gabby removed the wadded-up socks and tossed them into a corner. It was no use. Until she could convince the studio—and Viola—just how urgently she needed a whole new grown-up wardrobe, Eddie was just going to have to see her in something she'd worn before.

Sighing, she flung open the door of her closet, flicking dispiritedly through the tired, mostly pink dresses that hung there. The deep pink she'd worn to the Governor's Ball was way too fancy, her blue cotton check not fancy enough. She brushed past plaid skirts and white blouses, a polka-dotted two-piece with a bow at the neck, the burgundy crepe with the white collar she'd worn the first time he took her to the Dunbar, still draped in the sachets of lavender and cedar she'd hung all over it trying to get the smell of reefer out of the fabric before Viola caught on. When she came to a yellow silk print, she paused. It was a little . . . *sunny* for evening, but she could wear the black evening hat and black gloves Amanda had left her. Like Margo had worn with her yellow outfit at the bridal shop. It just might work.

Plus, to be perfectly honest, Gabby thought, gasping a little against the bodice of the black Mainbocher, *I can actually take a breath in it.* Should the opportunity present itself, she could get out of Amanda's dress—she just wasn't sure she could get back *into* it. She slipped the yellow dress off the hanger and tossed it onto the bed, then turned back to the dressing table, picking up the heavy lead crystal perfume atomizer to crush another pill.

"Gabrielle."

"*God!*" Gabby nearly jumped out of her skin at the sight of her mother in the doorway. "Don't you ever knock?"

"Why should I knock?" Viola raised an eyebrow. "What are you doing in here that you don't want me to see?"

"I don't know. Nothing," Gabby said quickly, putting down the atomizer and sweeping the loose pill and bits of leftover powder onto the floor with what she hoped was a surreptitious gesture. It wasn't that she was taking anything she wasn't supposed to be, she told herself defensively, just that she didn't feel like explaining to Viola the logic—or the inspiration—behind this particular *delivery system*. "But, you know, I could have been dressing. I could have been undressed."

"Oh, please. I used to change your diaper," Viola said, casting a critical eye over Amanda's black dress. "It's nothing I haven't seen before. Although obviously, I hope I can't say the same about your visitor."

"My visitor?" Reflexively, Gabby crossed her arms over her deflated, sockless décolletage. "What are you talking about?"

"That *bandleader*," Viola hissed. "He's here. Says he wants to see you."

Oh God. Eddie Sharp. In her house. Probably sitting in one of those horrible brocade armchairs that somehow always smelled of face powder and old soup, staring at Viola's humiliating collection of frolicking porcelain kittens and that photograph Gabby was always begging her to get rid of, the one of a chubby baby Gabby cheerfully lifting her sailor dress over her head to display a cloth diaper that Viola, for all her bravado, appeared not to have changed quite fast enough. Gabby had never had a boy show up at her house before, except for Jimmy Molloy, and even he had never been farther than the vestibule. What should she do? What would Amanda do in a situation like this? Or better yet—since Gabby had begun to wonder if maybe Amanda wasn't quite the expert in the field of male-female relationships that Gabby had assumed her to be—what would *Margo Sterling* do?

Margo would play it cool, Gabby decided. *She'd act like it didn't mean anything at all, like this was just the kind of thing that happened to her all the time.*

"Well, show him into the parlor, Viola," she said, in her best approximation of Margo's crisp, finishing-school diction. "Give him a drink if he wants one, and tell him I'll be with him momentarily."

"Show him into the parlor?" Viola said, goggling in disbelief. "What am I, your maid?"

No, Gabby thought meanly, *but somebody should be.* Viola was always going on about how expensive a maid was, and how she wasn't going to pay some stranger her hard-earned money—*her* hard-earned money, that was a laugh!—to hang around all day snooping, eating their food, doing things Viola could just as easily do for herself, but honestly, it was positively *humiliating* for someone in Gabby's position not to have any household help. Jimmy Molloy lived in a hotel half the time and still had a butler and a chef; Dane Forrest had a valet; hell, she'd even heard Amanda muse about hiring a lady's maid to help her with her hair and clothes.

"Just do it," Gabby said fiercely. "I'll be there in a second."

"Oh, yessum! I's go tell the young gentleman at once," Viola said, backing out the door in an obsequious imitation of an antebellum house slave. "And by the way, Miss Scarlett, you have lipstick on your teeth."

I bet Margo Sterling's mother never answered her own door, Gabby thought furiously as she turned back to the mirror to rub the scarlet stain off her incisor. Margo Sterling probably had a uniformed butler who said things like "she'll meet you in the library" and offered people brandy while they waited.

I need to make more money, Gabby thought as she slipped quickly into the yellow dress. No more Viola negotiating everything, being so pathetically grateful for any little crumb the studio deigned to toss their way. No. As soon as her contract was up for discussion, she was going to call Myron Selznick herself and tell him it was a thousand dollars a week or nothing, with script approval on a guaranteed three-picture-a-year deal. She'd get a big house in Beverly Hills with a big green lawn, a car of her own, a real housekeeper, and a secretary to answer her fan mail and read her scripts out loud to her to memorize. If Olympus wouldn't give her that, well, she could just go elsewhere.

And if Viola doesn't like it, she can go elsewhere too.

Eddie was in the living room, sitting in exactly the chair she was afraid he'd be in, the one with the dark spot that had been the preferred toilet facility of Piggy, Frankie's late cat, during the long years of his incontinent decline. "There she is!" he called, jumping to his feet as she entered the room. "There's my best girl!"

"Hi, Eddie." It appeared that Viola, Gabby noted with some displeasure, had not offered him a drink. Maybe it was just as well. If she was going to have any chance of being alone with him tonight, the safest thing was to get out of the house as quickly as possible, before Viola could put her foot down and/or invite herself along. *Besides,* Gabby thought as he leaned over to kiss her proffered cheek, *he smells like he's had a few already.* "You're early."

216

"Early?" Viola's ears pricked up. "What do you mean? I thought you were going out with Jimmy tonight."

"*And* Eddie," Gabby said quickly. "We were all going to see some music, isn't that right?" She shot him a meaningful look, praying he wasn't too tanked to play along.

"Uh, sure," Eddie said. "That sounds right."

"And Jimmy was supposed to pick me up," Gabby continued, "but obviously there's been a change of plan. Anyway, we have to go."

"Now?" Viola looked pointedly at the clock over the mantel. "It's not even six-thirty. I thought you weren't going out until seven."

"Well, now we have to pick Jimmy up, don't we?" Gabby said irritably. *Leave it to Viola to make you as grumpy about lying as telling the truth.* "And he's all the way at the studio, so we better leave now. You know how Jimmy hates it when you're late."

"Wait a minute." There was a suspicious look on Viola's face that Gabby didn't like at all. "May I see you in the kitchen, please, Gabrielle?"

"There's no time," Gabby whined.

"It'll only take a minute," Viola insisted. "Mr. Sharp, you'll have to excuse us."

When Viola got that tone in her voice, it meant she was about ten seconds away from causing a major scene. Unless Gabby wanted to risk being led away by the ear like a naughty little kid—in front of Eddie!—she had no choice but to obey.

"I don't like this," Viola hissed when the kitchen door had swung closed behind them. "I don't like this one little bit."

"And I don't see what you're getting so upset about," Gabby

replied, trying to keep as calm as possible. "It's just a change of plan. Big deal."

"Big deal?" Viola's eyes, fringed with their usual layer of ineptly applied false lashes, were practically popping out of her head. "*Big deal?* I knew it. I knew you'd been sneaking around with that punk behind my back, and now you're dragging Jimmy into it?"

"Keep your voice down!" Gabby begged. "He's right outside."

"You think I care? You think I care what he thinks of me? You know what I do care about? I've heard stories about that kid, about the people he spends time with. I care about what Larry Julius is going to say. What Leo Karp is going to say when he finds out you've been hanging around that"—she sputtered, trying to think of just the right word—"that *degenerate*. That *drug* addict."

"Yes, I'm curious about that too," Gabby said coolly, "since they were the ones who made me into the same thing. With plenty of help from you, of course."

Viola began to shake with rage, so hard that one of her errant eyelashes came loose and fell to the floor. It lay on one of the white linoleum tiles, curled up like a hairy bug. "*I will not be spoken to that way.*" She was trembling. "*You will not speak to me that way in my own house.*"

"Only it's not your house, is it?" Somehow, the more upset Viola got, the calmer Gabby felt. "It's my house. I pay for it, and for everything in it." She looked down at the eyelash, resisting the urge to crush it with the toe of her shoe like the smoldering butt of a cigarette on the sidewalk. "You're living under my roof, not the other way around."

"Gabby," Viola implored. "You don't know what you're talking about. You don't know what's best for you. You're just a child."

"Only I'm not, am I? A child is looked after by others. A child isn't expected to be responsible for feeding her family, or clothing them, or keeping a roof over their heads *or*," she added, unable to resist, "a Cadillac in their driveway. So since I'm not a child and this is my house, I think that from now on I'm going to do whatever I want. And what I want right now," she said, pushing casually past her gobsmacked mother, "is to go out with Eddie Sharp. Don't wait up for me."

"So that's your old lady," Eddie said when they were safely in the car, Viola's forlorn figure in the front yard growing comfortingly smaller as they drove away. "She seems like a handful."

"Tell me about it," Gabby said, reaching into the glove compartment for the fifth of Scotch he always kept there.

Eddie held up a neatly rolled joint. "Mind if I spark it up? I kind of need it after all that."

"Oooh, yes *please*."

He took a drag and passed it to her. She sucked the smoke, careful not to swallow so much that it set her throat on fire this time. *Let it never be said I'm not a fast learner,* she thought happily, pleased with her expertise. *Old One-Take Gabby. More like One-Toke.* She started to laugh, the smoke billowing from her lungs and settling around her in a sweet-smelling fog. *Green pills, Scotch, and reefer,* she thought happily. *The cocktail of the gods.*

"So where are we going?" she rasped, hoarse from the smoke. "Wherever it is, I hope it has a pay phone so I can call Jimmy and tell him not to come get me. I don't want him getting stuck as Viola's shoulder to cry on."

She giggled, but it wasn't actually a joke. Jimmy had always been a soft touch for Gabby's mother. If she got him in the right mood, she might talk him into telling Mr. Karp on Gabby, and that could be real trouble. Leo Karp didn't like to hear about anyone disrespecting what he referred to as "the sanctity of motherhood."

Still, Gabby thought, *motherhood is one thing. Mothers are quite another.*

"That's the thing, kiddo," Eddie said softly, steering the car up toward the hills. "We've only got a couple of hours."

"Why?"

"That's the thing. I meant to tell you . . . I've got a train to catch tonight."

A train? "What . . . what are you talking about?"

Eddie sighed. "Just hang on a second, okay?"

Eddie pulled the car over into a small, secluded dirt drive hidden from the main road by a cluster of cypress trees. They were looking out over the canyon now. The buildings of Hollywood spread beneath them looked as small as toys. Shadows from the tree branches played over Eddie's face as he leaned over to gently take the bottle of Scotch from the crook of Gabby's arm. He took a long drink and wiped his beautiful lips with the back of his sleeve.

"Where?" Gabby whispered. "Where are you going?"

"To New York," Eddie said simply. "We've got a gig at El Morocco, and then one at the Stork Club. The studio set it up. Big money, big exposure. Most of the guys left yesterday, but I stayed behind to tie up some loose ends."

"Like me."

"In a way." She'd never heard Eddie sound so earnest before.

Gabby swallowed hard. "Weren't you going to tell me?"

"I haven't known that long myself, and there was so much to do. I was going to tell you over the phone, but that . . . well, that didn't seem right." Eddie took another drink. "They've got me booked late tonight on the Super Chief to Chicago. I'll spend a night there with my folks and then hop the Twentieth Century to New York City and start rehearsals right away."

Gabby looked down at her hands. They were shaking slightly, as they always did from the pills. She clutched the right one in her left, trying to make them stop. "I didn't know your family lived in Chicago."

"Well," Eddie said, looking straight ahead, "now you do."

This little intimacy, however small, pleased her. She allowed herself a tentative smile. "I suppose Dexter is going with you?" *Odd,* she thought. She didn't know why Dexter Harrington should pop into her head just now. *I guess it's just something to say.*

"Dex?" Eddie snorted. "Who knows? He's supposed to be finishing up with Hawk at the Dunbar and then heading out, but I'll believe it when I see it. He's in and out like the wind, that guy."

"Aren't you all."

"Gabs, come on," Eddie said, laying his big hand over her trembling ones. "It's no big deal. It's just a gig. I'll be gone a couple of months, and then I'll probably be back."

"Probably?"

"As far as I know," Eddie said. He was getting a little impatient now. "That's the plan. And anyway, it's not like I'm going off to war. Nothing's going to happen to me. There's no need for the grand scene."

The grand scene. Gabby didn't need to channel Margo, or Amanda, or even to hear her own mother's voice in her head to tell her that was what men like Eddie dreaded most of all: the hurt recriminations, the hot floods of tears that left them feeling guilty and confused and, above all, furious at the person making them feel that way.

Of course, in the movies, all the heroine had to do was cry and the hero would take her in his arms and promise her the moon and the stars and that he would never leave her. Greta Garbo and Norma Shearer and Diana Chesterfield and Margo Sterling turned on the waterworks, and Clark Gable and Robert Taylor and Dane Forrest wiped them away with vows of undying love. But when was real life ever like the movies?

Gabby looked up at Eddie with a brilliant smile. "Oh no, I understand perfectly," she said sweetly, flashing her dimples. "It's just that I want to give you your going-away present, that's all."

"Oh?" Eddie looked amused. "What's that?"

This is it, Gabby thought. Either he'd think it was devastatingly sexy or off-puttingly forward, but she'd never know until she tried. Coyly, she looked up at him through her eyelashes, the way she'd seen Amanda do a million times.

"This," she whispered. Softly, she brought her lips to his, kissing him, pressing herself tightly against him so there could be no mistaking her intentions. She felt his body clench, and then thrillingly, start to respond. *It's happening,* she thought, dizzy with happiness. *It's actually happening.*

"Gabby," Eddie murmured, pulling away from her. "Wait."

"What's the matter?" she breathed. "Don't you want to?" *It certainly feels like you do.*

"It's not that. It's just . . . well . . ." He paused carefully. "I guess I don't know how experienced you are with this kind of thing."

"I'm not a virgin," Gabby lied. *He won't be able to tell, will he?* "And even if I was, it wouldn't matter. I want to."

"I don't mean that." Eddie looked pained. "It's just . . . I'm a musician, Gabby. I'm going on the road. And life on the road, well, it has different rules than regular life. I can't make you any promises. I can't let you think this means anything that it doesn't."

She put her hand to his mouth to silence him, loving the feel of his warm breath under her fingertips. "Don't say another word. I know all about that. It doesn't matter. We can worry about tomorrow later. The only thing I care about is today. Right now. This moment."

Eddie smiled with his lips against hers. "You're the best, Gabby. Did I ever tell you that? You're the best girl."

I'm the best girl. And as Eddie's arms tightened around her, the soft swish of the cypress needles the only music they needed as his mouth moved against hers, Gabby almost thought she believed it.

Nineteen

"Ginger!" Lucy shouted over the blaring radio turned up so high you could probably hear it all the way to Santa Monica. "What the hell are you doing here?"

Amanda's jaw clenched. *Funny,* she thought. *I was just asking myself the same thing.*

A year ago, she'd walked out of Olive Moore's house for what she thought would be the last time. She'd been so proud, so sure of herself, secure in her love for Harry and his love for her and her faith in the glittering, glamorous future that was finally hers.

And now I'm back with my tail between my legs. She remembered what Olive had said to her when she'd first told the older woman she'd won a contract at Olympus, and God willing, would never darken her doorstep again: "Seventy-five dollars a week? Seventy-five dollars a week isn't even going to keep a girl like you in lipstick and nylons."

And actually, it had been more like fifty dollars, all told. The concept of payroll taxes had never occurred to Amanda, who had spent her whole life working under the table—sometimes literally.

Not that the extra twenty-five bucks would have made a damn bit of difference. If a girl with a picture contract wasn't going to actually be in the pictures—and Amanda, if she was being honest with herself, had to admit that the looks that had the power to stun a room into silence in person didn't quite seem to have the same power on camera—then the best she could do was get photographed, and to accomplish that, she had to make sure she was something to see. She needed the hair, the makeup, the jewels, and enough suits and cocktail dresses and evening gowns to make a duchess weep. If she wore the same outfit twice, she wouldn't be photographed, and if she wasn't photographed, she might as well stay home listening to the radio in her bathrobe and bunny slippers. *And if you're going to be photographed,* Amanda thought bitterly, *you sure as hell better be wearing the very best.*

So she might have come by her expensive tastes honestly. That sure didn't make them any cheaper. She'd been braced—albeit lightly—for the eventuality of being unceremoniously released from her Olympus contract without so much as a penny to show for it. What she had *not* been prepared for was the letter she had received this morning by special delivery. It bore the postmark of the Olympus Studios post office, and she had assumed it was a check for her last two weeks' salary—a modest severance. It wouldn't do much in the way of clearing the overdue balances on her charge accounts at Saks and Bullock's Wilshire, but it would at least ensure that she could pay the back rent on her room at Mrs. O'Malley's boardinghouse and keep a roof over her head for the next couple of months, until she figured out her next move.

Instead, Amanda opened the pale blue envelope to discover a letter on legal letterhead informing her politely that no such check would be forthcoming. In fact, official payroll records showed that she had taken out so many advances on her salary over the eighteen months she'd been under contract that she was currently in debt to Olympus Studios to the tune of one thousand dollars. She was advised to settle with a single lump-sum payment, if possible; if not, she should contact the financial office immediately to work out a monthly installment plan at a special rate of 4 percent interest.

A thousand dollars. They fired her, and she owed *them* a thousand dollars. On top of all the money she already owed.

It was so absurd that Amanda's first impulse was to laugh. So she did. She threw her head back and let loose with a big, ugly, unhinged cackle that quickly devolved into heaving sobs that racked her body as she crumpled into a fetal position on the unswept floor of her crowded little room. Images flashed through her mind, images of Chanel suits and Caroline Reboux hats and enough tens and twenties surreptitiously slipped to buy the silence of hundreds of doormen and bellmen and lavatory attendants to form a pile for a gleeful gangster's moll to roll around in. "It costs a lot to be me," she used to say with a shrug when Harry or Gabby or Margo Sterling would question her extravagance, but she'd never stopped to think exactly how much.

It all seemed like such a good investment, Amanda thought, remembering the horrible day a decade ago when the stock market crashed and the cold gusts of the Depression began to blow. She'd been just a little girl then, no older than eight or nine. Her stepfather had gotten even drunker than usual that night. He hadn't yet started bothering her the way he would when she was older, creeping into her bedroom and trying to force his way under the covers before she woke up, but he could still hand out a beating when the mood struck him. That night, he seemed like he was in the mood to take a horsewhip to somebody, so Amanda—Norma Mae, as she was called then—had sneaked outside to sleep in the hayloft, figuring when he got back, he'd be too drunk to climb the ladder. In the morning, when she brought him his cold compress and his coffee with the slug of whiskey—"hair of the dog," he used to call it—she asked him what had happened that had made everyone so terribly angry.

"Bunch of damn fools up in New York City," he growled, the odor of the previous night clinging to him as tenaciously as if he'd just had a bath in gasoline. "Lost their shirts, along with everyone else's. Now the bastards are jumpin' out windows rather'n face the mob. Black Tuesday, they's callin' it."

Well, today's my Black Tuesday, Amanda thought, *and I guess I'm jumping out a window too. Here's hoping I land on my feet.*

"I need to see Olive," she told Lucy.

"What?"

"I said, I need to see Olive!" Amanda shouted. *"Is she here?"*

"Hang on, hang on," Lucy said. "Let me turn down the radio."

The jade-green silk train of her lounging kimono trailed behind her like a dragon's tail as she shuffled across the scrolled

227

carpet to a large rosewood cabinet inset with an elaborate pattern of mother-of-pearl.

"Isn't it swell?" she asked, making a big show of fiddling with the dial. "The cabinet is antique, but the radio is brand-new. Absolutely state-of-the-art. It's got, you know, the most powerful speaker *in the entire world*. It's a Zenith," she added proudly. "It's not even in stores yet. Olive had it shipped straight from the factory in Chicago. We might be the first people in California to even have one."

Olive must be doing well. "Is she here?"

"Who, Olive?"

"Who else?"

Lucy pouted. "Really, Ginge, you might at least try and make small talk before you go charging upstairs. Ain't I always been a friend to you?"

Amanda felt a pang of guilt. Not only had Lucy always been kind to her during their time together in Olive's stable of beauties, she'd never revealed the truth about Amanda's past to *Confidential* or *Broadway Brevities* or any of the sleazy gossip rags that would have paid a pretty penny for a scoop about how the girlfriend of the hotshot young screenwriter Harry Gordon could have once been your girlfriend too, as long as you had the dough.

"I'm sorry, Lucy," Amanda said. "We'll have a good catch-up soon, I promise."

Lucy wrinkled her pert nose. "That's what you always say, and we never do. You've never even come by here in all this time, let alone invited me over to your mansion."

"My mansion?"

"Sure." Lucy shifted her weight from one leg to another. "I've taken the bus tour of the stars' homes. Not to mention having seen quite a few of 'em from the inside myself, if you know what I mean."

Oh boy, do I. Amanda winced. This was hard enough without Lucy reminding her just what she was getting herself back into.

"I know how picture people live," Lucy continued, oblivious to Amanda's discomfort. "The least you could have done is had me over for a drink. Let me walk in the front door, like a lady. But I guess that's how it is in this town. You hit it big, you forget all your old friends."

"Lucy." As surreptitiously as she could, Amanda glanced at her watch. Time was running out. "I promise, promise, promise we'll get together very, very soon. Maybe not at my mansion . . ." She stopped herself. There was no need to go into any of that. ". . . but somewhere equally good. I just really, really need to talk to Olive right away. We'll make plans soon, okay?"

"I don't believe you," Lucy said, but she looked mollified. "Olive's upstairs. But I wouldn't go up there if I were you. Something's up. She closed the whole house up today; nobody who's got a date is supposed to bring them back here tonight."

"Good thing I don't have a date, then."

"All right, it's your funeral." Lucy shrugged, turning back to the radio. "But find me on the way out, will ya? I want to hear all about that snobby girl, Margo Whatserface, who got her hooks into Dane Forrest."

Amanda walked through the empty rooms to the big curving staircase at the back of the house. Devoid of its usual signs of lascivious life, Olive Moore's place looked more like a museum than ever. The flocked red wallpaper, the gaudy gilt sconces, the saucy Victorian engravings to put patrons "in the mood" on their way to "somewhere a little more private" were unchanged since she'd seen them last, as though they'd been preserved in amber. *Foolish,* she mused, her hand grazing the polished surface of the mahogany banister, *to think that just because you try to forget about a place, it will somehow go away.* It was like that French phrase Harry always liked to use when he'd had a couple of drinks and was feeling particularly urbane: *plus ça change, plus c'est la même chose.* "The more things change, the more they stay the same."

The door to Olive's office stood slightly ajar. Amanda rapped her knuckles against it lightly, calling out to her.

There was no reply.

Gingerly, Amanda pushed the door open a little farther and took a step inside. The lamps were lit. The big leather ledger books were spread open on the table. A cigarette smoldered in a cut-glass ashtray, and a mouthful or two of amber sherry glittered in a lipstick-marked glass.

"Olive?" Amanda ventured, her voice quaking. Why did it feel so spooky in here? "Are you there?"

"Amanda." Olive Moore suddenly materialized from behind one of the heavy velvet curtains that hung all along the back wall of the office, like the masking on the wings of a stage. "What on earth are you doing here?"

Her voice was low and her diction precise as always, but Amanda couldn't help feeling there was something off about her appearance. She was dressed in a neat, dark, expensive-looking suit, looking more like a soignée socialite matron than the movie colony's leading practitioner of what she primly liked to refer to as "a highly specialized concierge service," but the shoulders of her jacket seemed somehow askew, her makeup slightly smudged. A lock of hair had escaped from its lacquered chignon, dangling alongside the mysterious pink scar that ran the length of one cheek.

Oddest of all, she wore no visible jewelry, not even the little circular gold-and-pearl pin like the one Margo Sterling had that Amanda had always loved, the pin that in all the years she'd known Olive, she could never recall seeing her without. *Olive Moore without jewelry*, Amanda thought. *It's almost like seeing her naked.*

"Well?" Olive sounded impatient. "Is there something you need?"

"Money." *Why beat around the bush?* "I need money."

Olive's ice-blue eyes narrowed as a wide, Cheshire-cat grin spread across her face. "Well," she said. "Why don't you have a seat?"

"I'd rather stand, thank you."

"Oh, Amanda, don't be ridiculous." Olive sighed. "Sit down."

Hating herself, Amanda did as she was told. There was no point in grandstanding now.

"Sherry?" Olive asked, refilling her own glass.

"No, thank you."

"Suit yourself." Olive took a sip, her mouth puckering slightly from the dryness of the liquor. "Now," she said, putting the glass back down on the desk exactly where it had been. "Let me guess. The studio dropped your contract."

Amanda had told herself she wouldn't show any surprise in front of Olive. She swallowed hard. "How did you know?"

"Amanda, dear, let's face it. You certainly take a nice picture, but you haven't exactly been burning up the screen." Olive lit herself a cigarette from the gilt-edged box on the desk. "But you've been spending more than they paid you, and now you're into the studio for money and you've got no way to pay them back, is that right?" She sat back, arms crossed over her chest in triumph, puffing away.

Amanda looked down at her hands, her face flushed with shame. *How the hell does she know?* Olympus had promised not to make her termination public for a few more weeks—"to give you some leverage should you seek placement at another studio," the employment secretary had said benevolently, as though she were bestowing on Amanda some great kindness. Gabby, bless her self-obsessed little soul, had never bothered to follow up about the results of the meeting that had filled her friend with such terror that day on the Olympus lot. Harry was unreachable, Margo was remote. Dane . . . well, Dane Forrest knew. He hadn't offered any help, and she hadn't expected him to. But she'd never expected him to go blabbing it all over town.

Just goes to show you can't trust anyone.

"Oh, don't worry," Olive said, as though she could read Amanda's thoughts. "Nobody's betrayed you. It's just such an old story. So predictable that if it were a picture they'd send it in for rewrites. For a few girls, a studio contract is a winning lottery ticket; for most, it's a shell game. You come out worse off than you went in." Her words were hard, but her voice was not unkind. "How much are you in for? It must be quite a lot if you came to me."

"Six thousand dollars."

"What?"

"Six thousand dollars," Amanda said. Just saying the number aloud made her blush with shame. "And change."

"My God." Olive shook her head. "You've really gotten yourself into a pickle, haven't you?"

"I guess so."

"Well, I don't give gifts, Amanda. You're going to have to work for it. I want you back on the books immediately, and back in the house, where I can keep an eye on you."

"Fine."

"I'll give you a small allowance, for necessities. We'll deduct it from your earnings each week, and you'll be on every night until the debt is clear. And I don't want any complaints this time. You'll go with who I tell you to, and you'll do whatever they want." Olive's eyes glittered. "*Whatever* they want. Is that clear?"

Amanda swallowed hard, forcing back the bile that rose to her throat at the thought of exactly what Olive meant. The endless string of dingy hotel rooms; the sour breath and wandering hands. The smug, cruel smiles of men who thought they knew exactly what they were owed.

And worse—maybe worst of all—the expressions of everyone who saw her, their looks of disapproval and pity and disgust. The looks she wanted to punch right off their faces, the looks that made her want to scream and cry and spit *You don't know who I am! You don't know what it's like! You don't know what I've been through. You don't know anything at all!*

"Yes," she whispered.

"Good." Olive tossed off the last of the sherry and allowed herself a small smile. "You can stay here tonight. I'm afraid I've given Lucy your old room, but you can take Dot's at the end of the hall."

"What happened to Dot?"

"Dot?" Olive's smile disappeared. "To put it bluntly, Dot went and got herself knocked up. I do so hate to use such a *vulgar* phrase"—she gave a little ladylike shudder—"but when it comes to that girl there's really no other word for it. And since she refused to do . . . shall we say . . . the *practical* thing, there was simply no place here for her anymore. After all, she's no use to anyone in that condition."

No, Amanda thought, a shiver prickling her neck. *She's certainly not.*

"Now," Olive continued briskly, flicking past a few pages in the ledger as she picked up her fountain pen. "What would you like us to call you? Ginger, still? Or shall we come up with something else? Something to make our clients think they're getting someone new?"

Ginger's fine, Amanda was about to say, when suddenly, the door behind Olive opened and shut and the whole world changed.

It was only for a moment. And the door only opened a crack. Just enough for a brief glimpse of a platinum blond head, the silky sash of a dressing gown, a round blue eye stretched wide, as though wondering just what the hell was going on. But there was no mistaking who it was.

Diana Chesterfield. At Olive Moore's house.

And clearly *quite* at home.

From the look on Olive's face, she knew *exactly* what Amanda had seen.

And exactly what it meant.

"All right," Olive said in a low voice. Her lips pressed so tightly together they were almost as white as the cuffs of her shirt. "What do you want?"

What do you want? How much not to tell? How much to make sure that any breath of what you've seen never leaves this room? Olive was going to buy Amanda's silence, same as Amanda herself had done countless times. All those tens and twenties to bellmen and bathroom attendants finally repaid. All she had to do was name her price and she was free. *Careful, Norma Mae,* Amanda thought, steadying herself, her stomach churning harder than ever. *Don't lose your nerve, but don't overplay your hand.*

"I want a thousand dollars. Cash."

Olive let out a short bark of a laugh. "A thousand dollars? Darling, please. I could have you *killed* for a thousand dollars in cash."

Amanda's hands flew to her abdomen, as if to ward off an errant knife. "Five hundred, then." She wrapped her arms protectively around herself, doing the calculations in her head. *That should do it.* "Five hundred dollars. Right now."

Olive stared at her. Amanda felt her insides turning to water, but she forced herself to hold Olive's gaze. *Don't back down. Don't show weakness. Not when you're this close.*

Finally, Olive reached into her blouse and produced a small gold key, which she slid into the lock of her desk drawer with a smooth click. Wordlessly, she drew out a thick bank envelope and began to count out the crisp bills one by one, placing them in a neat stack in the middle of the desk.

"You know, Amanda," she said when she had finished. "You always were a terrible negotiator. I would have gone up to seven-fifty."

Amanda didn't bother to answer her, didn't bother to come up with some smart remark. She had already swept the precious

235

bundle into her hands and was running out of the room. Running down the big staircase with the wall sconces and the naughty pictures, through the parlor, pushing past the astonished Lucy with the radio up as loud as ever and out onto the street.

When she reached the dove-gray coupe parked at the bottom of the driveway, she doubled over at last, crouching next to the tires, heaving the contents of her churning stomach onto the gravel. *It's the past,* Amanda thought as she was sick again and again. *You're vomiting up the past. Go on. Get it all out.*

Back at the boardinghouse, the wretched Mildred was waiting for her, blocking her door like the strip of tape surrounding a crime scene.

"Mrs. O'Malley!" she screamed as soon as Amanda's green face appeared over the top of the stairs. "Mrs. O'Malley, she's here!"

The big Irishwoman popped out from behind a corner with surprising stealth for a person of her formidable size. "So, there she is," she trilled, wiping work-reddened hands on her calico apron. "All those bills and finally, the lady decides to grace us with her presence."

"Please, Mrs. O'Malley," Amanda begged, her hand clamped to her still unsettled stomach. "I'm in a terrible hurry. I just need to get a few things out of my room—"

"And sneak away in the middle of the night without coughing up so much as a cent? Do I look like I was born yesterday?"

Amanda closed her eyes tightly for a moment. *I have to get out of here. It doesn't matter how.* "How much do I owe you?"

Mrs. O'Malley and Mildred shared a triumphant look. Amanda couldn't help wondering just what Mildred was getting out of the deal. *Besides the satisfaction of seeing me busted.* "It's eight weeks you've gone without paying," Mrs. O'Malley said eagerly. "At twelve dollars a week. With laundry expenses and breakfast, not to mention the paper and ink for all those overdue bill notices," she added, "we'll make it a hundred dollars even."

A hundred dollars. Amanda thought of the wad of Olive's ironed bills in her purse. Last-minute passage on the Super Chief would be at least two hundred bucks. *And then there's a hotel once I get there, not to mention meals and clothes . . .*

"I'll give you fifty," she said firmly. "In cash. And I'll wire you the rest in a few weeks. With interest, of course."

"Nice try, sister." Mildred gave a cruel bark of a laugh. "Mrs. O'Malley, I still get first pick of her clothes, isn't that right? The hats and the bags I'll leave for you."

"Oh, hush up, Mildred," Mrs. O'Malley hissed. She took a step or two closer to Amanda. "With interest? And how do I know you're good for it?"

Amanda bit her lip, her mind racing, thinking of the one thing she could use as collateral. *Why not? Where I'm going, I won't need it anyway.* "I'll . . . I'll leave you my car."

Mrs. O'Malley's face stayed grave, but her eyes were suddenly lit from within. *Score.* "Your car? Not that little gray thing you're always speeding around in?"

"That little gray thing is a dove-gray 1938 customized Packard with all-leather interior and a state-of-the-art radio," Amanda said, picking up steam, "and it's yours until I come back for it. Unless I fail to wire you the money, in which case it's yours completely. Under one condition," she added.

Mrs. O'Malley's face was as alight with greed as Mildred's was with fury. "What's that?"

"The first time you drive it, it's going to be to take me to La Grande Station. The Santa Fe Super Chief leaves in an hour, and I'm going to be on it."

"Why?" Mrs. O'Malley was already taking off her apron, seeming, to Amanda's delight, quite swept up in the adventure. "Where are you going?"

Amanda closed her eyes. She could already picture the expression on Harry's face when he saw her, feel the warmth of his arms as he clutched her to his chest, never to let her go.

"New York City," she whispered. "I'm going to New York City."

And with just a little bit of luck, I may never come back.

TWENTY

"In the ballroom, you're in for a real treat. I think it's the most marvelous room in the whole gorgeous house."

The studio-appointed realtor's high heels clacked like the keys of a typewriter as she threw open the curved French doors and ushered Margo and Gabby through.

"There," she said happily, looking around with a triumphant smile. "Now does that deserve a 'wow' or does that deserve a 'wow'?"

Margo turned slowly to take in every inch of the cavernous room. The walls were the color of desert sands, with something mixed into the paint to make it glitter. Carved marble columns, inlaid with ornate mosaics of turquoise and jasper, rose to the midnight-blue ceiling, which twinkled with hundreds of tiny stars, like diamonds against a swath of rich velvet. In one corner, a huge golden fountain etched with mysterious hieroglyphics gurgled softly, sending crystalline jets of water down the proud face of a sculpted pharaoh.

"Wow." *Wow indeed. It looks like King Tut's summer home.*

The realtor—Miss Perkins, Margo thought her name was—looked pleased. "You'll note the Egyptian motif, of course, which was all the rage in the twenties but looks every bit as spectacular and unique today." She paused, as though to allow the profundity of this statement time to sink in. "Now, the floor of this room," she continued when she was certain Margo was sufficiently dazzled, "is particularly special. It's genuine obsidian tile from Argentina, installed by the original builders at the suggestion of screen legend Rudolph Valentino, who insisted there was nothing like a tile floor for a tango." She beamed, leaning forward as though she were revealing a wonderful surprise. "So in addition to being a stunning conversation piece, this floor is also of *great* historical import."

"What's the deal with the ceiling?" Gabby asked loudly, before Margo could respond. "Is it supposed to look like the one at the Grove or what?"

Miss Perkins regarded Gabby with the same look of anxious repellence she'd been fixing on the diminutive starlet since she'd turned up with Margo. It was clear the woman had no idea what Gabby was doing there or how she was supposed to behave toward her. Should she treat Gabby with the deference shown to an important star or the disdain shown to an unwelcome third wheel? Especially one whose playful presence (in lieu of any trace of the future master of the house) seemed to indicate that Margo was nowhere near ready to make the kind of financial commitment that would lead to a healthy commission? "Excuse me?"

"The Cocoanut Grove," Gabby said, even louder this time, as though Miss Perkins were deaf. "The nightclub at the Ambassador Hotel. It has a ceiling just like this."

"Ah. I see." Miss Perkins tried to smile, her lips pressing together in a thin red slash, as if she had an enormous paper cut on the lower half of her face. "Well, any similarity is *entirely* accidental, I assure you. *This* ceiling—like the rest of the house—was designed by the great Wallace Neff himself. It's an exact depiction of the night sky over Giza—which is in Egypt, of course—at the time of the pyramids."

Margo made a few throaty murmurs of polite appreciation. It seemed to be the only possible response. She might technically be the customer, a grown woman with an engagement ring on her finger and a huge line of credit with the Olympus bank, but something about Miss Perkins made her feel as though she were once again an Orange Grove girl in a navy boiled-wool jumper, being steered carefully (mind the nudes) around the Los Angeles Museum of History, Science, and Art on Mr. Howell's art appreciation class's annual field trip.

Miss Perkins swept ahead in a cloud of sickly sweet perfume. "And now, if you'll be so kind as to accompany me up the grand staircase, we can commence our tour of the private quarters."

"How did they know?" Gabby whispered as they followed the realtor back out the French doors and up the huge curving staircase.

Whispering so the teacher won't hear. Now we really are back at school. "Know what?"

"About the sky. How do they know that's what it looked like back then? In the time of the pyramids, I mean. There can't be anyone left who remembers. That must have been four hundred years ago."

"More like four thousand."

Gabby pouted, running her tiny hand restlessly over the polished mahogany banister. "Four hundred, four thousand, what's the difference? Dead is dead."

Margo dissolved into giggles. *Thank goodness for Gabby,* she thought, ignoring the look of alarm on Miss Perkins's face as she glanced back to see just what was so funny. *I don't know if she does it on purpose or what, but God knows I needed a laugh.*

"Thank you for coming," she told her friend sincerely. "I don't know how I could have faced this otherwise. It would have been too, too dreary on my own."

"Too, *too*!" Gabby said, imitating her. "La-di-dah. *Someone's* been spending an awful lot of time with Diana Chesterfield."

"*Honestly.*" Margo rolled her eyes theatrically. "Just when I said something nice."

"Aw, you know I'm just kidding." Gabby grinned. "Anyway, I was glad to come. I'm all done for now on the picture, and at least it gets me out from under Viola's nose for a couple hours."

"What picture?" Margo asked. "You didn't even tell me they put you on a picture! Gabby, that's exciting!"

"Aw, it's just a revue kind of thing. *The Madding Crowd,* they're calling it, although the title will probably change a million times," Gabby said, fiddling with the handle of her purse. "They're still shooting some of the big dance numbers and doing pickup shots, things like that. They just asked me to stick in two numbers at the last minute: 'I Cried for You' and 'Ballin' the Jack.'"

They had reached the top of the stairs now and followed

Miss Perkins down a carpeted corridor that seemed positively endless. *If this is the way to the bedrooms,* Margo thought, *I'm going to have to start carrying mixed nuts and a canteen every night.*

"The ones you did after the Oscars?"

"The very same. Same songs, same arrangements, same band. But we can't record the sound track until Eddie gets back from New York."

"They didn't make him finish the picture first?"

Gabby rolled her eyes. "Like I said, it was last-minute. And besides, it seems he's got some clause in his contract that says he can take off whenever he gets a live gig in a theater of a specific size. Addendum 'Music Comes First.'" She snorted. "God only knows how he swung that. I never could. He's never even been in a picture before." She shook her head furiously, her dark brown curls bobbing from side to side. "Damn men! They let each other do whatever they want. Meantime, if I gain so much as a pound over my contract weight, the studio is fully within its rights to tar and feather me and ride me down the middle of North Crescent on a rail."

Margo gave Gabby's arm a squeeze, although inside she was dying of jealousy. *God, what I wouldn't give to have a picture to worry about.* "I'm sure he'll be back soon."

"Yeah. He better be." Lifting her big brown eyes back to Margo's, Gabby gave a strange little laugh. "Anyway, in the meantime, here I am, your friendly real estate know-nothing. Honestly, Margo, I don't know the first thing about houses, or architects, or what you're supposed to look for, or what it's all supposed to cost. If it's got a roof and an indoor toilet, it all seems fine to me."

243

Margo laughed. "You should go live with Dane, then. The two of you will get along just fine."

"Don't go putting ideas in my head." Gabby looked at her carefully. "Still, it's too bad he couldn't come today. I mean, it's going to be his house too, isn't it?"

Theoretically. "Well, like I said, he's not too particular about this sort of thing," she said airily, waving her hands as though to swat away Gabby's questions before they were even asked. "And besides, he's got reshoots on that Western picture they loaned him to Metro for, and wardrobe for the mountaineering thing he's supposed to start right after the honeymoon. And with the wedding next week already, he's just got so much to do." She bit her lip. "I know he'd have come if he could." *Right?*

"Right," Gabby said, as though she could hear Margo's thoughts. "I'm sure."

They had finally reached the end of the corridor. Miss Perkins unlocked a pair of immense walnut doors. "Voila," she said. "The master suite."

Suite? More like a wing. Growing up in Pasadena, and now moving among the upper echelons of Hollywood, Margo had seen more than her fair share of lavish homes, but she'd never seen private quarters quite like this. Miss Perkins led them through a series of rooms that, judging from the dark wood finishes and rich, aromatic leather covering the walls, seemed meant for the man of the house: a sitting room, a library with a full bar built into the rolltop desk, a circular dressing room with an old-fashioned bellpull for the valet and a custom-built suit rack that rotated mechanically at the touch of a button.

"Yeah, it's nice," Gabby said as Miss Perkins was showing them the breathtaking view of the Pacific Ocean that was visible even from the gentleman's bed, "but I don't see the point of separate bedrooms. Kinda takes all the fun out of it, you know what I mean?"

Margo understood, even without Gabby's knowing wink, but the second they exited what Miss Perkins kept ostentatiously referring to as "the master's quarters" and entered "the mistress's," the separation made perfect sense.

The main bedroom was, quite simply, the most elegant, most feminine, most downright *beautiful* room Margo had ever seen. The gently curved walls were papered a gorgeous shade of robin's-egg blue, embossed with delicately drawn fronds in silver and pale gold. The round bed, covered in tufted lavender satin, was set against an iridescent headboard made to look like an open oyster shell. The chandelier—if you could call something of its splendor by so mundane a word—was made of thousands of ropes of gleaming pearls that stretched across the ceiling like a canopy. Unlike the hard reflective dazzle of crystals, the pearls seemed to absorb the light, casting a rosy, dreamlike glow over the entire room. Margo imagined lying in bed in the half darkness, looking up at them through heavy-lidded eyes as Dane lay beside her, took her in his arms, kissed her. . . .

"*Drat!*" Miss Perkins exclaimed, her composure rattled by the stubborn lock on an adjoining door. "The boudoir is right through here, but I don't seem to have the right key."

"It's okay," Margo said, almost relieved to be shaken out of a daydream that she had no business dreaming in public. "I don't need to see it."

"Oh, believe me, you do. If you think this bedroom is to die for, just wait until you see the bath. The right key has to be around here someplace. You don't mind if I go and make a phone call, do you?"

"Not at all."

Miss Perkins bustled out of the room, the plush carpeting mercifully muffling the click of her heels. Gabby sidled up alongside Margo, a mischievous gleam in her eyes. "You were thinking about getting Dane in here, weren't you?"

"What?" Margo felt her face flush. "What are you talking about?"

"Oh, Margie, come on. You can't fool me. I saw the look on your face right now, looking at that bed. You can't wait to see how that gorgeous husband-to-be of yours looks in it."

Giggling, Gabby flopped down on the satin comforter. *She sounds like her old self*, Margo thought. It was at times like this, when Gabby reverted to the funny, bubbly, instantly confiding girl who had made her feel so at home in her first lonely weeks at the studio, that Margo remembered why they had become friends in the first place. Before the Charles Darwin survival-of-the-fittest dogfight that was life on the Olympus lot had divided them.

Well, I guess she can afford to be nice now. Gabby's star was on the rise, and Margo's, which last year had blazed bright enough to blind, was beginning to fade. *She'll be Gabby Preston and win her own Oscars. I'll be Mrs. Dane Forrest and get to stand around and look at his.* Somehow, it didn't seem like a very fair trade.

"Believe me, I don't blame you," Gabby continued, curling her knees to her chest. "It's so amazing, isn't it? I mean, once you do it once, you just want to do it all the time. To be perfectly honest, I don't see how anyone gets anything else done."

"*Gabby Preston.*" A realization woefully late in coming began to creep over Margo. "You don't mean . . ."

Gabby wore the satisfied grin of a cat that had just licked up every last drop of the cream. *If she were wearing any buttons, she'd burst them.* "Eddie," she breathed, wrapping her arms tightly around her chest, her eyes shining. "Eddie and me. We did it. I went all the way with Eddie."

Of course, Margo thought irritably. *Of course she did. I'm not stupid. Why am I always so slow on the uptake?*

"Wow," Margo said, with almost exactly the same inflection with which she had acknowledged the dubious splendor of the Egyptian ballroom. Gingerly, she sat down beside Gabby on the oyster bed. "Wow."

"'Wow'? Is that all?" Gabby was practically jumping out of her skin with excitement. "Don't you want to hear how it was?"

"It seems like you want to tell me."

"Of course I do!" Gabby squealed, snatching up a shell-shaped pillow and clutching it to her chest. "Telling's the best part. Well"—she grinned sheepishly—"maybe not quite the *best* part. But a good part."

Margo smiled weakly. "Then I guess you better tell me."

"Well, it was all very spontaneous. Unplanned. I mean, I *planned* it"—Gabby wrinkled her pert nose prettily—"but not like this. I mean, I'd imagined I'd surprise him. I'd book some fancy suite at the Beverly Hills Hotel—"

"Not the Chateau?"

"Nah, something about that place makes me feel dirty." Gabby shivered. "Like you could murder someone and the chambermaids would just scoop the body into the incinerator, no questions asked. Besides, Larry Julius has practically the entire lobby staff on his payroll. All those newsreels about those men in the trench coats spying on everybody in Germany? Jeez Louise, they oughta hire *him*."

"I don't think Hitler pays quite as well as Leo Karp," Margo said tersely. It seemed churlish to point out that Larry lacked the specific, should one say, *ethnic* qualities the Nazi regime required in their minions.

"Well, anyway, I prefer the Beverly Hills. It's classier. So I had it all planned, how it would happen. I mean, since Eddie seemed like he was never going to make the first move. I thought I'd rent myself one of those fancy suites by the pool, maybe even a bungalow. Then I'd call him up and invite him to a drinks party, something that seemed like an occasion, so he'd be dressed up and looking nice. And then, when he got there, whoops! There's nobody else there. Like that trick Diana Chesterfield pulled in that picture she made for Metro, with Robert Montgomery—"

"*Move Over, Darling*," Margo replied instantly.

"Yes! Where she invites him to her room at the Plaza and gives him a glass of champagne and says, 'Oh, I'm *terribly sorry. . . .*'"

"'*The party is just you and me*,'" Margo finished along with Gabby, mimicking Diana's breathy murmur. *God!* She and her old friend Doris had seen *Move Over, Darling* at least four times during the two weeks it had played the Pasadena Rialto, and then sat at the soda fountain practicing talking with drinking straws clamped between their teeth, the way Diana did with her tortoiseshell cigarette holder in the picture.

"And now she's in your wedding," Gabby said, as though

once again she could read Margo's mind. "Funny how life works, isn't it?"

"Keep telling me about Eddie," Margo said, eager to change the subject. "You said he's in New York for a gig?"

"If you can call playing the Palace a gig," Gabby said proudly. "It's kind of like calling that diamond mine on your finger a ring. But like I said, it happened all of a sudden. It was Friday night. He was supposed to pick me up at Jimmy's bungalow at the Chateau to take me out, but he showed up at my house instead, hours early, and said it was important. He *had* to see me."

Her eyes took on a dreamy, faraway look. "He was supposed to catch the train that night, see, and he just couldn't go without saying goodbye. Well, Viola pitched a fit, as you can imagine. Gave me that whole over-my-dead-body, not-while-you're-under-my-roof song-and-dance. Mothers!" She rolled her eyes. "Can't live with 'em, can't be born without 'em. But she got it back this time, and good. Maybe it's these new pills I'm taking, or maybe it was having Eddie there. Maybe it was divine inspiration, who knows? But I told her as long as I'm paying, she's under *my* roof, and from now on, I'm going to do whatever I want and go wherever I want with whoever I want. And if she doesn't like it, then she can just go and find some other little singing and dancing meal ticket to exploit."

"Wow," Margo said dumbly once again. *I wonder what'll happen when Mr. Karp gets wind of that.*

"Wow's right," Gabby said with a proud nod. "So Eddie and I beat it, and we went for a drive in the Hills. He pulled over into this secluded spot, and that's when he told me how he was going to New York, and he'd be gone for a month at least, and well"—she looked up with a naughty grin—"I guessed I'd better give him something to remember me by."

"Gabby!" Margo's hand flew to cover her open mouth. "You mean . . . right in the car?"

"Yeah, like I said, it wasn't exactly what I'd been imagining. But still, it was awfully romantic in its way." Gabby's eyes were dreamy again. "We were up so high, nobody could see us, but we could see the whole city spread out in front of us. Like we were up in heaven or something. We were in a grove of cypress trees that smelled so good, and there was a cool breeze coming through the windows. Besides," she added quickly, recovering from her brief, uncharacteristic lapse into poetry, "Eddie's got one of those huge new model Lincolns. The backseat is practically as big as a double bed."

"Yes," Margo said, "but didn't it make an awful mess?"

Gabby frowned. "What do you mean?"

"Well, with, you know, the blood, or . . ." Margo trailed off.

"There wasn't any blood."

"There wasn't?"

"No. But I wasn't really expecting there to be. Amanda says it's a myth, about the bleeding. She says hardly anyone does."

"Well, I guess she would know."

Gabby shrugged. "It's not just Amanda. Pretty much everybody says that."

"Everybody?"

"Well, Dr. Lipkin, at least. I went to him a while back to see about getting fitted for one of those—whaddaya call it—that thing you can use—"

"A pessary," Margo said quietly, her cheeks burning with embarrassment. She might have recovered from most of the psychological injuries inflicted on her by the Orange Grove Academy for Young Ladies, but the scars never throbbed so hard than when she was discussing matters like this. *If only this were a real oyster shell,* she thought, *I could push Gabby out and slam the whole thing shut.* It seemed a more attractive alternative to the usual wanting to crawl into a hole to die.

"A pessary?" Gabby shook her hand. "No, I don't think that's right. Isn't that some kind of weird Australian bird?"

"You're thinking of a cassowary."

"Oh. Well, whatever it's called, he wouldn't let me have one. Said he didn't think it was moral for a girl in my situation, and I didn't want to press, for fear he'd go and blab the whole thing to Karp. But you have to have an examination, and he told me not to worry. That when the time came—when I got *married,* that is"—Gabby scoffed—"that it wouldn't hurt a bit." Her eyes glinted bitterly. "Remind me to thank that monster Tully Toynbee the next time I see him, will ya? Turns out he was good for something after all."

"What?" Margo asked mystified.

"All that dance rehearsal," Gabby said knowingly. "It makes things . . . you know, stretch down there."

"*Oh.* I see."

"Maybe you should have tried it," Gabby said cheerfully. "But I guess it's too late now."

"Too late?"

"Well, did you bleed an awful lot your first time with Dane? I mean, I'm *assuming* it was with Dane."

"Oh." Margo said again, paying very close attention to the complicated curlicues she was tracing on the bedspread with her finger. "I guess I . . . I don't remember."

251

"Don't remember?" Gabby cried. "How is that possible? The whole thing was pretty damn memorable, if you ask me. Unless you were really, really drunk. Or . . ." Suddenly, she clapped her hands over her mouth.

"Or what?"

"Oh my God. *Oh my God.* You haven't, have you?"

"What? What are you talking about?"

"You haven't done it yet." Gabby's eyes, always as wide as saucers, seemed to have grown to the size of dinner plates. "You and Dane haven't done it. You're still a virgin."

"No!" Margo exclaimed. "We have! Only . . . I mean . . . we just . . ."

Gabby leaned forward. "You just *what?*"

If it was possible to die of embarrassment, I'd be dead already, Margo reasoned, although she took significantly less comfort than one might have expected from this demonstrably true fact. "We *did*. At least, I think we did. Sort of. But it didn't . . . it didn't go very well."

That was all it took. If there was one thing Margo knew about Gabby Preston, it was that she took to the scent of trouble like a bloodhound on a trail. "What does that mean? Can't Dane . . ."

"No, no, Dane is just fine in that . . . in that department." Margo sighed. Did she really want to talk about this with Gabby? Did it matter? The door was open, and Gabby was going to charge through it whether she invited her in or not. "It's just . . . well, we tried one time, and it was just so hard, and it hurt so much . . . I guess I've just been too scared to do it again."

"*Margo*," Gabby said urgently, grabbing her arms. "You *have* to."

"I know." Margo looked back down at the bedspread, tracing her initials with her index finger. M.F.: Margaret Frobisher, her real name. She wiped them away as though the flat of her hand were a chalkboard eraser. "I know. But it's just . . . well, I didn't think it would be like that. That it would hurt that much. I mean, I don't know if it even really happened. If I'm still a virgin or not. Dane says . . ."

"What does Dane say?"

"Never mind." Margo colored. "It's just . . . I didn't think it was supposed to be like that, Gabby. What if there . . . what if there's something *wrong* with me?"

"You're going to go to Dr. Lipkin first thing in the morning," Gabby said firmly, "and you're going to have an examination. You're getting married, so it doesn't matter what he tells Karp. He'll take care of whatever it is. He can give you pills for the pain, muscle relaxants, whatever, so you won't feel a thing. Or sometimes . . ." She bit her lip. "Sometimes they can do sort of a little surgery, I guess. Right there, right in the office. There was this girl, Thelma, who had a tap act back when I was playing the Chicago Theater. She was awful young, maybe sixteen, seventeen, and she was going out with this wiseguy, one of those old bootlegger types. Well, it turned out she had kinda the same problem you have, I guess, and believe me, those Sicilian guys from the Outfit aren't inclined to be quite as understanding as someone like Dane Forrest. So she went to this doctor on the South Side, and he did a little bit of something in his office, I don't know what, and voila! The next time I saw her she was wearing a silver fox, and she said the whole thing took fifteen minutes and hurt about as much as a paper cut."

"Really? And what happened to her?"

"Oh, last I heard she wound up dead," Gabby said airily. "Two bullets through the head in a car trunk. But that's what happens when you get mixed up with guys like that; it's nothing you have to worry about, Margo. The point is, you have to get this taken care of, and quick. Otherwise, Dane is going to start looking for comfort elsewhere, if he hasn't already."

"Dane is just fine," Margo said hotly. "There's plenty of things you can do that aren't . . . that aren't *that*."

"But it all comes down to that, doesn't it?" Gabby asked. She sounded almost sad. "You've got to be realistic. You can barely expect a man like Dane to be faithful as it is. Don't look at me like that, you know it's true. What's he filming now, some Western?" Margo nodded. "Well, no matter how much he loves you—and I'm not saying he doesn't—every morning when he gets onto the set there's about a hundred gorgeous dames in saloon girl outfits who would give their eyeteeth to lure him behind a piece of scenery for a coupla sweaty minutes. And that's just the extras. When it comes to the leading ladies, that's a whole other ball of wax. You can't be in every picture with him. And the thing about pretending to be madly in love with someone five days a week, eight hours a day is that it can start to feel awfully close to the real deal."

And I know that better than anyone. Margo shivered, remembering her first screen test, when Dane's unexpected appearance had saved her from certain disaster as surely as if he'd ridden in on a white horse. The corny love scene they'd played had felt so real, the trite dialogue so imbued with genuine emotion, that it had cast a spell over her that lingered to this day. It was the moment Dane had gone from an untouchable idol with his picture hanging on her wall to a real living, breathing man she knew she had to have. *I can't lose him,* she thought. *Not now.* "So what do you think I should do?"

"I just *told* you," Gabby said. "Get it worked out." She shook her head from side to side, her dark ringlets bobbing prettily against her flushed cheeks. "I have to tell you, Margie, I'm still kind of in shock. I mean, everyone knows you'd been practically *living* together till the studio put the kibosh on it. I figured you must have been doing it all over the place."

"Gabby." There was something eating away at Margo, something she had to know. "If I ask you something, will you promise to tell me the absolute truth?"

"Sure. If I can."

I guess that has to be good enough. Margo steeled herself with a deep breath. "Was there anything to that gossip item about Dane and Amanda? Do you honestly think there's anything between them?"

Gabby leaned back against one of the shell-shaped pillows, looking thoughtful. "No," she said finally. "I don't think there is. They're old friends, I know that. And Amanda's never said anything to me, but I can't promise there isn't some history there. Two people who look like they do, how can there not be? But now? No. Besides, that girl is still so hung up on Harry Gordon it's almost funny. When she was staying with Viola and me, she used to lock herself in her bedroom every night and cry herself to sleep. I know she may look like bad news, but believe me, Amanda Farraday is a one-man woman." She chewed her lip. "I'd keep an eye out for Diana Chesterfield, though."

It was all Margo could do not to make her whole body recoil at the thought. "Why do you say that?"

"Oh, I don't think she's after him, exactly. In fact, there was always something a little fishy about that love affair, if you ask me. A little too perfect, you know what I mean?"

Oh boy, do I. "I guess so."

"But she did seem to make herself awfully comfortable at the bridal shop," Gabby continued. "It's like she's the first runner-up at the Miss America pageant. If for some reason you are unable to fulfill your duties . . ."

"No," Margo said. "Dane would never. Not after everything that's happened." *And not least,* she thought, *because Diana is his sister.*

"If you say so. Maybe you should talk to her, though."

"About what?"

"About your little problem." Gabby shrugged. "I mean, if nothing else *she* must know the way to keep Dane Forrest happy between the sheets. Plus, you'd be marking your turf. And maybe making an ally at the same time."

Talk about Dane that way with Diana. It was too, too terrible to think about. Margo suppressed a gag. She was desperate to change the subject. "Why do you care so much anyway?" she asked.

"Well, you know me, I love gossip," Gabby said. "And this is pretty damn good. Plus, we're friends, aren't we, and friends worry about each other."

"Even in Hollywood?"

"Who knows, maybe I'm getting soft in my old age." Gabby grinned. "But you know, I feel like I just want you to have what Eddie and I have. To be so in love with someone and be able to express it to each other like that, it's just . . ." Her eyes went dreamy. "All the pills, all the dope, that's nothing compared to this. I don't need any of it anymore if I've got Eddie. As long as I have him, I'll be all right. It's just the best feeling in the world."

Thankfully for Margo, Miss Perkins clattered back into the room before Gabby could go off on another unnervingly poetic reverie about the joys of lovemaking in the backseat of a Lincoln.

"A million apologies," the realtor said breathlessly, looking as though she were about to scatter the sheaf of paper affixed to her clipboard all over the floor. "I'm sorry to keep you waiting for so long. Unfortunately, the key to the dressing suite is nowhere to be found, and I haven't been able to reach the owner anywhere. I've already called the locksmith, though, and he should be here in a jiffy." She smoothed her hands over her smart green tweed suit. "While we wait, may I suggest another tour around the gardens? I'd love for you to take another look at the koi pond. And there is some statuary in the formal gardens that personally I'd have moved poolside, for a look of classical Roman decadence. . . ."

The realtor droned on, chattering about hydrangea bushes and artificial waterfalls, but Margo had stopped listening. She was filled with a sudden urge to do something, to *act. Everyone's done everything for me*, she thought. *Just like Dane said, it's like I'm a child. They tell me what to wear, where to live, whom to marry, what to say.* Walking out of her parents' house that night with Larry Julius was the last autonomous decision she had made.

Maybe that's what's been holding me back with Dane, Margo thought, looking around the gorgeous room at the oyster bed, the canopy of pearls. *It's not that there's anything wrong with me. It's that I can't be a woman until they stop treating me like a little girl.*

". . . and of course"—Miss Perkins was still talking—"the fact that the house is west facing means that you'll have a gorgeous view of the sunset during evening entertainment—"

Margo cut her off unceremoniously. "It doesn't matter. Call the locksmith and tell him he doesn't need to come."

"But the dressing suite—"

"Never mind about the dressing suite. I'm sure it's fine. I'll take the house."

Miss Perkins let out an audible gasp. "You . . . you will? But don't you . . . I mean, perhaps you'd better speak with Mr. Forrest. . . ."

"Mr. Forrest has perfect faith in me," Margo said smartly, thinking of the no-nonsense tone that had crept into her formidable mother's voice when she felt some tradesman or mechanic was trying to take advantage of her. "Besides, I'm buying this house myself. You can put all the paperwork in my name and send it to my bungalow in the morning. I'll be waiting."

She accepted the realtor's effusive thanks and excitement with gratification. It was time, Margo thought. Time to get out from under the thumb of the studio and have a house of her own, the way a woman, the way a *movie star*, should. Somebody had to make the decisions, and from now on it was going to be her. She'd make the house over in her image. Rip out that atrocious ballroom. Build a waterfall into the pool. Plant a privet hedge and flowering bushes all around until she felt as if she were living in a secret garden, like the book she'd loved as a child. She was going to have a home, and a life, of her own. She glanced back at the oyster bed.

And Dane is just going to have to learn to love it.

"Margie!" Gabby squealed as they made their way back outside. "This is so exciting! What a gorgeous house! We have to celebrate."

"Later." Margo glanced at her delicate diamond watch. It was almost five o'clock. "Right now, I've got to be at Schwab's."

"Oh, Margie, again?"

"Again," Margo said. "Every day until she comes."

"Who? Not Diana?"

"No." Margo felt filled with a new strength. *No more lies,* she thought. *From now on, I tell the truth to everyone about everything.* "My mother."

Helen Frobisher was an orderly woman.

Upon rising each morning, she washed her hands, then her face, in the blue willow pitcher-and-washbasin set that had stood on her dresser since her marriage, and on her mother's dresser before that. She combed and pinned her fading blond hair into a smooth and unvarying chignon with a marcasite comb as its only adornment, put on one of the fastidiously correct silk crepe dresses hanging in her wardrobe, daubed her wrists and temples with the lavender-scented eau de toilette the doctor had suggested could help alleviate her headaches, and put the stoppered bottle back in exactly the same position on her silver vanity tray.

In her drawing room, to which she retired at exactly

nine-fifteen a.m., after supervising Emmeline's clearing of the breakfast things and seeing her husband out the door to his club or his mistress's house or wherever it was he went when he pretended he was going to the office, she sorted through the household documents at a secretary with a neatly labeled row of cubbyholes: one for bills, one for invitations, one for personal letters. Everything had its place, from the comb in her hair to the feelings bundled neatly in her heart.

But the message Emmeline had relayed last week, along with her mistress's breakfast tray and a nervous curtsey, as though the old fool thought she was about to be fired on the spot—well, Helen Frobisher wasn't sure where she was supposed to put that.

She'd written it down. Written it down and then crumpled the piece of paper into a ball and stuffed it in the corner of the bottom drawer of the secretary. She retrieved it now and smoothed it out on the leather blotter, squinting at the spots where the decidedly *un*orderly creases had faded the pencil scratching.

Margaret. 5:00. Schwab's Sunset Boulevard. Please come.

All those years, all that sacrifice, and that was all the girl had left her. Taken everything Helen and Lowell Frobisher had offered her and thrown it back in their faces.

And now she's going to be a bride. Margaret was getting married. To some picture fellow. Some nameless slickster with no roots, no family, no identity apart from what the movie magazines made up for him. God knew where he came from, or who, or what. He'd have shellacked hair, a gleaming toothpaste smile, a light step on the dance floor—and absolutely no idea how to hold his knife or address a lady or what to properly call the lavatory. An upstart piece of trash, called a gentleman only by people fooled by the cut of his too-flashy suit.

Like mother, like daughter.

Maybe it was time to tell her the truth. If Margaret was really going to marry this fellow, if she was really going to fall forever out of the grasp of Pasadena and the Frobishers, she at least ought to know who she really was and where she really came from. Why their relationship had never been easy. Why Helen had been able to wave her out the door without the guilt or recrimination a normal mother would feel. A natural mother.

A real mother.

She ought to be told, Helen thought with a sigh. *And I guess I've got to tell her.* Schwab's was as good a place as any. It couldn't be tonight, obviously. The Frobishers had dinner with the Winthrops tonight. And dinner tomorrow with the Gambles and the McKendricks, senior and junior. Nothing was worth giving up a social occasion like that.

But the night after that. Or maybe the one after that. After all, Margaret had said she'd be there every night. There was plenty of time to tell her. So she'd know who she was and whom to trust and where she belonged.

So she wouldn't make the same mistakes the Moore sisters had.

TWENTY-ONE

"New York City!" The redcap's clear baritone rang through the car, loud enough to rouse any napping traveler. "All out for New York City, Grand Central! Welcome to the Big Apple, ladies and gents!"

New York City. At last.

Amanda gave her hat a final adjustment in the small round mirror affixed to the wall of the tiny sleeping compartment that had been her home for the past sixteen hours, since the Twentieth Century Limited had pulled away from LaSalle Street Station in Chicago. Three days on trains, watching more country than she'd ever seen in her life go past through the window, and finally, here she was.

She studied her exhausted-looking reflection, poking at her pallid cheeks, wondering if she could powder away the lilac shadows beneath her eyes. *The city that never sleeps,* she thought with a rueful grin. *Meanwhile, I look like I need to sleep for about five years.*

"Grand Central, miss." The redcap rattled the door with a knock that was polite but insistent. "Last stop."

Giving her hair a final pat, Amanda scooped up her leather traveling case and made for the exit. She stepped out onto the plush red carpet that ran the length of the sleek blue-gray train and onto the dim, smoke-filled platform. The sharp scent of diesel filled her nose as she pushed through the throngs of people waiting to embark for destinations north, skirting the uniformed porters struggling with piles of luggage, the little vignettes of joyous reunions and tearful farewells playing simultaneously all around her. *Like everyone is in their own little movie.*

When she emerged at last into Grand Central Terminal, Amanda gasped.

It looks like heaven. Like the beautiful watercolor of the gates of heaven in the big illustrated Bible her Sunday-school class back in Oklahoma had been allowed to take turns looking at as a reward for being quiet (and appropriately fearful) during the reverend's weekly sermon about fire and brimstone: the same radiant streams of golden light bouncing off arches of pale, pearly stone; the carved friezes of smiling cherubs and trumpeting angels; the celestial blue ceiling upon which heavenly bodies seemed to float.

The only thing different was the people. Streaming across the marble floor, never glancing left or right, purposeful as any crew she'd ever seen on a movie set. She stared at them in awe, eager to soak up every detail, like an anthropologist recording the rituals of an undiscovered tribe. The women's hair was sleeker, she noticed. Their coats were cut slimmer—the wasp waist was definitely back. The men all carried newspapers and wore snap-brim hats tilted low over their faces, as though to protect them from some imaginary torrent of rain. Did everyone in New York walk so fast? And how did they not bump into each other? It was like a dance, a vast number choreographed by some unseen, unknowable director. Like God.

Amanda giggled. *Funny how I'm getting religion all of a sudden.*

"Hey, watch it, will ya, toots?" The voice blared like the horn of car. Amanda scurried out of the way just in time to avoid being trampled by a mustachioed man with a bowler hat and a briefcase. Before she could apologize, he was already gone.

Wherever New Yorkers are going, Amanda thought, watching his figure recede among the teeming, speeding throng, *they all act like they're about an hour late.*

She finally made her way through the doors and out into the thrum of Forty-Second Street. In Hollywood, you always heard the East Coasters talk about how much they missed the Manhattan skyline, but from the sidewalk all Amanda could see was doors and windows and concrete and hardly a hint of sky.

And people. So many people, in every size and shape and color of the rainbow, united only by a mutual relentless hurry that seemed to preclude any eye contact or attempt at conversational engagement.

And yet, to her surprise, Amanda found she didn't mind. She didn't resent these swift-moving, smartly dressed people quite literally too busy to give her the time of day. Not at all. She wanted to *be* one of them.

She wandered over to a quieter block and stood on the corner, watching two or three people hail a taxicab before she mustered the confidence to flag one down and asked the driver if he might take her to a good hotel. He looked her up and down, sticking his head out the window like an eel peering out of its hole to check for predators, and suggested she turn around. Amanda did, and realized she had been standing all this time directly under the gilded marquee of the Waldorf Astoria.

A hotel. No wonder there are so many taxicabs.

Sheepishly, she turned to thank the driver, but he had already pulled away from the curb. She thought of a line from the script from the picture they were making at Metro, the one they'd sent to Gabby to read for before they gave it to Judy Garland, as everyone but Gabby had known they would.

"People come and go so quickly here," she said aloud.

Everything in the hushed lobby of the Waldorf Astoria, from the crystal chandeliers to the giant potted ferns to the exquisitely arranged groupings of antique gilt furniture, screamed money.

Or rather, it *didn't* scream; it whispered. This was not the flashy glamour of Hollywood, with its kidney-shaped swimming pools and plaster Corinthian columns as gaudy and hastily assembled as a set on a soundstage. This was *old* money, or at least as old as money got in the New World. The kind that was not earned but inherited, that by its very solidity had been burnished, not diminished, by the devastation of the Depression, that telegraphed a kind of aristocratic insouciance, a sort of "oh well, whatever happens, *we'll* never be poor." *Must be nice.*

Amanda approached the front desk, feeling shyer and less sure of herself than she had in years. *Like Norma Mae Gustafson, an Oklahoma rube in a tacky Woolworth's dress.* "Hello?"

The clerk, unexpectedly soigné in his dark green uniform, turned to examine her. "May I help you?"

"Yes. I'd like a room, please."

"Do you have a reservation?"

"No, I'm afraid not."

The clerk shook his head slightly, as though he couldn't believe anyone could be so colossally careless as to not keep a standing reservation at the Waldorf simply as a matter of course. "I'll have to see what we have available. Do you have a preference as to the kind of accommodation?"

The cheapest kind, thought Amanda, visualizing the rapidly thinning wad of bills tucked inside the lining of her black grosgrain handbag. She was trying to figure out the most discreet way of saying exactly that when she heard a voice call out to her.

"Red! Hey, Red, is that you?"

She was so surprised to see the boy bounding toward her, his porkpie hat pushed far back on his dark hair, his shirt open at the throat, that she didn't recognize him at first. Only when she noticed the battered trumpet case in his hand did she put two and two together.

"Eddie," she said, blinking stupidly. "It's Eddie Sharp, isn't it?"

"Sure is. And I know you too, Amanda Farraday. It's funny, huh? We've never been properly introduced—because believe me, sister, I'd remember—and we know each other anyway. Ain't it the darndest thing."

"That's show business I guess." Amanda fiddled nervously with the clasp of her handbag.

"Showbiz, yeah." Eddie looked at her appraisingly. "Now. Tell me the truth." He leaned in closer, as though he didn't want the desk clerk to hear. "What's a classy dame like you doing in a flophouse like this?"

Amanda laughed. "Fallen on hard times, I guess."

"Ain't it the truth. You oughta see my usual digs when I come here. They'd put, whaddya call it, Buckingham Palace to shame. But this joint?" Eddie cast a theatrically disgusted glare around the splendor that surrounded them. "Next stop, skid row."

"I guess your star must be falling."

"I guess so." Eddie lifted his cigarette to his lips—which, Amanda thought, were almost indecently full. A slow grin spread across his face as he exhaled. "So tell me seriously, what brings you to this neck of the woods. Business or pleasure?"

"Um . . ." *To be honest, I don't quite know myself.* "A little bit of both, I suppose."

"Good answer. I'm doing a little bit of both myself. My band and I are opening at the Palace in two weeks. But until then"—he smiled again—"it's all about pleasure. So let me know if I can give you a hand with that half of the equation."

I bet Gabby would love that. "I don't think so, Mr. Sharp."

Eddie whistled in dismay, although by his expression he seemed in no way deterred. "Wowee zowie, it just got cold in here. Look, sweetheart, I wasn't suggesting anything *untoward*. Just that this city can get real lonely real fast if you've got no one to see it with."

"Who says I don't?"

"Not me." Eddie held up one hand in a sort of truce. "I bet you've got truckloads of offers. But if you find yourself craving one of those fancy salads they got here and want someone to eat it with, you know where to find me. In the meantime"—he turned to the clerk—"you take good care of this young lady. Nothing but the best for her, and don't let her tell you different. This lady is a major Hollywood star."

Shamelessly flirty, Amanda thought as she watched him head to the door, *but I think he means well.* At least the hotel clerk was friendlier, now that Amanda had the official imprimatur of someone he recognized, although when the bellboy opened the door of the suite he insisted was the "only possible option" for a "special friend of Mr. Sharp," her heart sank. With its Aubusson carpets, gorgeous swag draperies, and magnificent green marble tub that was so deep you had to climb down three steps to get to the bottom, she didn't even want to *think* about what it must cost.

"Is everything all right?" the bellboy asked anxiously, mistaking Amanda's reticence for displeasure.

"Yes," Amanda muttered, struggling to keep down the remains of breakfast suddenly churning at the base of her throat. *Don't be sick,* she told herself sternly. *Not in front of him.*

"Good." The clerk gave a little sigh of relief. "And will your maid be arriving with your luggage?"

"No. No maid."

"I see." The clerk thought a moment. "If I may, we have an excellent personal maid service here at the Waldorf, with several ladies' maids trained in all the best houses of Europe. Might I take the liberty of selecting one of our more capable girls to attend you for the duration of our stay? It's a small additional daily charge, of course—"

"No," Amanda said too quickly. "No, that won't be necessary."

"Very well." Clearly, he was miffed. "I'll leave you, then. Please alert us if there's anything else you require."

Maybe it won't matter, Amanda thought as she grudgingly peeled off a few dollar bills for his tip. She'd find Harry soon, and when she told him, he'd take care of the bill anyway. *Or maybe I'll just have them charge everything to Eddie Sharp.* She giggled inwardly at the thought. *After all, he's the one who got me into this Popsicle stand in the first place.*

Left alone, Amanda stepped out of her dress, slip, and underwear and stood naked in front of the full-length mirror.

Thoughtfully, she peered at her reflection, running her hands over her pale body, trying to gauge its size. *Can you tell? Do I show?* Was her waist thicker? Had her hips spread? Her breasts seemed fuller, she noted with approval, feeling the unaccustomed weight of them against her palms. *Harry will like that.*

Smiling, Amanda cradled her still-satisfactorily flat stomach in her arms. "Hello in there," she cooed. "Hello. You can't hear me, but I know you're in there. And I'm out here, waiting for you."

Then she laughed at the ridiculousness of it all. *Look at me. Naked and talking to my stomach.* Hastily, she pulled her slip back over her head and went into the bedroom to unpack.

She'd found out for sure the first morning on the train. She'd slept in and gone to a late breakfast in the dining car, when she suddenly took a turn and collapsed into the aisle, upsetting a waiter with a huge serving platter of orange juice and scrambled eggs. "Fainted dead away," said the kindly porter who carried her off and summoned the train's doctor, an elderly gentleman with a faint Southern accent and a white handlebar mustache, who was sitting beside her when she came to fifteen minutes later, sticky with orange juice and studded with scraps of egg, on the cot of an unoccupied sleeping compartment.

His diagnosis hadn't come as a total surprise. *After all, I'm not an idiot.* She knew the signs. But she'd pushed it all to the back of her mind. Somehow, none of it seemed real until the nice country doctor took her hand in his and said, "Mrs. Gustafson"—she'd given him her real name, since they were traveling through Oklahoma at the time; the "Mrs.," bless his heart, he'd inferred all on his own—"Mrs. Gustafson, congratulations. You're going to have a baby."

A baby.

Everything she'd hoped for and everything she feared, all wrapped up in a single word. She was two months along. *Maybe there really is a God,* Amanda thought. Something, some force, had sent her to Harry just as she finally had a way to get him back once and for all—a bond between them that could never be broken. She'd always felt as if Harry were somehow inside her, in her blood, inhabiting her in a way she couldn't quite explain, and now he really was. It was like a miracle. *And not a moment too soon.*

Harry. Amanda hugged herself, tears springing to her eyes. She'd been crying an awful lot lately. On the journey, she'd found herself in floods at the littlest thing, whether sour or sweet: a woman in the club car who'd rudely snubbed her when Amanda had asked to borrow a pen; a child solemnly feeding a bit of stale cake to her much-loved doll. It was normal, the doctor said. Pregnant women felt things more. *So do women in love,* Amanda had wanted to respond.

What would Harry say when she told him? *It'll be quite a shock,* she reminded herself. Naturally, he'd be apprehensive at first. But then he'd remember all the talks they'd had, the kind that were all the more serious for their playfulness.

"We'll have two," he'd say, "a boy for you and a girl for me, just like the song says. With their father's brains and their mother's good looks."

"I like the way you look," Amanda would insist.

"Even now?" he'd ask, and pull face after face, crossing his eyes and puffing up his cheeks and forcing his overbite out over his chin until she about died laughing.

He'll remember that when I tell him. He'd remember the little black-haired boy or red-haired girl—or would the other way around be nicer? Amanda couldn't decide—they had both imagined more vividly than either could ever admit, and he'd take her in his arms and look down into her face with that burning gaze that was so warm, so deep, so full of love it almost hurt to look at it.

Amanda snapped open her traveling case. *It's all going to be wonderful.*

If she could just fit into any of her clothes.

TWENTY-TWO

The Martin Beck Theater was on Forty-Fifth Street.

"Easily walkable," said the concierge on duty, helpfully marking out the route on one of the miniaturized foldable maps the Waldorf Astoria handed out to guests. "Only eight blocks away."

What he had neglected to mention, however, was that while some blocks in New York City were so short you could see the next street from the corner, others seemed twice the length of a football field. Amanda had to walk three of the short ones and five of the long ones. By the time she arrived at her destination, her feet were blistered and aching, and she'd worn a small hole through the sole of her delicate kidskin pump. The New York girls who whizzed by her wore lower heels, she noticed, the kind of squat oxford lace-ups a glamorous Hollywood starlet wouldn't be caught dead in.

Well, this Hollywood starlet may have to reconsider. Amanda gazed up at the marquee.

THE GROUP THEATER PRESENTS: AN AMERICAN GIRL

She was dressed for battle, having managed to squeeze herself into a black linen suit with the aid of the torturous tight-lacing Mainbocher "cincher" her regular salesgirl at Bullock's had assured her—presciently, as it turned out—was "absolutely *essential*" for anyone who hoped to fit into the latest wasp-waisted fashions. The suit had a short-sleeved jacket, which in a sudden burst of inspiration she'd teamed with a pair of black kidskin evening gloves, carefully pushed down at the top. These left her arms totally covered from shoulder to fingertip except for a tantalizing three-inch swath of creamy flesh exactly where Harry would have to touch her if, as was his custom, he took her by the elbow for a private chat. Already, her bare skin prickled with anticipation at the thought of it.

Harry had never cared for her in hats, but without one her red hair seemed too conspicuous. The velvet Caroline Reboux beret Mildred had coveted seemed to do the trick. Tilted over one eye, Marlene Dietrich–style, it lent the outfit an appropriate bohemian touch.

Honestly, I couldn't have costumed myself better if I were Rex Mandalay himself. I hope he's being half as careful with Margo Sterling's bridal gown. She felt a sudden pang of guilt, thinking of Margo's certain panic when she realized that one of her bridesmaids had gone missing three days—or was it two?—before what the copy of *Picture Palace* Amanda had hastily picked up at the station in Moline was calling "Tinseltown's Royal Wedding," but she pushed the thought away. After all, Margo had only asked her to save face after the tabloids had made all those insinuations about Amanda's—wholly innocent—tête à tête with Dane. Once everything was worked out here, she'd send Margo a telegram to apologize.

And when Harry and I get married, I'll ask her to be a bridesmaid and she can stand me up.

Amanda had expected to have to sneak in the stage entrance, like one of those desperate starlet hopefuls who snuck into the offices of important producers disguised as prepubescent delivery boys or concealed inside enormous packing cases, usually wearing something enticing enough to be issued an invitation to stay—that is, if they didn't give the poor *schmuck* a heart attack when they popped out.

To her surprise, one of the front doors had been left ajar. She slipped under the beige brick Moorish arches that must have seemed the height of exotic chic to whatever gauche vaudeville impresario had built the place back in the twenties and proceeded into the slightly dingy lobby.

In the box office, a middle-aged woman sat playing a rapid hand of solitaire, a lit cigarette dangling from her lips. "You one of Stella's students?" she asked, barely looking up.

"What?"

"One of Stella's. Oh, dammit. Not a four of clubs." The woman groaned. "You can go on in. Just be quiet, will ya? They're all sitting in the back."

The theater was dark. Amanda slipped into a seat in the back row near a group of serious-looking young men and women furiously scribbling notes and all wearing what appeared to be matching pairs of tortoiseshell eyeglasses. On the stage, a young man in shirtsleeves sat at a card table set furnished with a few bare-bones props: drinking glasses, silverware, a couple of empty plates. A blond girl with short curly hair stood in front of him. She wore a plain skirt and sweater and a defiant expression as she spoke her lines toward the audience in a voice raw with emotion.

"And that day, I made a promise to myself that things were going to be different," the girl proclaimed. "That no one was ever going to make me feel like a nobody again. That someday, somehow, I was going to be *somebody*. No matter what it took. No matter what I had to do."

A faint sob crept into the actress's voice. The young people had stopped scribbling, seeming enraptured. Amanda looked around the theater, her eyes adjusting to the darkness. She spied a long table several rows down, near the front of the house, wedged into a small landing between the seats. Three men sat there. They had their backs to Amanda, but on the one on the left she could make out the shadowy outline of a very distinct head of unruly black hair. *Harry!*

"Look, I'm not a child," the actress was saying. "I know I can't snap my fingers and have every wish come true. But if I can't get what I want, at least I can be *wanted*. Isn't that the only real dream for a girl like me? For a girl like me, that's the only American dream."

She stared out into the audience for a moment, as though daring them to answer. Pens poised over their notepads, the bespectacled boys and girls seemed to hold their collective breath.

275

"Okay," came a voice from the table. "Very good. Let's hold there."

Somebody flicked a switch and the houselights came on. They were dim, but Amanda blinked anyway. The man who had spoken was scrambling over seats to the lip of the stage. With his messy dark hair and untidy clothes, he looked like a shorter, less handsome version of Harry. *He must be the director,* Amanda thought.

"Interesting work, Frances." He was close enough to the actors to whisper, but his voice boomed throughout the theater as though he were performing himself. *Perhaps he is,* Amanda thought. If the young acolytes around her had seemed transported during the actress's recitation, they now looked like they were about to take dictation from God himself. "*Very* interesting. How did it feel?"

The girl, Frances, scrubbed her hands roughly over her hair, seemingly heedless of her coiffure. Carefully adjusting the tilt of her hat, Amanda watched her with an odd mixture of disapproval and envy. *One more difference between Hollywood and the theater.* "I'm not sure," she said. "I suppose I feel . . . ambivalent."

"Good! Good!" the director bellowed. "Let's explore the ambivalence. And remember, ambivalence is not the same as apathy. It's merely an acknowledgment of conflict: the very essence, the absolute foundation of all dramatic art, of life itself. Without conflict, without that great chasm between what we want and what we have, without yearning, would we be human? I propose not."

Around Amanda, the pens were scratching away, sounding like an army of rats was scuttling between the walls. Her head was spinning. Never had she heard a director make a speech like this. In the pictures Amanda had worked on, she had rarely received direction with any more depth than "That's fine. Let's do it again with a little more leg."

But this guy . . . this guy sounded like a college professor, or a philosopher, or . . . *Harry,* she thought, looking at the head bent over the script on the table. He was writing something down. With the lights on, she could see the back of his neck just above his collar, that sweet patch of skin that had always felt so surprisingly soft against her lips.

"So, this ambivalence," the director continued, pressing his palms together thoughtfully, "this *conflict:* is it arising organically from the situation of the character? Or is some part of your preparation coming into contradiction with the demands of the text?"

"Um . . . I think it's a problem with the text, actually."

Amanda could see the glint of Harry's glasses as his head snapped up.

"Good," the director said. "What about the text?"

"Well, it's really just the last line of the last speech. 'For a girl like me, that's the only American dream.' It feels like it wants to be a declaration, a *manifesto,* if you will. A statement of intent. That's the beat I've prepared, but in the moment . . ." She twisted her hands. "In the moment, my impulse is to play it smaller. An intimate moment, a confession of sorts, between my scene partner and me."

"A confession. Interesting." The director stroked his chin. "Why don't we ask the playwright? Harry, what was your intention with that line?"

"My intention?" Harry's voice, softer than the others, seemed to pierce Amanda's heart like an arrow. "My intention was for it to be a joke."

"A joke?" Off to the side, a small, wiry man with a receding hairline and a fierce expression jumped to his feet. "A joke? But that requires an entirely different preparation. It changes the entire emotional honesty of the scene."

"It's not a laugh-out-loud, ha-ha joke, Lee," Harry said, with more than a hint of irritation. "I'm not talking about Laurel and Hardy. It's meant to be ironic, sardonic, whatever you want to call it. There's a disappointment there, a kind of fatalistic bitterness. But it's not entirely without humor."

"Bitterness." The man, Lee, rolled the word around in his mouth. He gave a terse nod. "We can find our way to bitterness."

"Good." The director was back in control. "Very good. Lee, you and Frances take a few minutes to find your way back into this, and then we'll start playing with the external physicality." He turned to address the group. "Everyone else, let's take five. Good work. Very brave, admirable work."

Lee vaulted up onto the stage, hustling Frances off into the wings. The group of note takers—the students of the mysterious Stella, Amanda had deduced—began filing into the lobby in pairs, pulling out cigarettes and lighters, talking in hushed, serious tones. Harry stood near the table, huddled with the director, jabbing his finger at something in the script.

I have to talk to him, Amanda thought, but she was nervous to interrupt. She dragged her sore feet along the carpet, waiting for the men to finish. She was halfway down the aisle before she mustered the courage to call out his name.

"Harry."

"A-Amanda." His face went pale with shock. "You . . . you . . . What the . . . what the hell are you doing here?"

Harry's fingers felt rough against her carefully bared sliver of skin as he grabbed her arm and steered her toward the side aisle and out of sight. It wasn't quite the welcome she had hoped for, but Amanda was determined to make the best of it. *He's surprised,* she reminded herself. *You knew he would be.*

She strove to make her voice as light as possible. "Haven't you heard? I'm one of Stella's students."

"Stella . . . you. You're studying with Stella Adler?"

"Well, that was the plan. Although, as it turns out, she says she has nothing to teach me. Apparently, I'm a genius. She's actually asked *me* to teach *her*, how do you like them apples?"

Harry's puzzled face relaxed into something that was not quite a smile. "You're joking."

"Of course I'm joking. I thought Stella Adler was out in Hollywood, anyway. Wasn't she making pictures for Paramount?"

"*Was* being the operative word. Now she's come crawling back to Broadway and is setting herself up as a teacher. She's been to Paris and studied with Stanislavski himself, and has been going around saying she alone knows his techniques as they were *meant* to be taught." His eyes wandered to the stage, where Lee, the man with the receding hairline, was saying something to Frances with a look of utmost concentration. "Naturally, it's been causing some tension with Lee."

"Naturally," Amanda said. She'd read an article once in one of the newspapers Harry used to have sent specially from New York about Lee Strasberg and the new acting technique he was inventing, all based on dredging up the most horrible things that had ever happened to you and reliving the experience

279

onstage. He called it "the Method." The idea seemed equal parts fascinating and terrifying to Amanda. On the one hand, it was comforting, even magical, to think that the awful memories that haunted you at night could somehow be repurposed into something beautiful. On the other, if she had to think about them more than she already did, Amanda was sure she would go raving mad. "Seriously, maybe I *should* see if she'd take me on. Apparently, I could use the lessons." She swallowed hard. "Olympus released me from my contract."

Harry looked away. "Yes, I heard about that. I'm so sorry."

"Oh, it doesn't matter. I mean, it has been a bit difficult, but"—Amanda forced the note of gaiety back into her voice—"it's certainly freed up quite a lot of time. So I thought I'd treat myself to a little trip. I've never been here before, you know. I thought I'd see the sights, do some shopping, maybe take in a show or two. And then when I happened by and saw the title on the marquee outside and the door open, well, naturally my curiosity was piqued. Can you blame me?"

If Harry doubted the veracity of this flippant little monologue, he was too polite to say so. "I suppose not."

"Obviously, I didn't realize you'd be in rehearsal or I'd never have dreamed of interrupting like this," Amanda said. "But I thought as long as I was here, it would be terribly rude not to say hello."

Harry sighed. "Where are you staying?"

Victory was in sight! "The Waldorf Astoria."

"The Waldorf." He sighed again. "Of course you are. Is there anyone with you?"

"Not a soul," Amanda declared. If he could ignore her obvious fib about just happening to find herself outside his theater in the middle of a rehearsal, she could ignore his insinuation. "I'm all by my lonesome, I'm afraid."

"Well, I suppose we should talk."

"Yes." Amanda looked up at him, her eyes full of meaning. "I'd love that."

"How about tonight? We can go have a drink at Twenty-One. Do you know it?"

"Only from the radio. It's where Winchell always seems to be, isn't it?"

"That's right. It's on Fifty-Second between Fifth and Sixth. You can't miss it, it's got all those lawn jockeys out front. Say eight o'clock?"

"Eight's fine."

"I'll be at the bar. I've got to go, we're about to start again." Awkwardly, he planted a quick kiss on her cheek. "I'll see you tonight."

Amanda spent the rest of the day in a cloud of preparations. First, a trip behind the legendary red door of Elizabeth Arden on Fifth Avenue, where solemn cosmeticians in awfully scientific-looking white smocks smoothed creams over her skin, set her hair in soft waves, and lacquered her nails in the latest shade of Jungle Red.

Clothes were next. She'd packed so quickly she didn't have anything that Harry hadn't seen her in before, and the Mainbocher waist cincher was only going to work for so long. *Not to mention it's pretty hard to take off,* she thought, with a wicked flicker of hope.

At the famous Hattie Carnegie boutique on Forty-Ninth Street, she selected day dresses, blouses, and suits, and, because she couldn't help herself, a red crocodile evening bag with a gold knot clasp, a pair of black-and-silver evening sandals, and some of the adorable little saucer hats with the built-in snood that had been the couturier's trademark back in her salad days as a Lower East Side milliner, in unexpected color combinations that would have made the old Amanda—the *sad* Amanda—blanch: violet and mustard, scarlet and shocking pink, Kelly green and robin's-egg blue.

Sure, it meant dropping a pile of money, but when she casually mentioned she'd like it all delivered to one of the penthouse suites at the Waldorf, the salesgirl was more than happy to let her have it all on credit. Besides, Amanda reasoned, it wasn't like she didn't *need* these things. In another month or so, she wouldn't be able to squeeze into anything she owned. Like most well-made clothes, Hattie Carnegie's creations had generous seams that could be let out as needed—hell, with a good seamstress, Amanda could make this new little wardrobe last months. *In the long run, I'll actually be saving money.*

And besides, when everything was all settled, Harry would want to take her to meet his mother. Maybe even in the next couple of days. She had to look respectable.

All settled. With that promising phrase in her heart, Amanda quickly added to the rapidly growing pile an ivory silk suit with a draped-front jacket and a cunning little matching hat with a blusher veil that looked as though it were made out of tiny flowers. *You never know. Better safe than sorry.*

For tonight, though, she needed something really special. After all, it could very well be a night she remembered for the rest of her life, a story she'd tell their daughter—it was going to be a girl, Amanda was sure of it—one day: how Mother came to New York to find Daddy, how he was suddenly so overcome with love he proposed right then and there. She'd leave out the part about the rather . . . *premature* conception, let alone how she'd gotten the money to make the trip; no need to confuse a nice, well-cared-for little girl like the one Amanda was going to have with a sordid detail like that.

To tell the story properly, she'd have to describe what she'd been wearing, so it had better be something worth the effort.

The salesgirl brought her an evening gown of ocean-green silk overlaid with black tulle. Artfully ruched, the tulle shrank her thickening waist and hips down to nothing. Above the silk, it looked like a shadow rising from the sea. The neckline was square, with delicately ruffled flutter sleeves of the same black tulle.

"You look stunning," the salesgirl said. "Absolutely stunning."

Amanda frowned. "Do you have a seamstress here?"

"Yes, miss, of course."

"Get her to take off one of the sleeves."

The salesgirl widened her eyes. "One sleeve? But that will throw off the symmetry. . . ."

"Yes, that's what I want. It looks like it's just set in. She can easily open the seam and close it back up again."

"But . . ." The salesgirl looked helplessly from Amanda to the vast pile of finery on the counter and back to Amanda again. "I can't just let you do that. Not unless you're buying the dress."

"Don't worry, I'm buying the dress. I just want to see what it looks like. If I hate it, the seamstress can put it back in."

The effect was everything she'd hoped for. The single ex-posed creamy shoulder set off her waist even more and made the graceful line of her neck seem to go on forever. She looked like some kind of seductively regal Greek goddess, invitingly sensual, half in and half out of her gown.

Amanda gave a little groan of pleasure. As earlier that day, with the little sliver between sleeve and glove, she felt a delicious tingle on her bare skin, as though it was already anticipating Harry's touch. "It's perfect."

The salesgirl agreed but insisted on fetching Hattie Carnegie herself from her atelier upstairs to give the final sign-off.

The famed milliner-turned-couturier was a tiny woman dressed in black, her hair parted majestically in the center like a wall painting of a Roman matron. An enamel cuff with a bejeweled Maltese cross adorned each wrist. She examined every inch of Amanda, poking at the bodice here, adjusting the line of the remaining sleeve there. In the crook of her arm, she cradled a fluffy black toy poodle with a gaze that seemed every bit as critical as that of his mistress.

Finally, Hattie Carnegie spoke. "You are a fashion designer?"

"N-no," Amanda stammered. "I just . . . like clothes, that's all."

"Well," said the couturier with a smart snap of the head. "If you decide you want to be, you know where to find me."

And she disappeared back up the stairs without another word.

After a day of such glamorous preparations, Amanda couldn't help but be a little disappointed by the ambience at 21. The exterior had been so promising, all wrought-iron balconies and colorful lawn jockeys standing in a row, like a sort of Manhattan version of an antebellum Charleston town house. But the inside bar area to which the maître d' guided her looked

284

like any other saloon where a nightclub act or an insomniac writer might grab a burger and a beer in the wee hours after a night's work, all scarred wood paneling and red-checkered tablecloths, like a cheap Italian restaurant, with an enormous fire roaring in a glazed brick fireplace off to the side. An assortment of odd items hung precariously from the ceiling, which was low enough to make you feel that at any moment you might get knocked in the head with a wooden ice skate or a dented old horn.

There wasn't a single man in a dinner jacket, and most of the women were no better dressed than an executive secretary on the Olympus lot. If any of them were famous, they were only New York famous—journalists, press agents, Broadway lyricists. Nobody Amanda recognized. In Hollywood, most everyone you saw out on a given night might be a nobody, but they were gorgeous nobodies, nobodies who looked like somebodies. At 21, the somebodies looked like nobodies. She didn't see a single face that had a prayer of one day gracing the cover of *Photoplay* or *Picture Palace*; in fact, Amanda noticed quite a few that, as Gabby Preston liked to say, "only a mother could love." For a girl accustomed to the glittering crowds and meticulously art-directed interiors of the Trocadero or the Cocoanut Grove, it was a little bit of a letdown.

Except for Harry Gordon.

There he was, in oft-repaired Harris Tweed. An already-emptied rocks glass stood on the tablecloth in front of him. *That's odd,* Amanda thought. In Hollywood, Harry almost never drank. Alcohol gave him a rash.

He half rose in his chair to greet her as she approached. "Amanda. That's . . . that's quite a dress you almost have on."

"Funny you say that," she cooed, presenting her cheek to be kissed. "Because frankly, looking around, I feel a little bit *overdressed*."

"Yeah, now that you mention it." Harry shrugged, looking around the room. "The real glamour-pusses hang out at the Stork Club, I guess. But you look beautiful. You always look beautiful."

"Oh, Harry, thank you." Her eyes shone.

"What do you want to drink? I'm having Scotch. I can have them bring a bottle. Unless you'd prefer a martini or something like that?"

"Oh, I'll just have a ginger ale," Amanda said.

"A ginger ale?" Harry blinked. "Don't you want anything in it?"

"No, just plain is fine."

"Are you sure I can't tempt you with something stronger?"

"Maybe I'll have something later." *A celebratory sip of champagne, maybe. But would that hurt the baby?*

Harry motioned to the waiter and ordered with an assurance he had never displayed in Hollywood. *It's like he feels at home here*, thought Amanda, with a mixture of pride and envy. *Like this is where he belongs.*

The drinks came quickly. Harry took a big gulp of his right away. Amanda sipped her ginger ale through a tiny straw, hoping it would help settle the butterflies in her stomach.

"I'm sorry if I was rude this morning," Harry said. "I think I was in shock."

Amanda smiled. "I figured you'd be surprised to see me."

"Surprised? You almost gave me a heart attack, just appearing like that in the aisle. I almost thought you were a ghost.

Broadway theaters are all haunted, you know." Harry took another gulp. "To be perfectly honest, I wouldn't have been thrilled to see anyone. Rehearsals aren't supposed to be open to whoever wanders in off the street."

"There were all those people there in the back."

"Stella's students. That's different. You could have been anyone. I mean, you're not, but you know . . . a critic, a reporter, anyone with some kind of agenda. . . ." Harry shook his head. "It's different out here. *The New Yorker, Vanity Fair* . . . the reporters here are real writers. They don't just type up whatever press release or glowing notice Larry Julius and his heavies hand them, under pain of death. They know what they're doing. And they can be vicious." He took another drink of Scotch.

Amanda gently laid her hand on his sleeve. "Harry, it's all going to be fine. You told me yourself the screenplay was the best thing you'd ever written. Why should the play be any different?"

"You don't understand. Whether the play is any good or not is beside the point. They have it in for me no matter what. Think about it: local boy makes it big in Hollywood, comes back to Broadway, flops. I'd be the laughingstock of business. How could they resist?"

"Stella Adler went to Hollywood," Amanda countered, "and she seems well respected."

"Stella Adler went to Hollywood and made one picture that nobody saw," Harry corrected. "Now that she's back, she can spin it like she was too good for the Philistines out there, and everybody nods and murmurs in agreement. Like butter wouldn't melt in her mouth. Like she was too good to succeed. They can forgive anything but success." He drank off the rest of

287

his Scotch and gazed at her with eyes that were just beginning to haze. "You know, I'm actually glad to see you."

"Well. Thanks a lot."

"No, you know. I mean, it's nice to see you. It's always nice to see you. But . . ." Harry looked down at his empty glass. "There's something I've been meaning to talk to you about. Something I need to tell you."

"Oh, darling," Amanda breathed, looking up through her lowered lashes. "There's something I need to tell you too. . . ."

"Harry Gordon, you sonofabitch!"

The man who blustered over to their table wore a dark gray three-piece suit. His fedora was tipped back on his head to reveal a face that would have been handsome if it weren't quite so shrewd. "You penniless playwrights are all the same," he crowed. "One day you're picking butts out of the ashtray, always hard up for a ten-spot. Then you jaunt over to the coast, come back with some dough in your pocket, and boom! You're sitting pretty with the prettiest girl in town. Honestly, I oughta come to you for tips."

"Hello, Walter," Harry said glumly. "I thought they banned you."

"Old news, my friend. And as they say in my business, no news may be good news, but old news is no news. Now, are you going to introduce me to this ravishing creature or am I going to have to be a heel and do it myself?"

"Amanda Farraday, this is Walter Winchell. Walter Winchell, Amanda Farraday."

"You're Walter Winchell?" Amanda couldn't help but let out a squeal. "Oh my goodness! I'm such a big fan of yours. I listen to you on the radio practically every day."

"Those words out of a mouth like that," Walter Winchell replied, grinning. "That's what a man works a lifetime to hear. But of course, I know all about you, Miss Farraday, from the picture magazines, or whatever you call those rags out on the Left Coast. Don't tell me I'm getting the firsthand scoop on the tender reconciliation?"

"All right, Walter, that's enough," Harry snapped. "Scram, will ya?"

"As a matter of fact, I don't mind if I do. I've got more congenial company waiting for me in the private dining room in the Vault tonight. Not quite in Miss Farraday's league"—his eyes lingered meaningfully over the neckline of Amanda's dress—"but she'll have to do. See you two lovebirds around."

"What was that all about?" Amanda asked when Winchell was out of earshot. "If you're worried about the press, Walter Winchell is the most powerful flack in the country. Maybe the world. It can't pay to be so rude to him."

"Ah, he's used to it," Harry said, waving her concerns away. "Besides, I didn't like the way he was looking at you."

Flushed with pleasure, Amanda smiled. *He cares how men look at me. He still cares.* "What was it you wanted to talk to me about?"

Harry sighed. "I'm not sure how to tell you."

"Just spit it out. It's easier that way."

"All right. All right. Here goes." Harry took another long drink of Scotch, gathering his courage. "Amanda . . . the whole thing about Olympus dropping your contract . . . it's all my fault. It's because of me. They were only doing what I asked them to."

Amanda felt like she'd just been shot through the heart. "You . . . you told them to fire me?"

"No! At least, not in so many words." Harry couldn't meet her eye. "It was . . . after that night we . . . spent together, after the Oscars . . . I just, I knew I couldn't control myself around you. I'd been trying so hard to avoid you. I thought if I didn't see you, I would get over you. That I would get you out of my system. But when I saw you at the Brown Derby that afternoon, and then at the Governor's Ball, I knew I never would. You're eating me from the inside out, Amanda. It's like a cancer; the only treatment is to just cut it out."

Amanda flinched, but Harry, looking at a spot somewhere over her shoulder, seemed not to notice. "So I called them that morning after we . . . well . . . and I begged them to help me. To fix it so I wouldn't have to see you anymore, wouldn't bump into you around the lot, or hear your name mentioned in meetings. And then, just to make sure I didn't see you around town, I came to New York. But I didn't know how they were going to do it. I thought . . ." He fiddled nervously with his glass. "I guess I don't know what I thought. I'm sorry. I know it must be difficult."

Difficult? Amanda didn't know if she wanted to scream, laugh, or cry. "Why stop at having them drop my contract?" she asked coldly. "Why not just have me killed?"

"Amanda, please . . ."

"Don't you 'Amanda, please' me!" She tried to keep her voice down. *God knows I'm conspicuous enough as it is.* "What I don't understand, Harry, is why you *have* to get over me. You know how I feel about you. You know how hard this has been for me. If it's been like that for you, then I don't understand what the problem is. I need you, Harry. We need each other. Why isn't that enough?" She was almost gasping now, choking with

290

the effort of trying to hold back her tears. "Why can't we be together?"

"Because of what you used to do," Harry said quietly. "Because of what you used to be."

"You mean . . ."

"You know exactly what I mean. What you did at Olive Moore's."

Of course. Amanda looked down at her hands. They seemed to dissolve before her eyes. *Of course.*

"I'm sorry," Harry continued. "I wish it could be different. I really do. But ever since Gabby told me that night at the party at Leo Karp's—"

If Amanda had already suffered one gunshot to the heart, this next shot went straight through her stomach. *"Gabby?"*

"Yes, Gabby Preston," Harry continued calmly, as if the world hadn't just caved in on itself. "I didn't believe her at first. I figured she was just angry about losing the part in the *An American Girl* picture and was making things up to hurt you. But then that sleazeball Hunter Payne confirmed it and, well . . ." Harry shook his head. "It was like the floor fell out from under me."

Tell me about it, Amanda thought.

"I loved you, Amanda," Harry continued. "I really did. I suppose in a way, I always will. But I can't deal with this. Believe me, I've tried. I've asked myself, what could make it better? What could wipe the past away? And it's no good. No good at all. I know myself. I know what I'm like. I'm a modern guy. I don't expect some unspoiled virgin. But this?" He shook his head. "I'd never be able to walk into a room with you without looking at every man there and wondering was it him? Or him?

291

Or him? Which one of you once ordered up my wife like a plate of eggs from room service in a hotel? Or was it all of you? I'd start to hate you, Amanda. And you'd start to hate me. And then it would be the end of the road for us. Better not to go any farther."

Wife, Amanda thought. He said *wife*. But the word bore little hope now. She felt like a marooned islander watching the ship that was supposed to save her disappearing over the horizon. "So you don't mind me doing it. Only that I got paid."

"Amanda." Harry looked at her reproachfully. "That seems a little unfair. Put yourself in my shoes."

Unfair? Amanda wanted to scream. *Why don't you put yourself in my shoes?* Did Harry have any idea—any goddamn idea—of what a girl could go through in this world? What could lead her to do what Amanda had done? The hunger, the fear, the cold nights sleeping on the street lying still like a possum, hoping that any predator that came along would think you were already dead? How relieved you were to be warm and fed and clothed and relatively safe, and to find out all you had to do to stay that way was the same thing men made you do anyway?

She was about to tell him that, and more, when the crowd parted and for the first time, she saw exactly what it was that kept making Harry's eye wander.

Sitting at the bar in a tight cocktail dress. With a cigarette in a long gold holder and blond hair set in curls so tight they looked like a devil's horns. It was Frances, that actress from the play. The actress who was playing the role Harry had written for Amanda. *The actress playing me.*

And suddenly, Amanda understood. She understood *everything.*

Pain coursed through her body, pain like nothing she had ever known. She felt as if she were splitting in two. She staggered to her feet.

"Are you all right?" Harry asked.

She didn't answer. Instead, she reached into her evening bag and pulled out the packet of letters. All the letters she had written him and never sent, tied with a pink ribbon torn from the dress he'd bought her. The letters of her life, of his life, or their life together. She held them up, taking a long last look.

Then she threw them into the fire.

"Amanda! What are you doing? Wait!"

"No!" she cried, pushing him away. "No. Leave me alone."

She pushed through the crowd, pushed past the maître d'. On the sidewalk, she doubled over in agony, letting out a small shriek. It was as if she were being ripped open from the inside, as if whatever was inside her were trying to gnaw its way out. It didn't matter now. She just had to get somewhere she could be safe, somewhere it would all be over.

So she ran. Blinded by pain, tripping over her hem, her heels; heedless of the taxicabs slowing at the curb at the sight of the half-crumpled girl in the evening gown clawing at her stomach and running as though every demon in hell were after her. When at last she reached her hotel room, she hurled herself into the bathroom and ripped down her underwear, bracing herself for the torrent of blood she was sure was surging out of her.

Nothing. Not a drop.

She collapsed to the floor like a rag doll, but the moment of relief soon gave way to vast, bottomless panic. So she still had the baby. What the hell was she supposed to do with it? What kind of life could she give it? Harry was gone. Forever. That had been made horribly clear. He didn't love her anymore, would never accept her for who she was—even worse, he was the architect of her destruction. *To fix it so I wouldn't have to see you anymore.* Amanda clapped her hand over her mouth to muffle her sob.

And Gabby. That betrayal hurt as badly as if not worse than Harry's. Amanda had thought Gabby Preston was her friend, someone she could rely on if things went bad. Gabby had welcomed her into her home, held her, patted her back while she cried, listened patiently to every raw detail of her heartbreak.

And Gabby knew all along. She knew all the time it was all her fault, and she never told me.

It was too much to bear.

Olive would take her in, sure. Amanda might even squeeze some more money out of her. But blackmail wouldn't work forever. Frankly, she'd been lucky to get away with what she had, before Olive realized Amanda couldn't very well compromise Diana without ruining herself. Besides, pretty soon, Diana's career would recover so much as to make her untouchable. And then Olive's hospitality would come with a price. Olive might pay her debts, but she'd see that Amanda paid her back, with considerable interest. "You can work it off," Olive would say, and Amanda would have no choice but to start back at the bottom of the ladder, seeing the men none of the other girls would. Men with cold voices and frightening desires who thought a fifty-dollar powder room tip didn't have nearly as favorable an effect on a girl as an unyielding pair of fists.

And when enough months had passed that Amanda's condition became apparent, the doctor would be summoned. Some bloodstained sheets, a few shed tears, and Amanda's "complication," as Olive liked to call it, would be decidedly less complex. She could be back to work in five days; hell, Lucy had been back on the job in three. And the entire cost of the operation, including pain medication and ruined linen, could easily be added to Amanda's tab.

I could say no, Amanda thought. *I could tell her I won't go through with it.*

And she'd be back out on the street before she even finished talking. Back to the fear, the hunger, and loneliness. The terrible loneliness that penetrated her more deeply than any cold night's wind could. The knowledge that nobody wanted her, nobody loved her, nobody cared if she was alive or dead.

"I'm alone," Amanda said to no one. "I'm all alone."

The marble tiles of the bathroom floor were cold against her bare shoulder. Shivering, she heaved herself up off the floor and crossed to the big picture window overlooking the street. *When God closes a door, somewhere he opens a window.* That was something she'd heard Margo say, although she dimly remembered hearing it before in some whitewashed clapboard prairie church a million lifetimes ago. Could this be the window he meant? *Norma Mae Gustafson.* Born in a hayloft in Arrowhead Falls, died on the pavement of Park Avenue beneath the open window of the penthouse suite in the Waldorf Astoria. In its own way, it was quite an ascent.

And quite a fall.

As mechanically as though she'd been hypnotized, Amanda undid the latch and pushed open the window. Could she really do it? The night breeze felt cool and inviting against her flushed face. The streetlamps made the pavement shimmer, like moonlight on a mountain lake. *It would be just like diving into a clear pool*, Amanda thought. One little jump and it would all disappear. The stacks of unpaid bills, the creditors and the threats. The nightmares of the heavy thud of drunken footfalls on the ladder to her hayloft. The dreams of being in Harry's arms, and the fresh, searing pain when she woke up to find he wasn't there.

Amanda looked around the sumptuous room, at the canopied bed she would never sleep in, at the glossy boxes of dresses she would never wear. She placed her hands on her stomach. "I'm sorry," she whispered to the child she would never meet, who would never be born. "It's better this way."

Slowly, she slid her leg over the windowsill.

And then there was a knock at the door.

Her first impulse was to laugh at the absurdity of it. To have a visitor at a time like this! But the knocking grew louder and more persistent, and for reasons Amanda would never quite be able to explain to herself, she found it impossible to ignore. *Maybe God doesn't open a window. Maybe when he closes a door, he just needs you to open it again.*

"Red!" Eddie Sharp's tuxedo was just disheveled enough to hint that he'd seen some real mischief that night and was looking to find some more. "They told me downstairs you were in. Thought I'd pop up and see if you were in the mood for a quick nightcap. . . ." The grin faded from his face as he got a glimpse of hers. "Holy hell, honey, what's the matter? You look like you've just lost your best pal."

"Eddie." Amanda looked up at him through lashes thick with tears. His eyes were dark and trusting. *Like Harry's used to be.* "Can I ask you a question?"

"Anything, Red. Anything."

"Say you loved a girl. Really loved her with your heart and soul. And then you found out she had . . . a past. There had been other men in her life. Quite a few men."

"If I really loved her with my heart and soul, it wouldn't matter the least little bit."

"Say it was worse than that." Amanda dropped her eyes to the floor. "Say . . . say she was a . . . a good-time girl. Then what?"

Eddie's voice dropped low, as quiet and final as the grave. "Well, then I guess she'd know how to show me a good time."

Letting out a cry, Amanda threw herself into Eddie's arms. She felt his astonishment, a tiny moment of hesitation, and then they closed around her, blocking out everything else. The danger had passed. Her mouth was on his, devouring it hungrily, and she took sustenance from a warmth, an ardor that quickly rose to meet her own. *Safe*, her heart cried out to itself over and over again. *This will keep me safe.*

In that moment, it wasn't Eddie Sharp she was kissing. It was life itself.

TWENTY-THREE

For once, Hollywood was in total agreement: it was the wedding of the year. Maybe even the century.

That is, they agreed as soon as they recovered their powers of speech. Then everyone in the movie colony was buzzing with all the romantic details, the sheer juiciness of which seemed to elevate the newlyweds to a level that neither had ever achieved on their own. About how it was love at first sight, eyes meeting across a crowded room—in this case, the crowded room of the Waldorf Astoria hotel, although the groom claimed he'd known she was the girl for him the moment she had briefly appeared in the doorway of the greenroom as he prepared to go onstage at this year's Governor's Ball. About how their mutual passion had been so strong that he'd paid a delighted cabbie five hundred dollars to drive them to Atlantic City in the middle of the night, where they could get married at one of those twenty-four-hour chapels without a blood test and with two down-on-their-luck poker players as witnesses. About how the bride arrived in a jaw-dropping black tulle evening gown with an unusually daring neckline that *Photoplay* claimed was "the thing that hooked her man," although she changed for the ceremony into a demure suit of ruched ivory silk with a matching veiled hat. Both ensembles were rumored to be Hattie Carnegie, although when reached for comment, the couturier would only say: "Miss Farraday makes her clothes her own." The House of Mainbocher, long associated with the famously chic starlet, offered no official statement from Paris, but as a representative in their Bullock's Wilshire boutique told *Reelplay*, "Mrs. Sharp is a cherished client and we look forward to providing her with many exquisite pieces for her new married life."

"I've never been so happy," said the radiant bride. "Eddie is everything I've dreamed of in a husband, and I'm determined to make him the perfect wife."

The dazed and grinning groom said simply, "I feel like the luckiest guy on earth."

At Metro, Paramount, and Warner Brothers, Katharine Hepburn, Claudette Colbert, and Bette Davis were all lobbying to star in pictures based on the Farraday/Sharp nuptials—the public frenzy over the elopement would surely translate into big box office, which all three stars could use.

Larry Julius was said to be fuming at having somehow been ignored despite his near-sacred jurisdiction over such matters, but ever sensitive to public opinion, he and his staff composed a statement for Olympus chief Leo Karp that was so brimming with "love conquers all" beneficence and fatherly pride in his wayward charges that it could have come from the desk of Walt

Disney himself. Every other flack and studio chief in town, however, was in raptures that the Omniscient One had finally been beaten—and by a girl he'd fired. Surely this was a sign that the tide was turning. Old Man Karp was slipping.

Margo Sterling, whose Wedding of the Year had just had the rug yanked cruelly out from under it—by one of her own bridesmaids, no less!—was diplomatic, but everyone knew the studio was going to make her postpone until she could win back the attention of the public. If Diana Chesterfield didn't win back the groom first.

The only comment from Harry Gordon, the bride's former flame, in whose company she'd been seen the night of her marriage by no less a reliable source than the legendary Walter Winchell, was a retort the editor of *Picture Palace* deemed unprintable in a family magazine.

From Gabby Preston, who had been seen keeping company with the groom during the past few weeks, there was no statement, printable or no, on the record or off. This was because just before the story broke to the press, a team of Larry Julius's goons arrived at the house on Fountain Avenue and, over Viola Preston's protests, cut the line to the phone.

It was just as well, really, Gabby thought as she snorted up another one of her crushed green pills from the dashboard of her mother's car.

After all, if they called now, what was Viola going to say? That the day it was announced that her underage daughter's bad-boy boyfriend had eloped with another woman, Gabby had stolen the Cadillac and driven off to parts unknown without so much as a word of explanation—or a license? The gossip rags would have a field day with that one.

300

But it's not like I had any choice, Gabby thought, swerving abruptly into the next lane. Angry honks went up from the car she'd just cut off, but she sped on heedlessly, barely noticing. She could run every automobile in Los Angeles off the road right now, and she wouldn't care. Gabby was a woman on a mission. The second she'd seen that blurry photograph of the man she thought she loved tenderly lifting the bridal veil of the girl she thought was her best friend, Gabby knew there was only one person she could talk to, only one person who would understand, who would be able to explain just what the hell was going on. *Only one person who might actually be my friend.*

She knew the only place to find him, too.

And there was no way in hell any studio chauffeur was going to take her there.

The famously rollicking sidewalk outside the Dunbar Hotel was almost eerily deserted by day. Gabby heard an ugly metallic crunch as she pulled the Cadillac up against the curb, but she didn't jump out to survey the damage. *There'll be plenty of time for that later.* Instead, she picked up the last bit of powder from the polished walnut dashboard with a moistened fingertip and rubbed it over her gums. *No sense in it going to waste.* But that made her heart race, so she swallowed one of the blue pills she had tucked into the glove compartment. *Two greens, one blue,* she thought, although today the magic ratio had been more like ten to three.

Or thirty to ten. She couldn't remember anymore. To be safe, she swallowed another blue pill. *Just to even things out.*

The slightly shabby lobby of the Dunbar was nearly as empty as the sidewalk. In the main dining room, where the musicians played, a couple of waiters were pulling the café chairs down from the tables. A janitor stripped to his undershirt, his suspenders dangling around his hips, was clenching an unlit cigar between his teeth as he ruminatively pushed a broom across the stage. Another man stood behind the bar in his shirtsleeves, carefully slicing citrus fruit with a small paring knife. He looked up at Gabby with an expression that might have been surprise if he weren't the kind of guy who had long ago made up his mind never to be surprised by anything.

"We ain't open yet," he said to her gruffly, still sawing away at the rind of a particularly recalcitrant lime. "Unless you're a guest of the hotel."

"And if I am?"

From the set of the bartender's mouth, he seemed to find this possibility highly unlikely. "Then you can go back up to the front desk and ask one of the porters to bring you a bottle of whatever you want."

"Actually, I'm looking for someone," Gabby said.

"Oh." His tone invited no further elaboration.

"Yes. A friend of mine."

"A friend of yours? Here?" Chuckling, the bartender shook his head. "Missy, I think you got the wrong place."

He can't give me the brush-off. Not now. Not after everything I've been through. "Dexter Harrington," she pressed. "He plays here sometimes."

The man's head jerked up from his lime. "Dexter Harrington?"

"Yes. The piano player. Although he plays a little bit of everything, I guess. Do you know him?"

The bartender put down his knife. "Maybe."

"Maybe?"

302

"I mean, sure. Sure I do."

"Well?" Gabby tapped her foot impatiently. "Is he going to be here tonight? Or do you know where I can find him?"

"Now, that I don't know. What does a girl like you want with Dexter Harrington?"

"What do you mean?"

The man's eyes flashed. "I mean, I aim to mind my own business, that's what I mean. So I ain't about to go running my mouth about Dex to just anyone. Least of all some little girl who, no offense, looks like she's going to be nothing but trouble. So I tell you what. You want to find Dexter? Why don't you write a note and I'll make sure he gets it. That way he can decide for himself whether he wants to be found or not."

Write a note? The mental image of this man watching her as she struggled to force a pencil to form the right letters sent a shudder of alarm through Gabby. "You don't understand," she insisted. "Dexter's my friend. He'll want to see me. He'll be angry that you wouldn't tell me where to find him."

Desperately, she scanned the room, a trapped mouse looking for a way out. A small stream of light shot through one of the shuttered windows and fell on a waiter setting up chairs, illuminating an unexpected reddish tinge to his close-cropped hair. "Him!" Gabby exclaimed. "I know him! I mean, he knows me."

"Rusty! Come here for a minute."

"Yeah? What is it?"

"This . . ." The man paused for a moment, studying Gabby. "This lady says you know her."

Rusty looked alarmed. "I . . . I don't rightly know."

"Sure you do!" Gabby exclaimed, extending a hand toward

him. "I'm Gabby Preston. Eddie's . . . Eddie Sharp's friend, remember?"

"Eddie Sharp's friend." His voice was mechanical, but a faint flicker of sympathy touched his eyes. "Sure. How you doing?"

"Oh, I'm fine." Her voice was artificially bright. "Just fine. Positively fine."

"Well, I'm glad to hear it." Wiping his hands awkwardly on the short apron he wore, he glanced anxiously back at the tables. "Now, is there something I can do for you, or . . ."

"As a matter of fact, there—"

"She wants to know where Dexter is," the bartender interrupted.

"Dexter Harrington?" Rusty whistled. "What the hell does she want with Dexter Harrington?"

"I'm right *here*," Gabby reminded them. "I can hear you. And I only want to talk to him." *Would tears help?* she wondered, looking from Rusty to the bartender and back again. "It's just that . . . with everything that's happened, I just . . . I need to talk to someone. Someone who might . . . understand."

And suddenly, without quite meaning to, Gabby Preston began to cry. The first tears she'd shed since the whole sordid mess of Eddie and Amanda came to light, and they weren't the winsome, pearly ones she'd been taught to let drop slowly down her cheeks by Olympus's most skillful acting coaches, the sort she'd always imagined might inspire the tenderest sympathy from all who saw them. This wasn't so much crying as awful, body-racking sobbing, the kind that made the tears pour down her face in torrents, disfiguring her features and leaving horrible streaks of Max Factor cake mascara behind.

Silently, the bartender poured a jigger of whiskey and pushed it toward Gabby. She gulped it down gratefully and slid the empty glass forward for a refill.

"There, there," Rusty was saying. "It can't be that bad. Eddie didn't get you into any . . . any trouble, did he?"

"No." Gabby shook her head, surprised to note that she was perversely flattered by the assumption.

"And Dexter?" Rusty asked carefully. "Did Dexter . . ."

"Aw, come on," the bartender snorted. "Dexter Harrington's got more sense than to fool with some little white girl."

"Dexter was always a perfect gentleman," Gabby insisted, trying to keep from slurring her words. The whiskey had made her awfully sleepy. She'd have to dip into her emergency stash of green pills for the drive home. *If I go home.* "I just wanted to talk to him, honest. Do you think he'll be here later?"

Rusty let out a slow hiss, like an ominously deflating tire. "Here? No. Not for quite a while. You see, Dexter's gone."

"Gone? What do you mean gone?"

"I mean, he's gone. All I know is he and that cat Eddie Sharp had some kind of falling-out. About what I don't know, although my guess is some chick. It's always some chick. Anyway, last I heard, he packed up and went back to Paris."

"Paris? Paris, France?"

"Far as I know, he ain't never been to Paris, Texas. He left a couple of weeks ago. Right before Eddie went off to play that gig in New York."

"But I saw Eddie right around then. He never said anything."

"Well, he wouldn't, would he? Like I said, it was a bit of a sore subject."

"He can't be in Paris," Gabby said flatly. "He just can't. There's going to be a war. Everyone says so."

"Yeah, well, you got me there." Rusty laughed. "Guess Dex figured he rather take his chances with Adolf Hitler than Eddie Sharp."

Gabby's hands were shaking. Dexter was gone. Eddie was gone. Amanda had betrayed her. *Nobody loves me.* The thought seared through her, as direct and final as a bullet through the brain. *Nobody wants me. Nobody cares if I live or die.*

"Give me a drink," she ordered the bartender.

"I just gave you two, and you ain't paid yet for either one."

With difficulty, Gabby undid the clasp of her purse and pulled out a crumpled ten-dollar bill. "That should take care of those and then some. So come on, fill 'er up. Unless you got something stronger behind that bar of yours."

The bartender froze, whiskey bottle in midair. "Stronger?"

"That's right. Whatever you have."

The bartender's eyes flashed dangerously. "I don't know what you're talking about."

"Oh, come on, sure you do."

"And I'm sure I don't."

"My God, do I have to spell it out for you?" Gabby yelled, lunging for the whiskey in his hand. "I'm looking for *dope.* Smack. Happy dust. *Anything.* Anything guys like you keep behind the bar so girls like me never have to feel anything they don't want to."

The bartender slammed down the whiskey bottle. "Get the hell out of my bar."

"*What?* What did you say?"

"You heard me. Get the hell out of here, before I throw you out."

"How . . . how *dare* you?" Gabby sputtered. "Don't you know who I am?"

"Believe me, sister, I know exactly who you are, and that's why I want you the hell out. Last thing I need is some junked-up Hollywood princess pulling a croak on my watch. So go on, get yourself gone before I call in someone to do it for you."

Rusty took her arm gently. "Come on, Miss Preston. You're not feeling well. I'll put you in a cab."

"Get your hands off me!" Gabby shrieked, jerking away from him as though he'd burned her. "Don't touch me! Leave me alone!"

She managed to snatch the bottle of whiskey from the bar before she was lifted aloft by a pair of massive arms—belonging to some previously unseen bouncer, it seemed—carried through the lobby, and dumped unceremoniously onto the sidewalk, where a small but curious crowd, lured by her screams, had begun to gather. *Great*, Gabby thought irritably. *Now everyone shows up.*

A man with a leering mouthful of gold teeth sidled up to her. "You lookin' to score, baby?"

Before Gabby could respond, she spied the telltale gleam of a camera lens in the crowd, leaving her no choice but to leap into Viola's Cadillac and peel away from the curb like a hit man fleeing the scene of a crime. In the relative safety and privacy of the speeding car, Gabby lunged for the glove compartment and emptied the remaining contents of both glass vials down her throat, washing the pills down with generous gulps of re-voltingly warm whiskey. Blue, green, the ratio of each to each, what did it matter anymore? She'd have to swallow an entire pharmacy to make a damn's worth of difference now.

The scenery was changing fast. *Amazing how quickly you can move when you decide to let the traffic make way for you instead of the other way around,* Gabby thought, taking another swig from the purloined whiskey bottle. *Maybe everything in L.A. really does take twenty minutes.* Already she could see the Hollywood sign looming before her like the gates of heaven. Or was it hell? Gabby wasn't sure anymore. She thought she saw Eddie's face as she came up Laurel Avenue and turned onto Sunset Boulevard. It was looming over the hills, smiling, beckoning to her. Then it changed to Dexter's face. Then Amanda's. Then some horrible amalgamation of the three.

"Please," Gabby said. "Please just hold still so I can talk to you for a minute. That's all I want, to talk to you."

What she didn't see was the other car. But she heard it. A sickening crunch of crumpling metal and shattering glass. The sound of everything bad in the world. The sound, Gabby thought, of death.

"Oh please," Gabby whispered. "Oh please, oh please, oh please."

She didn't know who she was talking to, or what response she expected. Dazed, she reached for the handle and forced the door open. In front of her was the crushed exoskeleton of what looked to have once been quite a nice car, bearing about as much resemblance to its former state as an exhumed corpse to a healthy human.

On a dashboard as littered with sparkling glass shards as any flashbulb-strewn red carpet, Gabby glimpsed a hank of yellow hair darkened with quickly congealing blood.

"Oh God," she gasped. "Oh God, oh God, oh God."

But if anyone was going to listen to her now, it certainly

wasn't God. Shaking, Gabby staggered to the pay phone on the corner and dialed the number she'd been instructed to remember as though it were her own name.

"Larry Julius's office."

"This is Gabby Preston." There was something warm and wet trickling down her face, filling her mouth with the taste of hot metal.

"Gabby, yes? Is anything wrong?"

"Yes. Oh, yes. Please help me. Oh please, oh please, oh please."

Then the receiver slipped from her hand as everything went dark.

TWENTY-FOUR

There was something peculiarly heartless about the weather in Southern California.

Sure, it was mostly wonderful to live in a place where it was blue-skied and beautiful all the time. But on the morning of Helen Frobisher's funeral, when one might wish for just a tastefully cinematic touch of melancholy rain, the relentlessly cheery sunshine felt like a stinging rebuke. *Look as solemn as you want in your black dress and heavy veil,* the dazzling rays seem to say to Margo. *We know it's all an act.*

It had been Larry Julius—appropriately enough, Margo thought, given the fact that he'd been the Pied Piper who'd led her away to this enchanted land in the first place—who had delivered the news that her mother was dead. "Car accident," he'd said brusquely, thrusting a handkerchief preemptively into her hand. "Some maniac was speeding around the curve on

Franklin and Sunset. Ran her off the road. She lost control and wrapped her car around a pole."

Margo twisted the monogrammed linen uselessly around her fingers. Her eyes were dry. "Did she . . . I mean, was it . . . ?"

"Instant?" Larry shrugged. "Who knows? Maybe it was the impact, maybe she had a heart attack when it happened. All I know is that by the time the ambulance got there, it was too late." His voice softened. "Do you really want to find out? If you do, I can try to get permission for an autopsy. Your father seems dead set against it, but if it's important to you . . ."

"No. What does it matter now? She's dead. Dead is dead."

"Duchess." Larry looked down at the hat he was twirling in his hands. "I know this must be hard on you. I'm awfully sorry to be the one to tell you."

"Nonsense. I'm glad it was you. No one else would have been so direct. After all, there was hardly any love lost between my mother and me. What use would it be to pretend?"

She held the crumpled handkerchief back out to Larry. He held up his hands. "Keep it. These things have a way of hitting you when you least expect it. I've seen you without a hanky when disaster strikes, and believe me, it's not a pretty sight." Sighing, he put his hat back on and adjusted the brim. "What I don't get is what the hell someone like your old lady was doing on Sunset Boulevard in the first place."

She was coming to see me. The message Margo had left with Emmeline that night had finally done the trick. After more than a year of total silence—and more afternoons than Margo could count spent sitting on the stools at Schwab's with her back to the door, waiting for the familiar click of footsteps that had never come—Helen Frobisher finally had something to say.

311

Whether their meeting was to have been a touching reconciliation or the final nail in the coffin of their estrangement, Margo would never know, but in her last moments, her mother had been thinking of her.

Margo wasn't sure if that made her feel better or worse.

At least the wedding has been postponed. Amanda Farraday had taken care of that with that stunt she pulled with Eddie Sharp. As Larry Julius had said over the phone the morning the news broke, from the studio's point of view, there was no point in getting married for publicity when another, far less proper bride was already lapping up every drop of ink in America. "Better wait until the fuss dies down," he had said, as casually if he were planning how to avoid the worst of the rush-hour traffic, "and the studio can recoup some of its investment, publicity-wise."

The idea that Margo and Dane might simply be in love and wish to be married for precisely that reason, and none other, never entered into the conversation.

"We bring nothing into this world, and it is certain we carry nothing out," Reverend Atkinson intoned, his voice just as spookily monotonous as when he used to threaten a misbehaving child with all the horrors of hell during catechism class. "The Lord gave, and the Lord hath taken away."

You got that right, Margo thought bitterly. *Some wedding it would have been anyway.* She was probably the first bride in history to have been jilted practically at the altar by her *bridesmaids.* Amanda had run off to New York without so much as a note. Gabby had been rushed to the hospital with acute uremic poisoning the same day Margo's mother was killed, and given the fact that poor Jean Harlow had abruptly dropped dead of the same thing just two years earlier, nobody in town was going to point out that it sounded like an awfully convenient euphemism for an overdose; at least, that was what Larry had hinted. Although, given the state of Gabby lately, Margo wouldn't be at all surprised if her kidneys were in an advanced state of shock.

As for the groom, that was a whole other can of worms. From under the veil of her hat, Margo stole a glimpse at Dane standing beside her. In his crisp dark suit with his appropriately somber expression, he looked perfectly cast in the role of the devoted and solicitous fiancé of a grieving daughter.

But is that what he is? He'd arrived just an hour before the funeral via Olympus-chartered train from the Sierra Nevadas, where he was shooting that mountaineering picture the studio had put him on as soon as the honeymoon had been canceled. Margo had hardly had time to accept a chaste kiss hello, let alone ask him the burning questions that occupied her mind even now: *Are we still getting married? Are you still in love with me? Were you ever?* Maybe it was the shock. Maybe now that the pressure of the wedding had lifted everything would go back to the way it had been before. But somehow, Margo couldn't help but feel as if something, something she couldn't quite name, were being buried today along with her mother.

No one else from Margo's world was in attendance. Lowell Frobisher had been unable to refuse Dane, who was, at least in a technical sense, almost family, but he had drawn the line at suffering the presence of a bunch of Hollywood types at an occasion as solemn as the interment of his wife. "I'm not going to have a bunch of Jews, Commies, homos, and gypsies leering down at Helen's coffin," he had declared, dribbling brandy down the front of his shirt. "It's the least I can do for her."

No, the least he could have done was to keep his mistress away from the funeral. There she was, on the other side of the bier, so far away that Margo doubted she would've been able to make out her face even if the woman hadn't been wearing the kind of heavy dark veil normally seen on the mysterious women who prostrated themselves at the tomb of Rudolph Valentino at the Hollywood Memorial Park Cemetery every year on the anniversary of his death. Clearly, she was trying to keep a respectful distance, perhaps even pass herself off as an unrelated mourner at some other person's grave.

She might have succeeded if not for the stipulation in Helen's will that the funeral be kept private. The woman who had set such store by appearances had liberated herself from them in death. There wasn't a Gamble, a McKendrick, a Winthrop, or a Nesbit in sight.

Just her father, looking older than she remembered and more bored than was seemly, flanked by a couple of ancient pallbearers in dusty suits Margo was sure had been hired directly from the funeral home. Two or three ladies she thought she remembered seeing play bridge in her mother's living room. Emmeline, of course, with a faraway look on her face that could have betrayed either a deep and profound grief at the death of her employer or a deep and profound concern over whether her stacks of premade sandwiches would still be fresh by the time everyone got back to the house for the funeral luncheon.

At least there were plenty of flowers adorning the casket, albeit sent mainly by the Jews, Communists, and homosexuals who had been forbidden to attend. A small wreath of Christmas roses—in red, of course—from Harry Gordon, which was awfully sweet and unexpected of him. A vast blanket of pale chrysanthemums—God knew where they'd come from, this time of year—from Leo Karp and family. The biggest, most lavish arrangement of all came with the simplest message: "Regards from Diana Chesterfield."

Easter lilies. Margo sniffed. *Mother would have preferred callas.*

"'Come, ye blessed of my Father, inherit this kingdom prepared for you from the foundation of the world.'" Reverend Atkinson was gearing up for the big finish. "'Grant this, O Father, for the sake of the same, for thy son Jesus Christ, our only Mediator and Advocate. Amen.'"

"Amen," Margo whispered.

No sooner had the reverend snapped shut his well-worn edition of *The Book of Common Prayer* than two cemetery attendants in coveralls sprang toward the casket, carefully clearing off the flowers and preparing them for transport. The rest of the assembled mourners were already making their way toward the line of black cars at the bottom of the hill.

Dane looked incredulous. "Aren't they even going to stay and watch the casket go into the ground?"

"Why should they?" Margo smiled sadly. "Why be sentimental when there's egg salad and gin waiting at home?"

Dane laughed.

"Are you . . ." Margo bit her lip. "You're not coming back to the house, are you?"

Dane looked apologetic. "The studio has a car waiting for me. I have to get back to the set. We're supposed to shoot night for day tonight."

"Oh. I see."

"Margo . . ." There was so much left unspoken in the way he

murmured her name; so much that might, in fact, be unsayable. He leaned toward her, his clear green eyes burning into hers like they had when she'd first met him. "Will you be all right?"

Margo squared her shoulders. "Me? Sure. I mean, what choice do I have?"

Dane caught her in his arms. She pushed her face hard against his solid shoulder, letting the scratchy wool fabric of his jacket sponge away the tears before they could fall. He pressed his warm lips against the top of her head just long enough for her to entertain a single, desperate hope that he might never let her go.

But then he was gone.

Margo turned back to the casket. It looked oddly naked now, divested of its blanket of flowers, balanced precariously over the grave on a hammock of canvas straps, like a suitcase on a luggage rack.

"Well, Mother," she whispered, "I guess you got what you wanted. You're all by yourself now."

But Margo wasn't. The mysterious woman in the dark veil was still there, closer than ever, lingering beside a marble statue of an angel with her arms outstretched. *She wants to talk to me,* Margo thought with horror, *and she's not going away until she does.*

Better to get it over with. "What is it?" Margo called, trying to make her voice sound as haughty and unappealing as possible. "Is there something you want?"

Lifting her veil, the woman came closer. She was older than Margo had assumed, but still a beauty: bright blue eyes, a warm, inviting smile. The only thing that marred her appearance was a faint pink line, like an old scar, running down the side of one delicately sculpted cheek.

"Margaret," the woman breathed, almost as though she were speaking to herself. "It's Margaret, isn't it?"

"Yes. And who are you?"

The woman ignored her. "You're even more beautiful than I imagined, my dear. Truly, your pictures don't do you justice."

"If you're looking for my father," Margo said coldly, "I believe he's already gone home. If you want to attend the lunch, I suppose I can't stop you, although I can't say I approve."

The woman hid a smile. "I don't think that would be a very good idea. Although I can't say I'm not curious. I haven't seen Lowell Frobisher for . . . God, it must be close to twenty years."

Twenty years? Margo sputtered. "You mean . . . you aren't . . . ?"

"A lady friend of your father's? Goodness, no. Although it certainly would have made things easier at times, wouldn't it?" *What things?* Margo wanted to ask. *How?* "Oh my," the woman continued, leaning closer, "what a lovely pin."

Margo's hand flew up to cover the little gold-and-pearl pin fastened to the collar of her black mourning dress. She'd pinned it on this morning almost as an afterthought, but once she had, she couldn't believe she hadn't thought to put it on sooner. It was the perfect occasion for it. A symbol of her mother, and of a life that was gone. "Thank you."

"I'm so pleased to see it on you. You haven't been wearing it lately, have you?"

"How . . . how did you know?"

"Certainly you know you're pictured quite often in the

317

picture magazines," the woman said pleasantly. "That's how I keep tabs on you, you know, I imagine in much the same way as your other fans. Besides, it could hardly fail to catch my eye. It's quite unusual, isn't it? And it suits you so well. Such a sweet signature."

"It's sort of a family heirloom."

"Oh, I know. You see, I used to have one just like it."

Margo felt every drop of blood drain from her face and plummet, one by one, into the pit of her stomach. "But you don't anymore."

"Of course not, dear." She paused for a moment, fiddling with the fine white handkerchief tucked into the cuff of her sleeve. "I sent it to you."

To me. The memories came back to Margo in a mad rush. The envelope left on the doorstep of the bungalow. The mysterious note signed only with the letter M. The overwhelming relief she had felt at the return of the precious object, as if someone were returning a piece of her.

Except it was never really mine at all. "Who are you?" Margo demanded.

The woman smiled. "Now, now. I think you've experienced more than enough emotion for one day. I know I have. In a few days, when you've gotten some rest, you'll come and see me and I'll tell you all about it."

"But how? How will I find you?"

"Simple, my dear. Ask any of your friends. Ask Dane Forrest or Amanda Farraday or Larry Julius or even dear old Leo Karp. Any of them can tell you where to find Olive Moore."

She pressed her cool hand against Margo's cheek with an expression of infinite tenderness. "Only don't wait too long, will

318

you, darling? I've waited so long to see you, and I've got such an awful lot to say."

She looks at me like she loves me, Margo thought. Almost like a mother.

And all alone at the graveside, for the first time in a long time, Margo Frobisher began to cry.

EPILOGUE

So many stars, Gabby thought, staring out the window. *You never see this many real stars in Hollywood.* There was too much sparkling chaos in Hollywood. When you looked up, you couldn't tell what was real and what wasn't.

But were these real? These stars, scattered like a handful of loose diamonds across the midnight-blue velvet of the night sky, were nothing but the reflected light of the real stars a million miles away, too far to ever be reached, too far to know whether they even existed. Maybe these stars were no more real that the painted ones on the ceiling of the Cocoanut Grove, twinkling down on the very different kind of stars below.

Maybe those were the real stars. Or maybe, just maybe, there was no such thing as "real" at all.

"I hope you'll enjoy your stay here, Miss Preston," the woman in the white uniform—Morisco, someone had called her—was saying. A couple of porters, also all curiously dressed in white, were making short work of the two small suitcases, hastily packed by Viola, that Gabby had been allowed to bring with her. *A funny kind of hotel that limits your luggage,* she had thought. "If there's anything we can get you to make you more comfortable, you just let us know."

"A record player," Gabby said instantly.

The Morisco woman—was she some sort of housekeeper?—stopped smiling. "A record player?"

"Yes. With an all-in-one radio. If you don't have one here, maybe you can send one of the porters to pick up my unit from home."

"Well, I'll have to talk to Dr. Allenby about that."

"Who on earth is Dr. Allenby?"

"He's the director here."

A director! Gabby brightened. "Then he'll understand. I have to have music."

The woman straightened her white cap. "We'll see. For now, I think it's most important that you have a nice long rest, don't you agree?"

Gabby was suddenly very tired. She looked around the room. The walls were apricot, like the carpet in her bedroom in the house on Fountain Street. The lace curtains were like a gauzy bridal veil around the face of the sky. "Yes," she said, more to herself than to the woman. "A rest sounds nice."

What a good idea this was. A little vacation, and no mothers or dance instructors or selfish friends or faithless lovers around to ruin it.

Morisco tucked the cool, crisp sheets around her as Gabby settled back onto the pillow, singing softly to herself. "You made me love you," Gabby sang. "I didn't want to do it, I didn't want to do it. . . ." If she couldn't have music yet, she'd just have to make her own. *Who can do it better than me?*

She'd have a nice long rest. And when she went back, Hollywood had better watch out.

Because when Gabby Preston got back, she was going to shine so brightly she'd make those stars in the sky look like painted dots on an old tin ceiling.

They might not want to love me. But I'm going to make them.

ACKNOWLEDGMENTS

So many people to thank, and no band to play me off! But for the sake of paper and ink, I'll try to be brief.

As always, gratitude goes first and foremost to my glorious agent, Rebecca Friedman, and my fabulous editor, Wendy Loggia, who are the best in the business.

Huge thanks also to Lauren Donovan, Krista Vitola, Dominique Cimina, and the whole gang at Delacorte Press for all their hard work and their belief in this project. Gratitude beyond gratitude to Joseph Papa, Bob Morris, Ira Silverberg, Dana Borowitz, Ember Truesdell, Jillian Larkin, Anna Godbersen, and of course to Michael Schulman, Lauren Marks, Suzanne Marks and Tony Nino, Peter Cook, Colin Shepherd, Alex Block, Laurie Henzel, Mike Edison, Judy McGuire, Billy Zavelson, Ben Rimalower, Dan Fortune, Nick Jones, Ariel Shukert and Jeff Wienir, and Aveva and Marty Shukert.

And to Ben, of course, who puts up with all of this nonsense.

ABOUT THE AUTHOR

Rachel Shukert is the author of *Everything Is Going to Be Great*, *Have You No Shame?*, and the Starstruck novels. She has been fascinated by the Golden Age of Hollywood since she was a girl, when she used to stay up all night watching old movies and fall asleep the next day at school. Rachel grew up in Omaha, Nebraska, and graduated from New York University. She lives in New York City with her husband. Visit her at rachelshukert.com.